TIME'S ALIBI

OR THE QUANTUM OF JAZZ BETWEEN THE SUN AND THE GRAVE

HUSKY HARLEQUIN

INSIDIOUS ALTRUISM

CONTENTS

HuskyHarlequin

Step into the void.
Crack the door to my mind's eye.
Dare to entertain.

Insidious Altruism

A flame in the black.
A hand in the sinking blue.
Caged in my wild mind.

For my parents, who belong in the Hall of Fame. For my lovely wife, who saved my life.

1 / BLACKBIRD

The last heir arrived ninety minutes late. Grandfather had been missing for more than a year, presumed dead. I couldn't believe he was gone. My mentor taught me many things about life. More than anything, he believed that music is the placeholder for life's moments. I can't listen to The Beatles' *White Album* without thinking about Grandfather because, for me, those songs are tethered to emotions and memories that are linked to him. He said he did his best thinking to music, and Grandfather always touted the creation of a soundtrack to facilitate creativity. "Genius inspires us to be the best version of ourselves," he would lecture. I spent the better part of the last year listening to his greatest hits compilation—the songs he would return to when he was trying to overcome his biggest challenges—in search of clues. *Disappeared.* If nothing else, I hoped the music would inspire me to write his story, *our story.* Even if no one read it, I could say that I completed something for the first time in my pathetic life.

I probably knew Grandfather the best, which is to say I barely knew him at all. *Can you ever really know a person?* All the same, I missed him.

The media, my family...I wanted to avoid all the chaos. Several news outlets had labeled some of us as sycophants, and it was hard to argue against their perspective. I wanted to be different; I needed to be different. If my tears weren't completely born from sadness, did it mean they were less authentic? *Maybe that made me the worst of all his heirs.* But we were all obtuse because while my family lamented in our own way his disappearance and legal death, Grandfather had fooled us all. If Grandfather was the center of our universe, you could say our lives began with a big bang.

I just wanted to say goodbye to the old man and smoke one more cigar with him. There is something empowering about smoking, at least when it is done right, sitting on a porch listening to some music. None of that *popular* nonsense that litters the radio today, but real material: An appetizer of Sam Cooke garnished with Bill Withers; a side of Marvin Gaye sprinkled with Etta James; an entrée of The Beatles sweetened by Nina Simone for dessert. Bon Appétit! Or if we were feeling adventurous, we would feast a little on Norah Jones. Man, her voice can take me to another world.

I parked my motorcycle and went inside.

"You're late," Dad said when I entered the law firm's boardroom.

D ozens of stares needled into my flesh. No response would placate my family's insatiable irritation. To be honest, I had become distracted by something unexpected, something unusual. I loathed tardiness.

"Glad you could finally join us," Aunt Hannah said. After three public divorces, three undisclosed settlement agreements, five children and countless trips to her therapist's couch, perhaps it was understandable that Dad's sole sister only knew bitterness and disappointment. Her lawyer's clever machinations were the reason we were gathered together, a flock of chicks without a hen. Rumors and whispers suggested that Hannah's modest trust fund had run dry.

The eighty-inch flat screen TV played a documentary about Grandfather produced by Aunt Hannah. She had secured a prominent director at a cutthroat rate. I'd seen it a half dozen times already: immigration from Europe with his mother after World War Two, the rise of Acheson Chemical Development Company, buying out his investors to avoid an Initial Public Offering on the stock market, and the production of a long chain of successful drugs.

But curiosity dictated that I watch the news. I stopped the playback of the documentary.

"Hey, what are you doing?" Uncle Albert asked. "We're watching that." I ignored him. Albert, Dad's youngest sibling, had been in and out of rehab, in and out of his lovers' beds, and in and out of court for failing to pay child support. One tabloid had numbered his offspring at seventeen and counting. At least he excelled at something.

I turned the TV channel to CNN. I needed an update on what was going on outside of the boardroom while we waited with our assorted attorneys for Mr. R. Sanderson Richardson IV, Esquire, to reveal the contents of Grandfather's Will to us. A global crisis had dominated the news coverage since a terrorist group had taken a Royal Circus cruise liner hostage ten days ago in the Mediterranean Sea. The ship was full of families who had hoped to enjoy a tour of Israel, Egypt, and Greece. Although a British corporation owned the vessel, the passengers held more than thirty different international passports, which made military intervention difficult, even though several dozen hostages had been executed.

"Crazy, huh, Andrew?" Dad said to me. I hadn't noticed that he had left his camp at the table and had slid next to me. It made me nervous. I wanted to remain independent in this meeting.

"Yeah, it's unbelievable. I was on the same cruise with Mom and her family last Christmas, same itinerary, same ship." To say I was obsessed would be an understatement.

"The world seems to take a step closer to insanity every year. I hope I'm not around when we finally lose control," he said.

"Grandfather used to talk about entropy all the time." I mimicked his voice, "The universe is always moving towards disorder. It is the natural course of nature."

"You sound just like him," Dad said, stifling a laugh.

"I miss him," I said. There was too much emotion in the room, and I sensed I stood on the edge of sentimental feelings, feelings I couldn't trust anyone in the room with.

"I do, too." I didn't believe him, but I knew at least a small bit of his soul mourned his absence.

"I can't believe it's been a year. I've been a mess without him," I said.

"Why don't we have a couple of beers after this meeting and catch up? We haven't talked much this last year. I know how much he meant to you," Dad said. I started to believe in his sincerity. *Maybe it wasn't an act? Maybe we could have a normal father and son relationship—whatever that is? Is it possible that my Grandfather had blocked my father and me from having a normal bond all these years?*

"Let's see how this meeting goes first," I said. "I'm feeling a migraine coming on." It was the type of headache only a smoke and a hammer to the head could cure.

"You know, I have a copy of his Will?" Dad said. His words fell on me like a steel sledge on an anvil.

"Viewers, I have just been told that we have a short broadcast from The Viper, the leader of the terrorist cell, The Midnight Veil, which has taken the passengers and crew of the Royal Circus cruise liner, The Hollow Moon, hostage," Leonard Cisco, the CNN newscaster reported. "We are going to play it live." The commotion in the newsroom threatened to distract me, but he had my attention. In a moment, The Viper's image filled the screen in the boardroom. She was unlike any terrorist I had seen or heard of. She looked to be in her mid-thirties, not too much older than me, but unlike me, she was domineering and seemingly capable of executing her plan.

"Citizens of the world, I am The Viper, the leader of The Midnight Veil. While some of you have labeled us a terrorist group bent on violence, I assure you we resent that characterization," she said in perfect English. "The Midnight Veil demands a violence-free Middle East. Our demands have remained the same from the beginning: the disarmament of all Mideast nations, including Israel, Egypt, Lebanon, Iraq, Iran, Syria, Jordan, Saudi Arabia, and Turkey, and the safe return of our compatriots being held in secret prisons in the United States, Great Britain, France, Russia, and China. These demands are non-negotiable, and until they are complied with, we will continue to execute the hostages on The Hollow Moon. We will throw every last body overboard if we must in order to achieve this goal. For far too long, the citizens of the Middle East have been subjected to unrestrained violence, brutality that has been precipitated by many of the governments who now have citizens in the custody of The Midnight Veil. We have returned this violence to your doorstep. Before you condemn us, before you label us as another short-sighted fanatic group, recall how Joan of Arc, Malcolm X, Abraham Lincoln, Harry Truman, and Nelson Mandela were willing to do whatever it took to achieve the peace they desired." With that, the broadcast from the terrorist ended.

"That is the latest from the Hollow Moon, transmitted worldwide just moments ago," Leonard Cisco prattled on.

"Will you just turn the TV off, Andrew?" Aunt Hannah demanded. "I don't want to see any of this right now. We have more than enough heartache to deal with in this room."

I didn't turn around and acknowledge her. *She has some nerve.*

"You need to show me some respect," Aunt Hannah continued. I guess your father never taught you that, did he?"

"You know you need to have a heart to feel pain, right Hannah?" Dad interjected. "But you wouldn't know that since you are a blood sucking vampire." He took the remote from my hand and turned the volume up. Way up.

"Folks, we are getting word from our crew imbedded on the carrier group that is flanking The Hollow Moon that military action has just commenced aboard the cruise liner. Stay tuned, we are about to receive live footage of the operation," Leonard Cisco said. Seconds later, The Hollow Moon and the serene blue waters of the Mediterranean were broken by the warships surrounding the vessel. The camera zoomed in on the cruise ship, and we watched commandos board it via what appeared to be a submarine. The commandos engaged the four terrorists that guarded the main deck. Gunfire rained down everywhere, and it was difficult to track which force had the upper hand. One of the commandos was hit, but the terrorist team was outflanked and overrun. The four dead terrorists were left on the deck while most of the soldiers disappeared from camera view below deck, but gunfire and screams were audible on the camera feed. The wait was as excruciating as watching a pregnant woman in labor with twins, but the deck soon erupted with the presence of hundreds of joyful passengers. Applause from the off-screen news crew could be heard in the background. "It appears that the rescue mission was a success," Cisco said. But the operation came at a price: Two wounded commandos and several injured women and children were helped onto the deck. Rescue boats and helicopters were on their way to the cruise ship when one of the commandos emerged onto the deck, frantically waiving his arms and yelling instructions. Confusion and panic permeated the deck. A massive explosion engulfed the cruise ship, sending people flying in every direction. "No, this is not possible," Cisco said. He lost his composure. The cruise liner sank into the sea within minutes, leaving only carnage.

"He left a copy of his Will in his office safe," Dad said, devouring the silence. "I had a locksmith open it about six months ago. I haven't told anyone yet." *Is there no end to my family's selfish behavior?* Then again, I supposed it might have been the responsible thing to do. Dad had to run the Company in Grandfather's absence, but it didn't seem right to invade a person's private places, even if he is dead. "Don't worry. Things look good for us. I guess the old man loved me after all."

"What do you mean?" He showed me a document neatly folded and tucked into the pocket of his Brooks Brothers suit jacket.

"He left everything to us. These clowns aren't going to get anything," Dad said. He seemed to relish the thought of finally being in control. Power really is the ultimate currency. *Maybe I was wrong about Dad after all. Maybe he loved power as much as Grandfather did.* "I have to commend the old man, though; he is leaving just enough to everyone to prevent a drawn-out lawsuit during probate. My lawyer says he must have spent years planning his estate with

Mr. Richardson in order to get this right." I couldn't believe what I was hearing. *Would Grandfather really leave everything to us?*

"How much is he leaving to everyone?"

"Eight figures to each of his children and another fifty million dollars in a trust to his grandchildren. You and I get the rest, which is considerable."

"How's work going?" Dad asked, as we stared at the eighty-inch TV.

"It's not the same without Grandfather. The lead scientist who took over the project I'm assigned to still isn't sure what he was up to," I said. Dad didn't seem surprised. The last few years I had been the subject of a side project at the Company. Grandfather said he was working on developing the ultimate sports supplement, and my job required me to train like an athlete. I ran on treadmills while technicians monitored my heart, lifted weights while they studied my muscle response, and ingested a steady diet of custom-made vitamins and protein bars while they took small quantities of sweat samples. Once a week I had to donate blood, semen, and urine to the cause. I felt like a bionic man. Whatever Grandfather was doing, it was working. I looked great, and I felt like I could respect myself someday in the future. The best thing about the job was that I could do most of it while watching TV or reading books. I rarely saw Grandfather in the lab; for him, it was just one of many projects. I didn't ask too many questions either because the technicians only spoke techno-babble. Looking back, it's clear Grandfather never gave them any details about what he was doing. They must have been afraid they could lose their jobs if they admitted their ignorance to me, as if my opinion mattered in the Company. The IT department worked overtime trying to recover the research from the Company servers. Grandfather was obsessive about encrypting all of his data. *Maybe there isn't any data. Maybe Grandfather just wanted me to be healthy?*

"It's better than that sports writing gig though, right?" Dad asked.

"I don't know, maybe. The pay's better at least." I loved baseball. I felt at peace on the diamond. Standing on the pitcher's mound was summiting Mount Everest for me. I was on top of the world there, whether I gave up a home run or managed a strike out. Dad did his best to come to games and cheer me on, especially after Mom left, but he never thought I had a future in it. At Grandfather's suggestion, I modeled my pitching motion, like many boys before me, after Nathan Levinson's, whose smooth delivery allowed him to pitch professionally into his mid-forties for the Brooklyn Dodgers. I even adopted his trademark wild hair, but unfortunately, I couldn't grow a beard to match Levinson's masterpiece. My junior year of high school, major league scouts were interested in my high-nineties fastball and overpowering curveball after I managed to pitch three consecutive no-hit games. I was untouchable. Then I tore my rotator cuff and the injury didn't heal in time for me to play my senior year. That's something I don't think I'll ever get over. With my mediocre high school grades, my only option to maintain my bliss was to attend a small local college. At nineteen years old, I walked onto the team at Montgomery Bucks Technical College, with a mid-eighties fastball and a developing change up, no longer able to throw my curve ball without putting tremendous strain on my surgically rebuilt and HGH mended shoulder. Grandfather had provided me with access to the best shoulder surgeon in Philadelphia and the human growth hormone treatment. The latter was enhanced and made undetectable in a Company laboratory. I didn't care if it was technically illegal, though. If it was all right with Grandfather, it was okay with me because Grandfather had taken an interest in my career. Even though Dad walked onto his university boxing team, I think Grandfather was surprised that an Acheson could do anything athletic. I think he was proud of me for discovering this about myself. On the days both he and Dad would be in the stands together, even their cheering for me took on a competitive nature. I only heard Dad from the stands on the days he was joined by his father. Fathers and sons: Is there anything more complicated? I'm sure they didn't realize it, but I won every game I pitched when they were in the stands together.

"If we don't start to make progress soon, to figure out your project, I'm afraid I'll have to reassign you," Dad said. "Have you taken a look at the Company job board lately? I know there are some entry-level jobs in finance if you are interested." The lab job was the best paying job I'd ever had, and I liked the results. I wasn't paid like a senior manager, but I wasn't struggling either, but the idea of working with numbers every day seemed an impossible consideration for me.

"I don't think I'm finance material, Dad." He had spent considerable time climbing the ranks of the Company and with great effort achieved the role of Executive Vice President, Grandfather's right hand man.

"Perhaps not. Would you like to come be one of my personal assistants? I could teach you how to be an executive. We could make a great team someday." Childhood memories of our Monopoly games inundated my emotions, how he paid himself an additional $600 salary every time he passed "GO" for being the Banker. When I'd complain about fairness, he'd say, *I'm working hard doing this job for the other players, son. In life, we can either be the guy following the rules, or we can be the guy making the rules.*

Mr. R. Sanderson Richardson IV, Esquire, blessed the boardroom with his presence and spared me from concocting an excuse.

"Everyone please take your seats," Mr. Richardson ordered with confidence. The curmudgeon had four decades of experience dealing with whiny, emotionally underdeveloped, rich people. Everyone obeyed. Dad turned off the TV. Despite the belief of many in the room, Richardson did not see us as a breed apart. I found my chair next to my attorney, Joe Howard. The poor chap was right out of law school and had an office across the street from my apartment building. He had agreed to work for me earlier in the day for a $500 retainer.

"Up until just a few days ago, I believed the latest version of David Acheson's Last Will and Testament was signed and executed about two years ago in my presence." Mr. Richardson had to take a pause. Something had thrown him for a loop. He actually had to sit down at the head of the massive conference table to deliver the remaining information. His reservation was not lost on the assembly. "However, in a most peculiar fashion, we received ten days ago a copy of his Will that was apparently signed and executed just days before he disappeared. Unfortunately for some of you folks, you're not going to like the changes he has made."

Aunt Hannah was livid. "What's going on? Is it a fake?"

"Why don't you provide us with a copy of the Will and the previous version of the Will he signed in your presence?" Hannah's lawyer demanded.

"Now just wait a minute, sir. I'm getting there. I want to tell you all that I've spent the last couple of days working to authenticate the Will. It was delivered with three affidavits certifying the authenticity. I've been able to track down the witnesses and interview them, and they confirm that they indeed were present for the execution of the document."

"Who were the witnesses?" Albert demanded. He and Hannah knew they were the most likely candidates to be disinherited.

"The President and Vice President of the United States of America and the Secretary of State. The Vice President delivered the Will himself," Richardson said. The air was sucked out of the room. *Why would they witness Grandfather's Will? He was rich and powerful, but this seemed outrageous.*

"Okay, everyone catch your breath. Let's get into the details. And let me assure you that the assets devised are real and set aside," Mr. Richardson said, calming everyone down. Dad looked nervous. *What could this mean for him?*

"Let's start with David's grandchildren," Mr. Richardson said. "Their situation is the least complicated." The boardroom was littered with my cousins. All five of Hannah's children were in the room. Six of Uncle Albert's progeny were there, too: The other fifteen or seventeen, who knew? "'To each of my grandchildren who can prove to be a blood relation via certified DNA testing within one year of the reading of my Last Will and Testament, I leave an equal interest in a trust account funded with fifty million dollars and created for their benefit. Such interest vests in each grandchild upon the condition that they graduate with a Ph.D. or M.D. from a university in the *US News and World Report* "Top 100 World Universities" and serve four consecutive years in the Peace Corp. Should one of my grandchildren die before vesting their interest in this trust, then their interest shall pass to the Philadelphia Public School System. I cannot tolerate ignorance in my family, not even from the grave.'" It was safe to say that my portion of this trust account would pass to charity.

"'To my children Hannah and Albert, I leave two hundred and fifty million dollars each. This money will be set aside by my lawyer, R. Sanderson Richardson IV, who will also serve as trustee in managing the separate Swiss bank accounts created for them. Hannah and Albert shall have the right to the interest earned on their trust accounts on one condition: They must sign a contract agreeing to leave the United States within twenty-four hours and never return to its shores for the rest of their lives. Should they return to the United States, they shall forfeit their interest in their trust accounts with the remainder going to the Children's Hospital of Philadelphia. They've needed a fresh start on life since their mother died, and they will not find it in this glorious country. Lastly, if Hannah and Albert do not sign the conditional contract obligating this performance before leaving my attorney's law office on the day this Last Will and Testament is read or they contest the validity of my Last Will and Testament, then they will forfeit any interest in their trust accounts and will receive only a twenty-five million dollar cash inheritance.'"

Hannah and Albert cried. They vacillated between happiness and grief. Despite the obvious slight, their inheritance was secured. Mr. Richardson passed contractual documents to each of them. "The law office closes in an hour, so you have to make up your mind quickly. I'm sorry." Hannah and Albert consulted quietly with their attorneys.

"Shall we move on?" Mr. Richardson asked. Dad and I both nodded. "'To my son, Peter, and my grandson, Andrew, I leave one hundred million dollars each in a trust account for their benefit and a forty percent interest to each in the Acheson Chemical Development Company. These gifts are given on the condition that the Company is never sold to a third party or taken public via a public offering of stock. If the Company is sold or taken public, any stock or cash due to Peter and Andrew resulting from such sale will be forfeited and devised to the Foundation of Brotherly Love. Furthermore, if Peter and Andrew do not sign the conditional contract obligating this performance before leaving my attorney's law office on the day this Last Will and Testament is read or they contest the validity of my Last Will and Testament, then they will forfeit any interest in Acheson Chemical Development Company and will receive a twenty-five million dollar cash inheritance.'" Mr. Richardson handed us both contracts to examine. I passed my copy to my new lawyer. The glassy look in his eyes indicated that he was over his head. That made two of us.

"'I leave a twenty percent interest in Acheson Chemical Development Company in trust to the United States General Fund. The President of the United States will serve as Trustee for this twenty percent interest.'" Mr. Richardson chuckled. "Always the humanitarian."

"What about his personal property?" Hannah asked.

"Yes, one last item. 'All my real property, personal effects, remainder, and residue, I leave to my grandson, Andrew.' Here you go, kid." Richardson tossed me a set of keys. "Your grandfather's mansion is now yours. Go take a look around," Mr. Richardson said to me softly. "You must have been his favorite. I hear he has a nice collection of vintage cars."

Mr. Richardson smiled at me.

"That's so unfair," Hannah said. "He's my father. You're just his grandson." I shrugged my shoulders.

"Please consult with your attorneys and make a decision on whether you will sign your respective contracts within the hour," Mr. Richardson concluded.

Dad signed his agreement and stood up. "Well, this isn't exactly what I expected. Whether you like it or not, son, your inheritance makes you an executive now. We need to talk. Give me a call when you're ready."

"I haven't even decided if I'm going sign my agreement yet," I said. Joe Howard, my inexperienced attorney, started to laugh.

"Listen to your attorney. He will give you sound advice," Dad said.

"I advise you to sign. You have nothing to lose," Howard said. And with that, my attorney earned his $500 retainer. I executed the document and got in line behind my aunt and uncle to hand my documents to Mr. Richardson.

"You better watch yourself, kid," Albert said. "The world is a dangerous place and it would be a shame if something happened to you. You wouldn't be able to enjoy this inheritance that just fell into your lap."

I nodded, acknowledging the threat.

"Don't worry, I'll make sure my lawyer writes you into my will," I said careful to slather on the sarcasm. "And Aunt Hannah, too." I handed my paperwork to Richardson and departed the building.

5 / EVERLONG

I went to go see the one person in this world I completely trusted, Jennifer Dennison, who lives about two blocks from the University of Pennsylvania. Like many old and prestigious schools, the socio-economic elite do not surround the Penn campus. But graduate students are left without many options—live at home, live with five roommates, or live in an apartment the size of a bathtub. Jennifer chose door number three.

Love is the inexplicable force that both draws us together and sends us scattering in search of its existence, the elusive filling that if found, promises to make us whole. I am not sure if I really know what love is beyond what I have seen on the movie screen and in the numerous books that have kept me company. *Can love even be real?* I know what a broken heart feels like, Jennifer made sure of that. She is pure, from the bounce of her thick blonde hair to the fleck of green energy in her eyes, but the righteousness of her smile is what communicates the essence of her benevolence. I was always too afraid to touch her, to know her, to let her love all of me for fear that I would somehow contaminate her beauty. Some say our beauty is found in our flaws. How many flaws does it take before we are no longer beautiful?

Jennifer and I were friends since our introduction at the Company daycare. We spent countless mornings sipping juice and playing. We did everything together: Blocks, house, peanut butter and jelly, and nap-time on adjoining carpet pieces. Any attempt to separate us in those early days was akin to nuclear fission. Every afternoon at the end of the workday when her father would arrive to take her home—he always arrived before my dad—she would force the whole room to endure our private Chernobyl Incident. I made lots of noise with her, mostly because I was happy to be wanted so badly. The rhythm of tears quickly and tragically singed away the comfort her smile would bring me. Her father and the Company daycare attendants would work relentlessly to calm Jennifer when she would leave each evening. The same effort was not made to soothe me in her absence.

Our childhood friendship could best be described as a patch covering up a hole on an old pair of comfortable jeans, which were worn thin from years of intense companionship. The simplicity still baffles me. We were inseparable. *How could she grow out of needing me?*

It took me fifteen minutes to get to Jennifer's apartment on my Vincent Rapide Series B motorcycle that was a gift from Grandfather on my eighteenth birthday. I didn't call ahead; I figured I would just surprise her. I needed to unload the weight of the day's events. I pressed the button on the intercom for her apartment.

"Hello?" It was Jennifer. She sounded spent.

"Hey, it's Andrew. Can I come up?" She didn't answer; she just buzzed open the door. I took the two flights of stairs up to her place and she let me inside. Her puffy eyes indicated that she had been crying.

She hugged me. It had been a month since we had talked. School kept her busy, and she often disappeared in her studies for extended periods of time. Even so, the hug had more meaning than usual. I noticed the TV across the room was on CNN. It made sense; she had been my guest last Christmas on the family cruise aboard the Hollow

Moon. Jennifer needed a break from school and has always been close to my family.

"I haven't been able to pull away from the TV all day," Jennifer said. "It could've been us. We could've been killed on that boat today. You should have never invited me on the cruise last year."

"It's terrible, I know."

"What's wrong with humanity? Why do we insist on killing innocent people?" I didn't have an answer for her. I could only hug her with more urgency. We moved over to the couch and sat down. I held her in silence for fifteen minutes. In moments like that, I wonder why things have never worked out between us. I loved her. But she is in love with her professor. I could never seem to take her off the pedestal that I thought she belonged on, and Jennifer would never forgive me for thinking that she's perfect.

Geoff Henderson thinks she is perfect, too. Dr. Geoff Henderson. Professor Geoff Henderson. She doesn't hold his beliefs against him, though. Why would she? He is smart, sophisticated, and good to her. Geoff gives her things that I will never be able to: Consistent intellectual stimulation and an understanding of her need to obsess with history and all of its details. This common ground is everything for them. A couple can have every ingredient necessary for a good relationship, but if they are lacking a common passion, they will never have that vibrant perfection that transcends human understanding. It can be faked for a while, but soon the relationship becomes threadbare. A friendship can be built upon a tattered yet shared temporal existence. That is what Jennifer and I have, just a well-worn and comfortable familiarity. Our relationship will never be content as anything more.

It's not that I don't like Geoff; he tried to be my friend. I helped him move into his new high-rise condo last year after he hurt his back playing racket ball and needed some last minute help. Geoff tried to give me some cash for my effort. When I refused, he sent me passes to the Philadelphia Zoo that he'd been holding on to. As a grown man, I wasn't sure what I was supposed to do with them. *Maybe take a date, someone other than Jennifer?*

"Why isn't Geoff here?" I said, conceding the end of our moment. I stared at a picture of the two of them on the wall. He was too good looking. Even his singular physical imperfection—a tiny mole under his right eye—couldn't shatter the made-in-a-factory look he cultivated.

"He was earlier. He got called down to DC an hour ago. The Philosopher's Cave has asked him to come down to sit in on a meeting."

"The Philosopher's Cave?"

"You know the famous think-tank?" I didn't. "They consult on tons of government and military projects. Geoff has been contracting with them for the last two years because of his work on the history of terrorism. They've been pressing hard lately for him to come in and take a larger role. He said he didn't feel like he could say 'no' anymore."

"Is this a permanent move?"

"I don't think so. No. He'd never give up his tenured position on the Penn faculty."

"Not until you graduate at least." She didn't like the fact that I was right and ended our embrace. At least we remained nestled on the couch, and this gave me that tiny bit of hope that everyone holds onto, that little fragment that helps us survive at night when we are acutely aware of our inescapable solitude.

"Have you been crying today, too?" She studied my face.

"A little bit. Today was the one-year anniversary. The lawyers read Grandfather's Will. So now that he is legally deceased, his assets were divided up according to his wishes."

"Are you happy with what he left you?" Jennifer probed. I loved making her pursue me because her concern for me felt genuine.

"I don't know. Why don't you come take a look with me?"

We rode on my Vincent to Grandfather's mansion—to my mansion—in Villanova. It gave me time to think.

What was I going to do with all of this money? How was I going to help run a company? Could I just stay in the background where I belonged and forge my own plans for my life? Grandfather was foolish to place any trust in me with his company. It was the one thing that he was most proud of. Was he really dead? Our private investigators and the FBI never produced any credible leads concerning his disappearance. I still half expected him to walk into the lab every morning to see how I was doing. How did he become acquainted with the President, Vice President, and Secretary of State? Grandfather is important—yes. But *that* important? Why would they be interested in the contents of his Will? He has always been generous, so maybe the politicians took an interest in his gift to the hard-working folks of the United States, I thought.

Jennifer's father passed away in a workplace accident during her freshman year at Princeton. She considered a transfer to a more affordable school, but Grandfather stepped in and gave her a scholarship covering the entire cost of her education. She didn't even have to ask for help. I think he wanted to love those that I loved. His generosity made some sense, but there were so many questions without answers on the horizon.

Yet, everything felt right to me on my bike with Jennifer's arms wrapped around my waist. Simplicity. Why couldn't I stay in this moment forever? This moment could last as long as there was fuel in my gas tank. I decided to take the long way to my new residence.

My new twenty thousand square foot home sat on fifteen acres of land. Thankfully, Grandfather's small staff of housekeepers and landscapers had agreed to stay on since his disappearance. Dad had arranged for everything in Grandfather's absence. Still, I popped in from time to time; I couldn't keep myself from searching for metaphorical ghosts.

Jennifer and I turned on the lights in every room we entered on the way to the massive garden. Even on this late October night, the evening was quite cool. We walked the mazes of rose bushes and oak trees, just like we did when we were young. I wrapped her in my coat to keep her warm, and for a while, I was the center of her universe.

"Grandfather left me all of this," I said, boasting a bit.

"You were always his favorite, Andrew," Jennifer replied.

"Second favorite. He loved himself more," I said in jest.

"Well, third favorite then. He loved his Company the most." We both laughed a bit. The best jokes have at least a hint of truth.

"He left me more. I'm the proud owner of a forty percent stake in the Company, too." She seemed happy for me, but not particularly surprised. "And one hundred million dollars." Her eyes lit up.

"Wow. What're you going to do with all of that money?"

"I don't know yet. Do you think it is possible to spend all of it in one lifetime?" I asked.

"You wouldn't dare waste it. I hope you are above a life of decadence."

"I don't know if I am. This is all new to me," I said, an honest answer. Despite the fact that my family was wealthy, I was never encouraged to consider that a portion of their hard-earned assets could be mine someday. In fact, the opposite landscape was routinely painted for me.

"Why don't you share it with me?" I suggested. This was the best offer I was ever going to be able to make her.

"What?" she asked, her reaction incredulous. "What do you mean?"

"I need a partner. Someone I could marry. You know, someone who could help me be a better person." It was not the best marriage proposal, but I was doing better than Mr. Darcy in *Pride and Prejudice*.

"Andrew, you could have any woman in the world with what you have to offer. You don't need me," Jennifer answered.

"But I want you." We stopped our trek through the garden, and I pulled her in closer to me.

"Andrew." She couldn't find the words.

"Yes." I did my best to be charming.

"What about Geoff?" Jennifer asked.

"What about Geoff? He could have any woman in the world. What does he have that I don't?" My desperation escaped my lips.

"He has my heart, Andrew." With that, I released her from my grasp.

"Was there ever a time when I could have won you?"

"Andrew." She didn't want to have this conversation.

"I need to know. I need to have answers if I have to let you go."

"Let's go inside. It's getting too cold out here for me," she said. We entered the greenhouse. We were like prehistoric elephants caught in a tar pit, struggling against the inevitable, hoping to outmaneuver fate. The tar, like the past, could be overcome, but our dual freedom might have a cost. We could be too weary to continue on living and collapse on the shores of liberty, our friendship the price tag for our emancipation. *My emancipation.* I never considered the fact that I had led my friend to this bleak condition. It would have been best for me to muster my strength and push my friend free before succumbing to the sticky shallows. *At least one of us could survive whole.* But my damaged soul preferred the dark shadows of purgatory and its undercurrents.

Grandfather's tobacco grew inside. The good stuff that he had engineered to be free of nicotine and most of the carcinogens.

The humidity and heat hit us and chipped away at the chill. I examined the plants. "These are ready," I said. I picked up a knife from the tool rack and cut away a half dozen large green leaves. The delicate process was an art form. Jennifer watched me with curiosity.

"I've never seen you do this before," she said.

"I know." I cut one more leaf away. "It's something we shared."

"You've kept his greenhouse going the last year?"

"Yeah. In a weird way, I wanted to be prepared in case he ever came back. Now, it's more like a mausoleum. I can feel him with me when I do this."

She nodded her head, and I gathered the clipped leaves together.

"Let's go," I said.

We raced through the cold October air back to the mansion. I led Jennifer down to the basement to Grandfather's garage and workshop. She snuggled into a blanket on the old couch.

"I'll be right back," I said. I left the tobacco leaves on a workbench and walked upstairs. In the kitchen, I found some Hershey's cocoa in the cupboard and prepared some passible hot chocolate on the stove.

I took my time and let Jennifer simmer in her thoughts before rejoining her. If she was going to reject me once and for all and close the door to hope, then I needed to make her tell me the reasoning behind her feelings, if indeed logic could be attached to emotions.

I handed her a cup of cocoa and settled in under the blankets next to her. "Look what I found," I said. She sniffed the mug.

"Hot chocolate. My favorite. Are you sure it is safe to drink?" she asked. "Who knows how long it has been sitting in there."

"I checked the expiration date. It's fine; no worries," I said with a smile even though I hadn't checked. "So."

"So," she repeated. Jennifer put her cocoa down without tasting the drink. It was up to me to chase her for an answer. Even though she prayed like prey for relief, I would not give up my pursuit.

"Have you thought about my last question?" I left the blankets and returned to the workbench.

"Andrew, are you really going to make me do this?" Her pleading would have no effect on me this time. Jennifer perceived my resolve. It's a rare moment when I'm willing to fight for something.

"You're my oldest friend. You know that, right?" she asked.

"Yes. You're probably my only friend, Jennifer." Grandfather had an elaborate set up for processing the leaves. I placed the new clippings inside the drying box close to the heat lamp. I checked the temperature and humidity gauges. They looked good.

"I love you. I really do," Jennifer added. "But as a brother." I sensed her earnestness. This wasn't easy for her to say. It wasn't easy for her to hurt me.

"I know, but was there ever a chance at anything more?" I asked. I examined the leaves that had been in the drying rack for several weeks. Some were ready. I separated the perfect ones from the imperfect ones.

"When we were children playing in daycare, I used to imagine us married one day."

"Come on. What about after that?"

"There was a time in high school, but it all fell apart. I came to understand that you are possessive."

"What do you mean? I don't understand."

"Like when your mom moved to Rome," Jennifer said.

"I fell apart. Aren't all boys supposed to love their mothers?" Mom left Dad when I was twelve. An Italian director she met at the Cannes film festival swept her away. She moved on and produced three new children. I loved Rome and my half siblings, but I never felt comfortable since I don't speak Italian. Mom tried to remedy that with a gift of Rosetta Stone software, but I couldn't bring myself to use it. A dark part of me reveled in my isolation and the pain it brought, not only to me, but the rest of my family.

"It's kind of more than that, really. It's like how you are being now. I can sense that you feel the need to own me," she said.

"What? How can you say that?" I asked.

"You want to possess me for your vision of me. You want to put me on this shelf that you have created for me in your mind. You have this need to worship this image of me that you have created."

"No, that can't be what you think of me."

"What I need is to be treasured. This means loving me, yes. But this also means giving me the freedom to wander and explore who I might become and for you to learn to enjoy this journey with me."

"You don't think I'm capable of this?" I asked.

"No. No, I don't," Jennifer whispered. She seemed unsure how to disclose the thoughts I had long desired to know. "You're possessive about other things, too. This forces you to be comfortable only in the status quo. You won't allow yourself to discover the possibilities that might come with change."

"I don't understand."

"You have many addictions. First and foremost is your dependence on suffering," she said.

I cut the vein from a flawless wrapper leaf.

Jennifer was right. I do have addictions. I am addicted to her effect on my life, but I have weightier addictions, too.

The first time I gave in was a couple of years after Mom and Dad divorced. I was a teenaged boy who couldn't deal with the reality of separation from my primary caretaker and champion. The robbery of her constant affection introduced me to the reality that darkness can be as intoxicating as the light.

Their divorce sent me into depression, and I spent most of my ninth grade year in my bed under the covers, far from the sun. I shaved thirty pounds off of my already frail frame. Dad didn't want to take me to see a psychiatrist because he didn't want *his* dirty laundry being discussed with anyone outside the family. When Mom protested from Rome, he insisted that my problems were derivatives of his problems. I suppose he was embarrassed by my lack of fortitude for emotional disillusionment. "Life is full of disappointment, son. Best get used to it," he would offer, always the fatalist.

I made it back to school towards the end of the first month of my sophomore year. The home-school teachers that were sent by the superintendent had become dull, and I began to see my way through my overwrought sadness. It was short lived. A chance encounter in the boy's locker room after a game of dodge ball in PE introduced me to heroin. *Love at first taste.* It wasn't the elation and invincibility it gave me while I was high, but the intense depression that always followed that hooked me. When I was low, I could feel. Feeling sadness is better than feeling nothing at all.

In between my bouts of depression, I courted my mistress, Heroin. Whenever I called her name, she never left my side. She provided me with thrills, and the higher the highs, the lower the resulting plunges would be. The farther I was from my emotional center, climax or gorge, the better I felt.

And the lows lasted longer.

Then I ran out of money, and my mistress left me. It happens to all users. I began to ask Dad for extra allowance money, but when he started asking questions, I had to get creative. I would sell things from around the house: Items that wouldn't be missed like old clothes Mom left behind in the attic. But I got sloppy, and the probing questions from Dad returned. So I resorted to stealing for the chance to dance with my lady of the night. He was too busy to notice my further weight loss and punctured flesh, but not the disappearance of his old Breitling wristwatch. He hadn't worn it in years, but I had forgotten it was a wedding gift from Mom. That's when everything got out of control.

Rehab lasted seven months. That is its sterile, white washed, suburban name. Detoxification more suitably captures the violence. My favorite *brand* of heroin, while unusually potent, was apparently laced with heavy metals. Restoration required that my soul be sucked from bone and sinew. The flavor of depression it provided was not pure sadness, but a tortured endurance race through a basin saturated with inescapable agony and deafening defeat. I couldn't even recognize myself in the mirror. What sort of decision-making process led me to such ruin? *Was I even human anymore?* These questions could not be answered without inviting more destruction.

I was delivered to a place of beauty. Upstate New York. The green leaves, the naked hills clothed in green grass, and a creek babbling in the forest welcomed me. But it was the horses that spoke to me. An equine therapy ranch was where I began my ascent back to the land of the living.

Bubba was my daily companion for three months. To a horse breeder, he may not have amounted to much, but to me, he was magnificent. Every morning at dawn, I would get up to feed him and brush his hide. After breakfast, I was given the privilege of riding him. Those moments of responsibility provided me with the opportunity to discover his personality and to develop a true friendship. Somehow, Bubba could tell that I was working through something bigger than myself. Thankfully, he was up to the task of leading me to a better place. On occasion, early in my stay, I would show up late to the stall to care for Bubba or I would give him half-hearted attention, but Bubba would not tolerate such treatment. He would kick the ground, nip at his own skin, and our rides would not be pleasant; he would look for low-lying trees to try and knock me out of my saddle. And that was my answer: A man requires maintenance, and I had denied myself proper care. The result was melancholy and discontent. Such feelings, if left unpruned, fester and become wounds that do not heal on their own. Whether man or beast, we are kept functional through relationships of mutual responsibility. I suspect all horses have the same divine ability to instruct. I suppose that's why all little girls fall in love with them. I will never forget my friend. It was in the middle of this education that Grandfather found me walking Bubba through the glen.

Jennifer wept. My inquisition had its price.

"It's okay, you can stop," I said. I prepared a less perfect leaf as the binder and poured in tobacco I chopped and dried last week, a different tobacco variety Grandfather had developed for fuller flavor.

"No, I need to finish now," Jennifer answered. I had forced her to defend herself like a cat backed into a corner. "I love you. For our whole lives, I have loved you. You're the one I spent my childhood imagining a life with. You know how girls are," Jennifer continued.

"Yes. I think I understand." Foolish words. *What man can truly claim to understand a woman?*

"But you changed when your parents broke up. I had a front row seat. You're no longer joyful. Nothing excites you anymore."

"You excite me," I said.

"No, I don't think so. You've just become possessive. You can't stand to think about someone else loving me like you love me," Jennifer said to me. Her unbearable stare underscored her point. "I've seen firsthand what you are capable of. You took something from me that can never be replaced."

"I thought we were past this? I thought you had forgiven me?"

"I have forgiven you, but I cannot forget. You stole from me the one physical thing that mattered to me in life, and I never want to feel that way again." I started rolling the binder leaf with the filler material.

She's right. I had robbed her. During the dark days of my addiction, I took her necklace. Not just any necklace: Her mother's diamond pendant necklace. Jennifer's mother died giving birth to her. Her father had bought her mother the gift to commemorate Jennifer's debut into the world. When his wife passed, he gave the treasure to his daughter instead. To Jennifer, the jewelry embodied the very essence of her mother, and I took that from her. How could I dare to ask her forgiveness when I cannot forgive myself? *Of all the things I wish I could change, it would be this moment.* I cannot imagine the separation from someone you should know intimately but never had the chance to meet. I suspect it is a wound that never heals. I had been at her house doing homework; I often met her there after her afternoon lacrosse practices. Dad had been on my case about his watch disappearing, and I was desperate for a fix. Her necklace, sitting on her desk seemed to offer me salvation. She was so focused on our trigonometry exam that was looming the next day that she didn't even miss it until the next morning.

I traded it for one hundred dollars at a pawnshop in the city on the way home from Jennifer's house. That was probably less than a tenth of what it was really worth. The tweak that followed was the best I ever had. So good, it nearly killed me. Needless to say, I didn't make it to the trig test. Dad broke my door down that night after Jennifer called him at work. He didn't even notice that I hadn't gone to school. How could he? He left our house each morning before I did. Near death, my guardian angel had saved me. You might think it was Jennifer, but I'll always give credit to her mother. They weren't able to trace what happened to the necklace when I was aroused from my coma three days later, but I believe her essence left the locket and watched over me that night. Mrs. Dennison saved my life that day. How else could you explain my ability to survive? I don't believe it was luck as everyone in detox liked to suggest. It was intervention.

"I am sorry I am such a disappointment," I suggested to

Jennifer as she cried. I hadn't done heroin since. It has been four-teen years, fourteen very long years. Not a day goes by when I don't think about a reintroduction. The thirst will always be with me.

"You're not. You are not a disappointment," Jennifer said. I couldn't really believe her since they are words that echo from my own psyche every day. "You just need to take this opportunity to strike out on your own. You need to discover something that inspires you to live, something that inspires you to create a better life for yourself."

"What about you?"

"You are so blind. Your love for me hasn't gotten you anywhere. We're thirty years old now. I haven't inspired you to grow beyond the disappointments of our childhood."

Maybe she was right. I had been stuck. At least my disastrous existence had pushed her towards something fresh. Someone new. Someone good. Then it hit me.

"Without you, I have no one," I said.

"You still have your Dad," she said.

"He's never been there for me."

"And maybe that's your first problem. You're so selfish. Have you been there for him lately? Your grandfather is legally dead now. You and your Dad need each other more than ever." I rolled the interior tube with the wrapper leaf into a perfect *parejo* cigar and sealed it with glue. Grandfather always appreciated my technique, my devo-tion to detail. I placed the finished product into the humidor, next to the dozens I'd rolled over the last year.

I thought about Jennifer's words. *How could I be so blind?* She was right; I needed to see Dad, right away. I kissed Jennifer's cheek: One last moment between friends. Things would never be the same after this night. For once I was able to see what she had been seeing for years.

"I'm sorry I couldn't be the kind of man you need," I said with all the sincerity I could summon.

"There is someone else out there for you, Andrew. Go out there and figure yourself out. She'll be there when you do."

"Thanks," I said. It was all I could produce.

"And I'll always be here for you. I will always love you."

We mounted my Vincent one last time, one last time with her arms around my waist, one last time with her head resting on my back. I took the long way back to her apartment. *When was the last time I had a woman's arms around me?* I couldn't recall. It was probably my mother last December. *When would be the next time?* I didn't walk Jennifer to the entrance, but I watched her disappear behind the door. If I didn't let her go once and for all, I would be stuck here in this moment forever.

I sped away to the nearest gas station and checked the time. 10:47 p.m. It was late, but I knew Dad would still be up. I grabbed my cell phone from my pocket and dialed his number.

"Dad. This is your son." Loud blues music played in the background.

"Hey, Andrew," he said. I could tell he was preoccupied by the dismissive tone in his voice. I had heard it a million times. It was his default telephone voice.

"Dad, you still up for that drink tonight? I know it's getting late," I said.

"Um, yeah. Sure."

"Well, where are you?" Maybe this was a bad idea so late in the day, I thought. He had probably been out drinking since our meeting with Richardson had ended in the late afternoon.

"I'm on my way to Franklin's Pint," Dad said. I could hear him speak to someone nearby. I figured he was whispering instructions for more drinks to a young woman he had just met at the bar. He had no shame anymore. "I'll be there in about twenty minutes, I think."

"Okay, Dad. I'll see you then."

Franklin's Pint is a dive that the kids attending the swank colleges on the Main Line love. Cheap food. Cheap beer. Cheap hookups. It's Dad's type of place during midweek when he doesn't want a challenge. If Franklin's Pint were a baseball diamond, he would be slugging a thousand. In there, he was Babe Ruth and could survive on his good looks and his fat wallet.

I flowed through the river of people dancing and sailed as far away from the stage as possible. Dad wasn't at his reserved table in the back. In his old age, his ears couldn't handle the loudness of the music as well, but he was addicted to the atmosphere. I anchored myself in position to see the TV array nearby, not that I could hear anything above the local blues band banging away on stage. It didn't matter. The reporters on ESPN were commenting on the tragic events on the cruise ship in the Mediterranean. They were old enough to remember the paranoia that came in 2001, but the folks in this place obviously didn't care about the atrocities that were occurring around the world. Maybe that was the point; they needed the distraction from another conflict, from another act of terrorism. These events were becoming too commonplace for the younger generations. It was just another blip on the social media network, something else to ignore in the face of their own life challenges. The world in turmoil paled in comparison to their crushing student debts, a shrinking job market, or a love life in disarray. These were sentiments I could relate to after my day, sentiments which fostered guilt within my weary and defenseless mind.

Then I saw Dad. The pretty, young, multi-ethnic woman woven into his overcoat excised herself from his grasp when she saw me across the room. She was as skinny as a match. Dad wasn't embarrassed, not even a little. I had witnessed this a hundred times before. They joined me at his table, and immediately a waiter presented himself.

"Bring us a couple of Yuenglings," Dad said to the waiter.

"Anything for you, Andrew?" the waiter asked.

"I'll take an ice water and some hot wings if you've got them," I responded.

"You sure you don't want anything stronger? It's been a hell of a day," Dad asked as the waiter lingered.

"I'm fine," I said. One drink is a gateway for me, a waterslide to an ocean of debauchery.

"I'll take a cheeseburger, if that's okay," Dad's date added. We both looked at her. Despite the fact that she was beautiful, I had forgotten she was there, and I felt bad about it. I don't like being flippant.

When the waiter left to deliver our orders, we let the next few minutes pass while the band played on. By her body language, I could tell Dad's date could not stand to sit in silence for very long. She had to initiate conversation, and when the band's set ended, we had no choice.

"Are you two related?" she asked. This was the best she could come up with.

"Yes, Andrew is my son."

"Nice to meet you," I said. She had a nice smile, a smile with genuine kindness. Maybe she cared about Dad, I thought.

"Alyce is a student at Villanova."

"Really," I said. I tried to sound like I cared. I wanted to care. I wanted Dad to think I cared. "What are you studying?"

"International business and economics. I want to travel the world."

"Has my dad offered you a job yet?" I wasn't beneath being coy.

"I should. Alyce is a National Merit Scholar with minors in Spanish, French, Korean, and Arabic."

"And a four-point-oh student," she added, clearly proud of herself. Pretty and smart: There always seemed to be a shortage of girls in that department because they don't stay on the market very long.

"I feel like I'm on a job interview," she said.

"Maybe you are, Sweetheart."

"Would you rather work at Dad's hedge fund or the Company?" I asked. Dad looked irritated.

"Definitely the Company," he said. "I'm going to wind down the hedge fund. It was just a side project anyway. A way of proving a point to your Grandfather."

"Ten years is a long time to prove a point," I said. He smiled at her.

"Definitely the chemical company," Alyce said. "I have lots of ideas."

Dad kissed her lips then turned to me. "We've been seeing each other for five months now, Andrew." Our food and drinks arrived. *Is Dad getting serious with Alyce?* I took a bite of one of my wings for momentary respite from the conversation. They caught Alyce's attention.

"Do you mind if I try one? They look delicious," she said. There was an innocent quality to her.

"Sure, they're pretty spicy, though."

"I like hot food." She took a wing, dipped it in the extra hot sauce, and took a bite. She was trying to impress me.

"Andrew, Alyce is the first woman I have loved since your mother," Dad said, squeezing Alyce's hand.

"Oh, Peter, you are so sweet," she said.

"Well, we've been talking a lot lately about the future, our future, and Alyce and I have decided to get married. I wanted you to be the first to know," Dad said.

"Peter! You mean...the topic has come up a few times, but I didn't think you were seriously considering marriage. Not yet at least. You're serious?" Alyce asked.

"Yes, I am. It has been that kind of day for our family." She leaned into him and gave him a protracted kiss.

"So, that's a 'yes' then?" Dad asked her.

"Yes. I could *never* say 'no' to you." She gave him another long smooch and afterwards, Dad became aware of how awkward things had become for me.

"Let's cool things down a bit in front of Andrew," Dad continued. "Why don't you take your phone over to the bar and search online for an engagement ring while Andrew and I have a father-to-son chat?" He stood up to escort her.

"Okay," Alyce said, happy to comply with his request. He walked her to the bar, and she gave him three short kisses.

"I love you," he said. Dad turned and began to walk back to where I was seated.

"Peter," Alyce yelled to Dad when he was almost to our table. He turned around in time to catch her as she ran into his arms. "You never gave me a budget for the ring," she continued, after a long, passionate kiss.

"Surprise me."

"Really?"

"Yeah. What can I say? I've completely fallen for you," he told her. She released him and he finally sat down at our table.

"Congratulations," I said.

"Thanks, son."

"No budget? You are getting soft in your old age."

"Not hardly. It's a test. She is an economics major, remember," Dad explained.

"What do you mean?" I asked in response.

"Well, relationships can be understood in terms of economic concepts like supply and demand. The give and take or push and shove is what makes a relationship work or not work, just like any country's economy," he explained.

"I don't follow you."

"It's a test because Alyce has to choose a ring, but I didn't give her a budget," Dad said. "If she chooses a ring that is too cheap, then it tells me that she doesn't value herself properly, and sooner or later, I'll begin to see her as a bottom dollar acquisition. It's an invitation for exploitation. On the other hand, if she chooses a ring that is too expensive, then eventually I'll see her as high maintenance because it'll put stress on our relationship, our personal economy, if you will. If I start to feel that the cost of maintenance is too high, I'll have to address things in a manner that'll shift control to my advantage, either by making certain demands, which you can think of like taxes or other regulations, or by breaking off the relationship completely if the strain becomes too great for the price tag required."

"Okay," I said.

"Alyce has to think and get this right, not only this time, but every time because our relationship is in constant flux. She has to identify the variables that matter and keep them in equilibrium, or we won't be happy together. She understands; she knows there are rules."

"And she still wants to be with you?"

"Yes. You see, the rules exist for everybody whether we believe it or not. That's where your mother and I went wrong. The economics of our marriage became irreversibly imbalanced, and no bailout could save us," Dad said.

"I still can't believe you are engaged," I said. "She's young enough to be your daughter."

"What's wrong with that? She's beautiful and smart. And we get along," Dad answered.

"How old is she, twenty-one?"

"Twenty-four. She needed more time with all of those language minors. Listen, I really like her, so make an effort for me, okay?"

"I will." I meant it, too. Even if we didn't get along, I wanted Dad to be happy. "Acheson men aren't very good with women, are we?" I asked.

"What do you mean? I'm doing okay." He seemed offended by my comment.

"Well, Grandfather never remarried after Grandmother Maria died, you and Mom couldn't work things out, and I can't attract the only woman I've ever had feelings for."

"Did you see Jennifer today?" he asked.

"Yeah. I dropped in to check on her. She's taking the terrorist attack on the cruise ship hard. I should have never invited her to join us on the family vacation with Mom." I paused. "I asked her to marry me. Sometimes it scares me how similar our behavior can be."

"What? Isn't she seeing someone? That Geoff guy, right?"

"Yeah."

"Son, you can't be so desperate. It comes across as pathetic."

"About as pathetic as a rich man marrying a girl half his age," I countered. He gave me a stern look but otherwise ignored my comment. Only a small part of him really cared what I thought of him, and that piece was buried deep beneath many years of self-righteousness.

"Look, Andrew, no matter what anyone tells you, women want men who are strong and confident, not men that grovel at their feet. They want a guy who is strong enough to leave them behind when they are acting crazy."

"Sometimes, I wonder if you are a misogynist."

"Please. I have been good to every woman who has been in my life, even your mother. In fact, she is the one who actually left me, but let's not get distracted, son. You have to think of it like this: You are a misogynist if you are weak because women do not need weak men."

"Now you're talking crazy," I said.

"Think about it: Women destroy their lives by committing to weak men. When we decide to be weak, we willfully destroy every woman linked to us."

"Just like Mom. You never appreciated her."

"You're right, just like your mother, but I'm different now. You know that," Dad said. He was proud of who he had become. "How about you?"

"What do you mean?"

"Are you weak? Are you a misogynist?"

"I don't know," I answered.

"Well, now that you are working with me, I will teach you to find your inner strength. Who knows, maybe one day Jennifer will see you differently?" I wanted to believe him, but that was a dangerous thought. Even though most young men fantasize about being the kind of man that women love, I didn't want to be a consumer of women like Dad. *But engagement...maybe he had changed? But the heart is a dangerous battlefield best left to poets and musicians.*

I took a long drink from my recently refilled ice water and prepared for the rising inferno.

"Dad, why haven't we ever gotten along like a normal father and son?" I asked.

"What do you mean?"

"We've never been close. I've never felt close to you."

"I've always done the best that I can, son," he offered. He seemed to really believe what he was saying.

"Then why have I always felt alone? You've always put work and your own life first."

"Are you going through something right now? Is this about your grandfather?"

"I don't know. Have you ever really felt close to me, Dad?"

"You're my son. Of course I feel close to you. I've raised you the best way I know how. Dad was always hard on me. And it's the only way I know. I've always felt that it was my responsibility to work hard and put food on the table, to try and forge the best life possible for us," he said.

Suddenly, I couldn't take my attention off of my glass of water. It was a nervous habit: Spinning it around and around on the table.

"Listen, starting tomorrow, we are partners. It is a second chance for us," Dad continued. "I know I wasn't around much when you were a kid, but we are going to be together every day now. Father and son. You are going to like working in management because a lot of exciting things are happening at the Company. We have a few break-throughs that we are preparing to announce to the public. The world is about to change, and you get the opportunity to be a part of it."

"Why didn't you even try when I was a kid?" I asked.

"I don't know that I didn't. Your mother was always the nurturer. When she left me, I was lost. I let your grandfather step in. I grew up without my mother and I survived. I knew you would, too," Dad said. "Even after your problems with drug addiction, I knew you would be okay. You always found a way to cope because you have the Acheson inner strength."

"You sound just like him."

"I know. He was really proud of our family, of what we've been able to accomplish," he said, ignoring his siblings' vast failures.

"I really miss him."

"I miss him too, son. Even though we never got along, I just wanted him to be proud of me. Things are going to be different between you and me now," Dad said.

"I still don't understand what happened. Why hasn't his body been found? Why aren't there any leads?" I asked.

"Son, we worked very closely with the FBI, you know that. We also hired our own investigators and spent several million dollars trying to find out what happened," Dad said and then paused to take a sip of his drink. All of this seemed difficult for him to put into words; it was his father, after all. "There is a lot about your grandfa-ther that you don't know. He was involved in some crazy stuff with people that do not take 'no' for an answer."

"What kind of stuff? What people?"

"I don't know exactly. Everything is just incomplete. I'm not sure we will ever have answers."

"Do you think he was murdered?"

"Maybe. It is a real possibility, Andrew."

"Why didn't you tell me?"

"I don't know. I know how much you loved him. I wanted to have something concrete before coming to you," Dad stated, but it wasn't comforting.

"Are there any reports I can look at?"

"Yes, there are reports from the FBI and from our PI firm. I'll make sure you get copies tomorrow."

This was all too much for me. Too much information. Too much confrontation. Too much failure.

"There is also the possibility that he just disappeared," Dad added.

"But for this long? Surely he would have shown up to ask for help before today, right? He's legally dead now. His will has set things in motion that cannot be changed now even if he is still alive." A flicker in his eye, a mood change, made me shudder.

"Dad, are you glad that he is gone?"

"Why would you ask that?"

"You like being in control of the Company. It is what you always wanted, right?"

"I don't like where you are going with this, son. I want him back as much as you do. I wish our last conversation had been different. We had a disagreement, and he left the office in anger. I never got the chance to make things right."

"What was your conversation about?"

"It doesn't matter now, just a work disagreement. I wish I'd handled myself better. I was so angry with him at the time. Now, my anger with myself grows with each passing day."

"When are we going to do a funeral?" I asked.

"Well, several months ago, your aunt, uncle, and I decided to do it one week from the reading of the Will if nothing developed in the meantime. But now, your grandfather has given them twenty-four hours before he reaches out from the grave and sends them into exile," he said and paused.

"So, now what?"

"I guess we probably won't have a ceremony now."

"That's unacceptable. He deserves some sort of send off, Dad."

"Son."

"Can't we move up the ceremony or something?"

"Listen, Albert and Hannah aren't answering their phones. I've already tried."

"You need to try harder. Go over to their homes and try to get this set up for the morning. If we aren't proactive, we are going to have another shared memory we regret at the graveyard next week when Grandfather's entire family isn't present to lay him to rest," I said. I pushed my chair away and stood up with the flair of a seven-year-old girl. I didn't care if anyone noticed; I was ready to leave.

"That's not how we were going to do it, Andrew," Dad said. I was shocked. *No graveyard service? How were we going to say goodbye then?* "We were going to plant an orchard in his honor." I could live with this concession: A service that utilized the imagery of life from death made sense to me. "That's not exactly something we can do a rush job on."

"Well, you better figure something out then," I said, pulling on my jacket.

"I'll let you know what the plan is at work in the morning. Prepare yourself for something involving just the two of us. Your great aunt Eva is supposed to fly in next week, but I guess everything is up in the air now." Eva: Grandfather's half sister that he raised as a young man. I'd never met her. She'd moved to California to attend college and never came back east.

"You can't be serious about work. We're never going to get along."

"Maybe you need to take your own advice and try harder. Everyone is counting on you now."

"See you in the morning," I said. I looked over at the bar and made eye contact with Alyce, waved goodbye, and left the building. For her sake, I hope Dad wasn't going to put her through one of his *xanax romances*, a crash course in artificial bliss. I hoped love between them was authentic.

I decided to sleep in my old apartment that night for one last time. In my meager means, I could only afford a modest one-bedroom downtown. It's always a mess, and I couldn't seem to bring myself to keep it in order. It didn't matter, I told myself. I wouldn't have to worry about it anymore because I could now spread out my chaos in the expanse of Grandfather's estate.

I parked my bike around the corner from my building in my usual spot and walked up to the outer door. Out of the corner of my eye, I saw them, but it was too late. I took a heavy fist to the jaw and stumbled sideways, dropping my keys. It took all of my strength to keep my temper from erupting.

"What took you so long to get home?" my cousin, Eduardo asked. He's college age, built like a bodybuilder, and one of uncle Albert's many children. Two of his half siblings accompanied him. The oldest girl is in her mid-twenties—Amelie. But I couldn't remember the younger girl's name. She's thirteen or fourteen—*Sandy or something like that?*

"What did I do to deserve that?" I demanded.

"You know, we don't like your attitude, cousin," Eduardo answered, bowing up to me like a gorilla. "We don't think it's fair that you got so much more from Grandfather than us. What makes you so special?"

"Well, that's not my fault. I was just as surprised as you were today," I said.

"That's bull and you know it," Amelie said. "You know that most of us don't stand a chance of qualifying for the grandchildren's trust. I'm not smart enough to get a Ph.D.".

"I'm sure you'll figure it out," I suggested and started to look for my keys on the ground.

"No, you don't understand. Teaching at university is a dream of mine. I've already applied to a dozen schools, but no one will accept me," she continued.

"And I've just been dishonorably discharged by the Army for fighting," Eduardo interrupted. "No G.I. Bill for me now, man."

"What do you want me to do about it? I didn't ask for all of this. I would trade it all just to have him back," I said. I found the keys on the stoop and bent over to retrieve them. Eduardo saw the opening and seized it, pushing me to the ground. My anger smoldered.

"You can give us some of your money for starters," he demanded.

"And jobs," Amelie added. "You've had all the advantages; now you can help your family out. Our dad says that you should feel obligated."

"What about your dad? He's rich now. Ask him to help out," I said. I found my feet and buried my motorcycle helmet deep into Eduardo's stomach. With the wind knock out of him, it was his turn to kiss the ground. Amelie rushed to his side. Sandy looked like she wanted to fight, but I wanted no part of hurting a kid.

"You want some of this, Sandy?" I said, hoping to scare her. She kicked me in the shin and then in the balls: hard. I joined Eduardo back on the ground, and I had to admit, I probably deserved it.

"You're so mean. And I'm Sasha. *Sandy* is our little sister," she said, standing over me. *Can't I get anything right?*

Amelie helped Eduardo to his feet, while I writhed in pain.

"No, our dad says that we are on our own. It's just like it's always been," Amelie said. She helped her siblings into her beat-up sedan, and with some effort, she got the engine to turn over. "Listen, I'm sorry about all of this, Andrew. I'd like to talk to you about this again later. Please, make time for us. Please." She drove off.

"You okay, man?" I looked up and saw a bum in the street staring at me.

"I hope so."

"If you want to call the police, I'd be happy to be a witness. I saw everything," the bum continued. He left his shopping-cart-suitcase in the road, extended his hand, and assisted me upright.

"No, that's okay. Family issues." He accepted the few dollars I found in my wallet.

"Thanks. Thanks a lot, man. I really appreciate it," the bum said. I gave him my gratitude with a customary nod.

Finally in the safe confines of my apartment, I needed to find a way to decompress. I turned on an old Bruce Lee kung fu film and punished my body with alternating sets of pushups and sit-ups. Bruce epitomized the classic underdog hero with his unassuming stature yet invincible persona. *Underestimate him at your own peril.* The film made me feel I had the potential to overcome any obstacles life placed in my path. The world was robbed of witnessing Bruce's greatest achievements when he died at the age of thirty-two under mysterious circumstances. Like the John F. Kennedy assassination, there is no shortage of conspiracy theories regarding his death.

When the film finished, I was inspired by my frustration, and even though it was 2:00 a.m., my electric guitar called to me from the corner of my living room. *Will I always get joy out of playing distorted power chords? Would I even like music if hard rock and grunge didn't exist?* For me, angst was the gateway to all music, and I am thirteen all over again. No prescription is more effective for disappointment than a musical creation. Somehow, the promise to play for only fifteen minutes turned into two hours; my blood pumped, and my mind galloped along paths of sharp regret, misery, and the hope for a satisfied life so big that it could not possibly come true. Failure always lurks in the shadows, but for a moment, my musical high diminished my insecurities.

In my exhaustion, I overslept. Noon. Not a good way to start my first day as an executive. *Was I really going to try and make this work?* The Company needed to get used to my patterns, and it might as well start from day one. I flicked on the news station on my shower radio while I washed away the stale crust of yesterday's adventures. President Jackson had declared war this morning on The Midnight Veil and any nations harboring them and promised retribution, American vengeance, on any parties involved in yesterday's atrocity. It was an off-the-shelf serving of political saber metric psychobabble. I didn't vote for Jackson. I didn't vote for anyone in the last election. All politicians were the same opportunistic egomaniac to me. They just happened to come in different shapes and sizes. But they all wanted the same thing. Power. The more, the better, and their avarice was insatiable. But Jackson was right; The Midnight Veil should be brought to justice for murdering all of those innocent people on the cruise ship.

The local news segment reported that Grandfather had been declared legally dead. Hannah and Albert had called a press conference this morning disclosing the information and had taken the opportunity to announce that they were both moving to Monte Carlo. They failed to mention that this was a condition of their inheritance, but it was a good choice for them. *Perhaps they could avoid some estate tax liability as citizens of the glamorous city-state.* Odds were a tax would be levied at the craps table every time luck was against them. I couldn't help but be jealous. They had no responsibilities.

By 1:00 p.m., I made it to the Company's building downtown. The security guard at the checkpoint in the lobby informed me that my office upstairs had been prepared for my arrival. The elevator provided me transport to the lofty heavens of the 30th floor and the Executive Suite.

Upon disembarking from the elevator, I was greeted by Grace, who was to be my new executive assistant. For how long was the question. She appeared to be about seventy, but she was experienced, as she had worked for Grandfather for as long as I could remember. I was shocked when she led me to the old man's office.

"This is mine? I'm not sure I'm comfortable with this," I said. It was bigger than my entire apartment. Some of his personal items were boxed up and deposited in the corner of the room, giving a feeling of finality to all of this. Why wasn't I more prepared to deal with it?

"Do you want to use your Grandfather's furnishings or would you like to start from scratch and order something new?" Grace asked me.

"I don't know. What do you think I should do?"

"You should do whatever you want, son," Dad said. He had entered into the room undetected behind me.

"Good morning," I said.

"You mean, good afternoon. I'm glad you made it in today," he said with a thick slice of sarcasm.

"Well, it's your first day. There's no point in getting crazy."

"Maybe I should let you boys talk," Grace said.

"No, that's okay; I just wanted to pop in. Andrew, why don't we set a meeting for eight a.m. tomorrow to start working through things," Dad said.

"Okay. I'll try to be in that early."

"You'll get used to the new schedule. I won't make you work my crazy hours, but I will have to insist that you keep regular hours. We'll talk about it in the morning. Oh, I almost forgot. I'm meeting with your aunt and uncle tonight at seven p.m. at the airport. We're going to have dinner and a little ceremony for Dad before they leave. If you want, you should come."

"Okay," I answered. Dad left the room, and I was relieved for the reprieve.

"Peter offered to let you have his office if you would rather trade with him," Grace said.

"That's not a bad thought, I guess," I said.

"His office is about the same size of this one, but the view is better here," she said.

"True." Dad's office has a view of the city, while Grandfather's has a view of the river. "I think I'll stay here." I knew the choice would irk him a bit. He must have had his eye on Grandfather's office.

"And what about the design?" Grace asked again. My phone buzzed. The call was blocked on my caller ID.

"Why don't you come up with several suggestions for later? I'm going to take this call."

"All right, I'll have something prepared then," Grace said. She left me alone in the office.

Even though it was against my personal protocol to answer blocked numbers, my gut told me to answer the phone. "This is Andrew."

"Mr. Acheson, it is important that we meet immediately," the voice on the other side said.

Traffic was heavy on I-95. My Vincent motorcycle zipped between the travelers enslaved inside their hybrids, busses, and eighteen-wheelers. On my bike, I felt exposed, but free in the autumn breeze. Mr. Richardson, Grandfather's attorney, had given me some instructions. Apparently, Grandfather rented a room year round at the Renaissance Hotel in Manhattan, a secret room that Richardson just discovered. Now that Grandfather was gone, someone needed to go and collect his personal effects. In a private memorandum to Richardson, Grandfather insisted that the existence of this room remain secret upon his death to everyone except me.

There were so many questions. What could Grandfather possibly need a private hotel room for? Did he keep a mistress? Was it a secret rendezvous point or just a private retreat? The possibilities accumulated faster than the number of vehicles on the highway. Would I even be able to tell what was going on once I got into his room?

Thankfully, it is just a 100-mile trip between Philadelphia and New York City. I found a parking space in a nearby alleyway; no need to pay the sixty dollars a day Times Square rate for parking when you have a bike. I pulled the keycard from my wallet once I was in the bustling lobby. Room 1807. I found the elevators and got to the eighteenth floor. To my surprise, the key card worked without any hitches, and I entered the room.

It was a basic corner suite with two bedrooms and a nice common room, not very large, but lush in design and sparkling clean. Inside the closet of the first bedroom, I found some of Grandfather's clothes. The lone standout, his old leather jacket that he loved, hung on a hook. It wasn't your standard cowhide or lambskin, but rather thick horsehide. *The only leather that is waterproof,* he would educate anyone who showed interest. He took pride in them; he had a new one ordered every three years. I tried it on like I did so many times when I was a boy, a bit small for me now, but I could make it work.

Over on the desk, I found some newspapers and mail. The most recent newspaper was dated just over a year ago. A small brown package sat at the bottom of the pile, and it had *my* name on it. In thick blue ink, in Grandfather's scrawl, my name stared at me. *Andrew Acheson.* Its presence on the perfect brown paper was almost profane. *How long had this package been sitting here?* The package was unaddressed. *Was he going to mail it to me or give it to me personally? What happened to the old man?*

I picked up the parcel. It was solid, but not too heavy, just about a pound. It didn't feel right opening the package because it had never been given to me. But my name was on it. *Did Grandfather want me to find it here?*

The paper yielded to my will as I tore it away like a baby on his birthday. I couldn't believe what I found inside. Grandfather's cigar box. And inside the box, among other things, was a note addressed to me.

My thoughts drifted to Bubba at the equine therapy ranch. It's been nearly fifteen years, and the horse may not even be alive anymore. I should have given a better goodbye, but our final moment consisted of Bubba eating an apple out of my hands, an act repeated nearly every day of my stay. But our simple relationship was made complex by the guarantee of routine. The day that Grandfather met me in the fields of the Back in the Saddle Ranch set me on a path that changed my life because it instituted a new routine, a routine built upon human frailty.

Grandfather had confronted Dad about my extended therapy. The two heavyweights went at it for weeks. The continuous sparring exhausted Dad, and he agreed that Grandfather would take over my reconstruction. That's when my time on the porch began with the music, the philosophical discussions, and Grandfather's outpatient drug addiction therapy. Grandfather's unorthodox methods worked. He believed that if he could guide my mind to a place of transcendence, I would no longer need heroin.

At first, it was the music that lifted me. It pleased him when I loved a song that he treasured, too. What is it about human nature that when someone loves the things we cherish, we get a sense of pride that only the creator should feel? After a few weeks, he incorporated discussions on philosophy, religion, and science. His approach was methodical, but with the unpredictable improvisation of jazz. *A mind put to work on the problems of the world is a productive mind indeed.* Soon, the memories of my mistress, Heroin, faded into the shadows that inhabit the frontiers of the mind. Grandfather gave assignments like *if you could redesign the United States Government from the ground up, what would it look like? If you were exiled on a desert island and could take three studio albums of music, what would you take? Or was the invention of the pencil more important than the invention of the Internet?* All assignments were taken seriously. If I couldn't respond to his satisfaction, then it would become a written homework assignment. Desperate to please him, sometimes I feigned ignorance just so I could take an assignment home. *Did he know that?*

We met every evening for two hours until I graduated from high school. After that, it became more infrequent, but we tried to meet at least once a week. I adored Grandfather, but the therapy sessions on his porch transformed me. The more I was with him the more I loved him. I wanted to be just like him. I worshiped him.

I remembered my eighteenth birthday, the day Grandfather first offered me one of his cigars. He had boasted about its serotonin-boosting properties, a pure and natural high. I asked him one time why he never marketed it to the world. "There are some creations so beautiful that they should only be shared between loved ones," he answered.

I never missed him more than in that moment, in the hotel room, opening his cigar box. I hadn't indulged in one of his "classics" in more than a year. and there weren't any inside the old cigar box in my hands. But along with the letter, another curiosity hid in the hand-made oak container.

"Dearest Andrew," the letter began. "I know how much this old box meant to you. I had hoped that one day I would have the chance to teach you how to make your own. But these are difficult times, and I am honored to give you mine. I know no one will appreciate it quite like you do. I need you to sit down for what I have to say next."

Why do people always say that?

"I am in trouble and I need your help," the letter continued. My legs turned into a pile of Cheese Whiz. *What is going on?* I found the bed before my face found the floor.

"Evil forces are at work that I cannot discuss. It would be too dangerous to put into writing. I'm not sure who I can trust beyond you, my boy. I need you to look deep into your soul and understand what I'm asking you to do. Inside this box, you will find one green pill. It is full of very dangerous drugs, chemicals that I have spent my life designing, but they have a beneficial side effect. Ingesting this pill would likely kill most people. But not you. You are strong and come from good stock. You are an Acheson. I need you to take the pill and then come and find me. With any luck, I am still alive and I will explain more when we are reunited. Burn the letter before ingesting the pill. Burn it. If you decide not take the pill, flush it down the toilet and tell no one about the contents of this box. But know that you will go to your grave a great disappointment to me and to yourself. Your loving Grandfather, David."

How loving indeed. I took the singular green pill out of the envelope in the box. Inside on a slip of paper read, "Be precisely 187.0 pounds when you take this pill. Find the scale under the bed." I looked under the bed and sure enough, I found a scale.

Beyond being bizarre, how could Grandfather ask me to take *dangerous* drugs...*kill most people?* He knew everything I had been through.

He must be in trouble. He must still be alive. I wanted to believe it. My heart required it, but this was too much to ask of anyone. I stepped onto the scale. 190 pounds. I decided to weigh myself naked. *Was I really considering doing this?* I came in at 187.5 on the scale. That is the exact weight I had checked in at for the last three years at work. Well, a mile of running would probably burn off some water weight, I thought. And running would give me a chance to consider all of the possibilities.

But I didn't have any exercise gear. I searched the drawers and found some running shorts and a t-shirt. In the closet, I found a pair of running shoes. They were exactly my size. Grandfather had planned for every contingency and clearly expected me to follow through; he didn't want me to find any reason to back out. *Couldn't someone else do this, I wondered? What about Dad? Should I just call him? What about Sanderson Richardson IV? Surely he would know what to do.* But Grandfather said to trust no one. *What would Jennifer do?* I felt like an orphan.

I realized that I wasn't going to make it to the Philadelphia airport to see my Aunt and Uncle off to Monte Carlo and for whatever ceremony Dad had been able to put together. I decided not to call Dad and give him a heads up because I didn't want to have to explain. I turned off my cell phone.

After changing, I took to the streets, but Manhattan at 4:30 pm on a Friday is not a good place to get into a running rhythm. For forty minutes, I desperately did my best to work up a sweat while dodging hordes of tourists and droves of workers released from the dam of gainful employment. In between weaving, I attempted to make sense of everything, but resolution seemed like a fairytale dangling from the horizon. Life is oppressive. *No one should ever need to count on me for anything.*

Only love could save me from such disastrous decisions, but Jennifer didn't love me. She couldn't love me in the way I needed her to. Mom. A mother always loves her son, but the distance and years between us had exacted a toll too heavy to recover from. She wouldn't understand. Dad. I know he cared, but love isn't what drove our relationship. Grandfather loved me, but it had been a year. A very long year. I couldn't be certain he was even alive. Besides, my heart told me that familial love wouldn't be enough anymore. I needed a muse, someone to push me to greatness. But there was no one for me. I felt there would never be inspiring moonlight in my midnight of despair.

I returned to the hotel with a heart full of obligation. My life was not my own; my family had staked a claim on it a long time ago. There was nothing left to do but strip down again and return to the scale. 186.60 pounds. I cursed myself for running too long. Could I drink a liter of water to make up the weight? *How was this supposed to work?* In my experience it was never a good idea to take drugs on a full stomach, especially a stomach full of liquid.

I burned the letter and note regarding the pill with Grandfather's custom lighter that sat in the cigar box. What did I have to lose? If I died, at least I wouldn't have to go back to the office and work. The thought brought major relief. Maybe I always preferred death. *Besides, Jennifer doesn't love me.* I put my clothes back on. If I was going to die, I wanted the hotel hospitality crew to find me looking my best. Wearing Grandfather's jacket seemed apropos.

I put the pill in my mouth and swallowed it down with a quarter liter of cool water from the mini-bar. Instantly, the only thing I could think of was how bad a decision this was—college graduates are supposed to be able to think rationally. My mind spun a million miles a minute: This wasn't a recreational drug; it was engineered. Was it addictive? I would never survive another round of detoxification. It could be worse: Grandfather said I could die. *Death*. I wasn't ready to die. I'm too young with too much I dreamed to experience. I should have thought about this more; I should have put days into the decision if necessary. "Only fools follow," Grandfather used to tell me. Then I felt the sensation. Exhilaration. Elation. Invincibility. A familiar feeling, yet exponentially deeper, like I could feel every bit of matter within my body. Then it happened. At first I thought it must be an effect of the drugs. The skin on my hands disappeared, evaporated away like a glass of water on a hot day. I ripped off Grandfather's leather jacket and my dress shirt. I watched my bones pop out from underneath my musculature, but the feeling remained fantastic. I had never felt this pleased in all my life. *Even if death awaits me, it was worth it to feel this way, even if it was only for a single fleeting moment.* I saw the remnants of my fleshy smile in the mirror before everything went florescent red.

The sensation dissipated, and I felt free. I looked down at myself and noticed my nude body. *What happened?* Everything was surreal. I looked into the mirror; I looked okay. Everything seemed normal about my face and body, and all of my bones appeared to be in their proper places. Other than a thin haze in my mind, I felt normal. I felt strong.

Where are my clothes? I looked around the room. The style had changed, everything from the bed to the curtains. *This is some trip Grandfather has put together.* He must be laughing about this somewhere, I thought. Then, I started to second-guess myself. Was I even in the same room? *Where are my stupid clothes?* I tore through the drawers and closets. Nothing. In the other bedroom, to my relief, I found some a single pair of crispy, new boxers, a pair of faded jeans, a Blues Breakers t-shirt, and a pair of sneakers all in my size, yet retro like the room's décor. *They will do until I can find something more suitable.*

A set of papers on the table stared at me. When I picked up the document on the top of the stack, I almost choked. Led Zeppelin. In concert. Nassau Coliseum, Uniondale, New York. June 14, 1972. *Could this be some sort of joke? Zeppelin hasn't toured in years.*

Underneath the concert ticket was a copy of the *New York Times*. In pen, next to a headline about strife in the Middle East, the date was circled and the following phrase was scribbled in bold writing: "Follow the White Rabbit".

I must be in some sort of drug-induced dream state. I looked outside my window. Times Square still bustled, but the streets were filled with people dressed as if they were filming a movie from the 1970s. Even the cars were authentic. I took pride in my mind's ability to create such a vivid fantasy.

Back on the table, I found a set of directions to the Coliseum and ten twenty-dollar bills. The cash was in the old style I remembered from my childhood, all dated before 1970. I figured I had nothing to lose if this was a dream. *Might as well see how far my mind would take this before I wake up.* The directions were in feminine handwriting I did not recognize.

I grabbed the key from the table and tested it on the front door. It worked. Cash in pocket and directions in hand, I ventured out of the room. I avoided contact in the lobby, and everyone seemed content to ignore me. This was New York, even in my dream, and everyone was content to let me be a part of the dynamic background, as long as I didn't get in the way. The doorman informed me that it was 5:47 p.m. and that it was indeed Wednesday, June 14, 1972. He didn't bat an eye at the strange nature of my questions. *Hey, it's New York.*

I looked for my motorcycle parked behind the hotel. It wasn't there. I thought of filing a police report, but curiosity propelled me forward. I needed to see how far this dream would go. The subway took me to Penn Station. The directions said to take the Long Island Railroad to Hempstead Station. I used some of the vintage cash to buy a ticket.

The train ride gave me time to think as the cityscape rolled by my eyes. *What was going on? What was Grandfather trying to accomplish with all of this? Why was it so important for me to take the pill? When was I going to wake up?* Led Zeppelin is one of my favorite bands. In the broad importance of rock and roll, they are in the pantheon right next to The Beatles. Their influence could be heard everywhere from Metallica to Lenny Kravitz to Coldplay. Every rock fanboy wanted to play like Jimmy Page and sing like Robert Plant. Just ask Slash and Axel Rose. *Why was my dream taking me to this place?*

The train reached my stop on Long Island. I hopped a bus for a short trip to the stadium. When I stepped off of the vehicle, my mind focused on the ultimate drug. Music.

My seat, located front and center of the energized arena, waited for me. *Why would my mind have it any other way?* I was relieved that I hadn't missed anything, but of course, my mind would always wait for me. I prayed that it wouldn't wake me before the conclusion of this glorious dream.

An uproar of appreciation shook the room as the band took the stage. They looked as I had always imagined them, skinny and dressed in tight flamboyant costumes. They were already damp with salty saturation. I wondered if they smelled.

Bonham wasted no time getting started. His sticks and skins exploded to life, leaving no doubt of their masculinity. Page and Jones followed with the unmistakable riff from "Immigrant Song," its power pulsing through the eager audience. By the time Robert Plant began his trademark wail, my heart threatened to implode within my chest like I was a thirteen-year-old geek at a midnight show of the latest *Star Wars* flick.

The crowd sang in unison. While our lungs fought for the air needed to fill the arena with our sonic jubilations, our posteriors never found the comfort of our expensive seats. From the fury of "Heartbreaker" to the ubiquitous "Stairway to Heaven" to the groundbreaking "Dazed and Confused," the band was flawless. *Should I have expected anything less?*

More than anything, I wanted Robert to acknowledge my existence. Did that make me a common school girl? Maybe. But this was my dream, *and who was ever going to find out?* I got my wish during "Moby Dick." Page was busy setting the atmosphere on fire with his phat instrumental riffing, and Robert engaged the front row, squeezing as many hands as possible. When he reached my hand, it almost felt like a bit of power transferred his greatness to me. Perhaps every rock lover kneels in the presence of his hero, no matter how irrational the act seems? But I couldn't escape how *real* his hand felt.

After the concert, I splurged on a cab and made my way to my room at the hotel. Music buoyed my mind as I drifted in the chaotic flow of New York City at night. My smile spiked my blood stream, and soon unconquerable thoughts flowed outward as I observed sanitation workers, third-shift laborers, and women of the night navigate the artificial light that penetrated our communal shadows. *Darkness can be empowering.* Some of us are programmed to run from it. *Good for them.* Others openly seek it, blinded by its cloak of endless pleasure, which feeds a concealed and insatiable appetite for inevitable and perpetual spiritual suicide. But folks like me have no choice because the darkness is woven within us. There's no place we can run that the shadow doesn't follow us: *Light provides no sanctuary.* We have to learn to harness the shadow and transform it into something beautiful or we will be devoured by it. Some of us can achieve this by experiencing music, but for people like me, music can only offer a temporary respite. Upon opening the door to my room, in the penumbra, where the shadow finds the light, I was slammed with the biggest surprise of my life.

"How was the concert?" Grandfather asked as he rose from his chair in the hotel room. "Maybe you will agree with me now that Jimmy Page is the best guitarist of all time? Or do we need to go visit Jimi Hendrix to settle this once and for all?"

What's going on? The only thing I could do was hug him. As I inhaled, the familiar smell of tobacco invaded my sinuses, giving me a tickle, as fumes escaped from his old fashioned double-breasted suit.

"I can see that you're speechless, but if we are going to settle this argument, we will have to go back in time since Jimi died a couple of years ago," he continued.

"It's really you? You're still alive?" I reluctantly released him from my vice grip hug and looked him in the eyes. *How was this possible?*

"Yes, Andrew, my boy, I have achieved time travel."

"Am I high right now?"

"Well, yes...and no."

I had to be high because *this was impossible.* How could time travel be a reality? I knew Grandfather was a genius, but this achievement flew beyond mankind's capabilities.

"Whoa," I manage to say. I had the vocabulary of a stoner.

"Andrew, please take a seat, and I'll to fill you in all the details and answer all of your questions," Grandfather said as he led me by the arm and escorted me to a chair. He had a way of getting exactly what he wanted. That's when I noticed that we weren't alone in the room.

She was short, late twenties, and *maybe* slightly overweight, depending on the standard of beauty. The bellbottoms and floral top made it clear that she tried to fit into the crowd, but it was obvious that she was a nerd. The blending of her features maximized her cuteness.

"Who's your friend?"

"My name is Rose. Rose Montoya," she cut in. She had a soft southern accent.

"Actually, it is Doctor Rose Montoya," Grandfather said.

"But you can call me Rose. I don't allow anyone to call me "Doctor" outside of academia. I work for your grandfather. And no. Before you ask, we are not lovers. I just wanted to clear that up. He has been the perfect gentleman." Though awkward to admit, even to myself, she was right, I was curious. I had never seen Grandfather in the company of a woman. In that moment, my heart broke for him. *Why not find a new love?* I had never considered the possibility.

"I plucked Rose out of her post-doctorate program at Duke University to help me. She was the top of her class," Grandfather said. He glanced at her. He was proud of her, and I wondered if he did have feelings for her. "She's the best at what she does."

"And what is that exactly?" I asked.

"I'm a synthetic chemist. I make drugs," Rose said.

"She's a genius," Grandfather added.

"Like you." I'm the only non-genius he regularly associated with.

"Obviously."

I started to feel light headed, and the world grew faint. I fought to stay conscious, but my body wouldn't cooperate. The last thing I remember, Grandfather rushed over to me, and Rose frantically moved around the room as Grandfather barked orders at her. I'd never seen him so fiery before, and I was flattered that it must have been on my account. Of course, under the circumstances, that wasn't a good thing.

My head throbbed like an overfilled helium balloon being squeezed by an unrestrained toddler. I opened my eyes: I laid on a bed with IVs hanging out of my arm. Rose and Grandfather were at a table across the room having a quiet yet intense discussion. *So this wasn't a dream. What Grandfather said must be true.* The moan I bellowed drew their attention, and they joined me at the bed.

"The pain will pass in a few minutes, Andrew, just try to remain still," Grandfather said.

"What is wrong with me?"

"Well, nothing unexpected. We just have to get you acclimated."

Rose drew some blood from my arm. She had decent bedside manner; the needle didn't hurt too much when it hit my vein. Or maybe I was just used to it after being a lab rat in a cage at the Company the last few years. A piece of equipment started to buzz across the room. Rose went over to retrieve the printout.

"Look at this, David," she said to him. I had never heard anyone refer to Grandfather by his first name, especially an employee. "What do you think of the numbers?" He studied it for a moment.

"He is going to be okay, thank God. His blood's returning to normal," Grandfather said. He came over to the bed and squeezed my arm. "I actually thought I might lose you, Andrew."

"What do you mean? I thought you said nothing was wrong?"

"Well, I don't know how to tell you this. You have cancer."

"What! You have to be kidding me! How can I have cancer?" I was screaming. I tried to stand up, but Grandfather, Rose, and the pain in my brain subdued me.

"Because I gave it to you," Grandfather said.

"What?" I was livid. *How and why would he do such a thing?*

"Listen, you will be fine. I have everything under control. I know what I'm doing."

"Then why do I feel like my head is about to explode? How could you do this? When?" Tears formed in my eyes and threatened to flow with learning of this betrayal. I loved Grandfather more than I loved anyone else on this earth, and this is not the way to reciprocate love.

"I did it because I knew you could handle it. I did it because I need you. I need your help."

His desperation seemed to embarrass him. Grandfather had never needed anyone's help before. He couldn't possibly need mine. I was a failure. Completely average at best. *If he needed me, he better be prepared for utter disappointment.*

"I don't understand. How did you do it?"

"Listen. If you calm down, I will try and explain everything," he said. He attempted to pacify me.

"How could you be so selfish?" I looked at Rose to see if she could offer any sympathy. But she stayed out of the discussion and pretended to hide behind of mountain of equipment and a stack of readouts. *Definitely a nerd.*

"Don't be so silly. You aren't the only person in the room with cancer. That's how it works."

"What?"

"The time travel phenomenon...I have the disease, too, my boy."

"This is crazy. I feel like I'm in an episode of the *Twilight Zone.* I'm getting out of here." I struggled to get up once again, but I was too weak.

"I wouldn't do that if I were you. You need me now more than ever. If you don't stay here with me, you will surely die. If the cancer doesn't kill you, our enemies will if they find you. And make no mistake, they're looking," Grandfather said.

"But why me? Why would you want my help? And wait, who's looking for me? I don't have enemies. I haven't done anything wrong." I had many questions and no definitive answers.

"Let's talk about it after we get something to eat. You need to keep your strength up."

Rose and Grandfather dragged me to the deli across the street from the hotel. A twenty-four hour joint, and at three a.m., I was surprised to find it devoid of people. It shouldn't have been; it was New York.

The recent revelations fostered a terror within me that I hadn't felt since my heroin days. Everyone we passed became a suspected enemy. I couldn't help but stare, but in New York that is never a good idea. Grandfather ordered a pastrami and Swiss cheese on rye for me with a glass of water. Neither he nor Rose joined me in this feast. Rose had to lift the sandwich to my mouth. After a few bites, I felt my strength returning to normal levels as the sandwich's distinctive flavors danced their way through my palate.

Rose slid several white pills across the table.

"What are these?"

"Life savers," she replied. It didn't matter. I had to follow along. Compliance was the only thing I excelled at. I swallowed them with a gulp of water. "It's actually just a bit of something to take the edge off of the pain in your head. Is it still bad?"

"Yeah."

"Good, the aspirin should help. It's a miracle drug," she said with a wink and a smile. At least she tried to help me acclimate to this new reality.

"I've got lots of questions."

"And I have lots of answers for you," Grandfather said. "But not here. You must be suspicious of everyone now. You never know who is watching. Paranoia is your best friend." And with that, Grandfather and Rose left the table and exited the building. I had no choice but to follow.

We didn't return directly to the hotel. Grandfather wanted to make sure that we weren't being followed. After an hour, he was satisfied. The roundabout trek gave me a chance to sort out the day's events. *Could I even call it a day?* I was in the past, in a time before I was born. The feeling of seeing Grandfather was indescribable, but the reality of my situation went beyond surreal. Time travel. Mother-flipping time travel. *Grandfather invented time travel. This is the stuff of science fiction. How could this be true? The company I now owned invented time travel. The possibilities...I'm not the right person to be involved in this sort of thing.*

Back in the confines of our hotel, I realized it was too late to get into further discussion. Grandfather and I shared the suite that I had traveled back into, while Rose was set up in the suite across the hall from us.

"Goodnight, David. Goodnight, Andrew," she said and lingered in the hallway. "Welcome to 1972 and welcome to the team."

"See you tomorrow, I guess. Or is it yesterday?" I said. She giggled at me.

"You'll get used to it. I promise," she said before disappearing behind the anonymous doorway.

Once we were inside our suite and alone, Grandfather grabbed me by the arm and pulled me aside with surprising force. "Never trust a coworker, my boy. They can turn out to be the worst enemy."

"Do you mean Rose?" I asked, startled.

"I mean any person you work with, especially those you think you ought to be able to trust. Rose, she may be okay, but you'll never really know. She may end up being just a sweet and naïve scientist that has been swept up into an exciting game of cat and mouse. But the stakes are too high to know until we are at the point of no return."

He gave me a well-meant hug.

"I love you, Grandfather." Overwhelmed, I neared tears. The day had taken its toll.

"I know you do, Andrew. That's why I brought you here." I released him from my grasp and let him go into his own room for the night.

Outside of my room, on the streets of New York below, the world was alive. Somewhere out there, the sun was preparing to shine on a new day. It was real. The past was now my present. For some reason, I couldn't get Grandfather's warning out of my mind. Trust no one. *Could I even trust Grandfather?* He'd gotten me into this mess, and I had the feeling that whatever was coming next could be more devastating than today. I just wanted to go home.

When I stumbled out of my bedroom in the morning, I discovered Grandfather waiting in our common room. He sat at the table before a spread of food.

"I went ahead and ordered lunch for you. I figured you'd be hungry," he said.

"Thanks." He was right. I needed to eat like crazy. I joined him at the table and filled a plate with a little bit of everything: ham, bread, a hamburger, French fries, a banana, and an apple.

"I'm glad to see you still have your appetite. You'll need it."

"I'm sorry if I seem a little slow. My brain feels like it is a few steps behind right now," I said in between bites.

"Well, you will get used to it. I promise. I did. It just takes a few days."

"Okay, I guess I have to take your word on it. I'm in the dark here."

"To be honest, I'm surprised that you made it at all," Grandfather said.

"To breakfast?"

"You mean lunch?" He had a love for precision and accuracy. "No, I was talking about the past. Here to me. You're my only hope.

I've been preparing you for this potential outcome for a long time, but to be honest, I wasn't sure my best would be good enough in the end. But, thankfully you took the pill and here you are."

"Grandfather, why can't we just go home?" I asked.

"Andrew, I hope in due time we can, but that remains to be seen."

"Ok."

"Why don't you fill me in on what happened the last few days?"

"Well, Aunt Hannah has made quite a stir over having you declared dead since you have been missing for over a year now."

"That's not surprising. She's desperate to get her hands on my fortune."

"Yeah, it seems so."

"How did everyone take the reading of the Last Will and Testament of David Acheson?"

"Well, some folks took it better than others. You made the news, of course, but I really didn't catch the full blurb on TV yesterday. Sorry."

"That's all right. Go on," he said. He leaned forward.

"It was really hard to focus. Mr. Richardson took his time, but we were all forgiving under the circumstances."

"What do you mean, Andrew?"

"Oh, of course, how could you know?"

He looked at me funny.

"On the day of the reading of your Will, there was a terrorist attack on a cruise ship in the Mediterranean, northeast of Egypt. The exact number of casualties isn't known yet, but the news media is saying around four thousand people are dead."

"That's terrible. Very, very terrible," Grandfather seemed to take this new information rather hard. "What about your father, how is he taking all of this?"

"He seemed pretty confident, up until the end. I don't think he was expecting to share power in the way you set it up. I think he may even miss you a bit, Grandfather," I said and paused. "Can I ask you something?"

"Of course," Grandfather said.

"Well, why did you insist that Aunt Hannah and Uncle Albert leave the country as a condition of their inheritance?"

"Andrew, I can't expect you to understand what it is like to be a parent, more specifically, what it is like to be good at nearly everything except the things that really matter. I'm a terrible father."

He was right; I didn't know what it was like to be a father, but I sure knew what it was like to be the child of uninterested parents.

"Andrew, they are not capable of taking care of themselves. I insisted that they leave for their own protection. And not a moment too soon, I'm afraid. War is coming."

After lunch, we joined Rose in her suite. Much to my surprise, she and Grandfather had turned it into an improvised lab. She wore a nice late 1960s style flower dress that was mostly covered by her well-worn lab coat.

"Good afternoon. Glad you could join us," Rose said with a little edge in her voice. She took off her goggles and shook my hand again.

"Hello. Sorry. I'll set an alarm or wakeup call or something for next time," I offered. *She would learn soon that I was not someone to be counted on for anything of importance. I would only be able to let her down.*

"Well, let's get down to the nitty-gritty, shall we?" Her enthusiasm showed, but I was too disjointed for her eagerness to be contagious. I wondered if she dreamed about her work at night like other nerds. She handed me a two large pills and a Styrofoam cup.

"What's this?" I asked, in a more belligerent manner than I intended.

"It will save your life. Now drink it immediately, Andrew," Grandfather said. I swallowed the pills without further delay. Lukewarm tap water. I guess bottled water hadn't become popular yet. At least I didn't immediately transport to another time period, I thought.

"What have you told him so far, David?" Rose asked. She must have been surprised at my cavalier attitude.

"Not much, we were just catching up on some family business. Sit down, Andrew. Let's get started," Grandfather said.

"Mind if I butt in real fast before you get started? I need to get his morning data," she said.

"But it's not morning, it is afternoon," I said, trying to both irritate and entertain her at the same time.

"Wise guy, huh?"

"Rose, it's fine, of course," Grandfather consented. With that she took my blood pressure, pulse, and a small vial of blood from my vein.

"Ok, I am going to run this through the spectrometer. Let me know if you need me for anything, David," Rose said. She walked over to one of the machines and prepared the blood sample for some sort of technical analysis.

Grandfather and I settled into two leather chairs away from the lab area. "Should we get started?" he asked after some time.

"Grandfather, are you ok?"

"Sorry, you know that I'm not usually at a loss for words. You would think that after all this time, I would know where to start."

"How about at the beginning," I suggested. I think I detected a stifled giggle from Rose across the room. Grandfather didn't notice, though, or I am sure he would have been irritated. *What was the arrangement between them anyways?*

"Ok then. That will do. We'll try that," he said and steeled himself for what was to come. "You never knew your grandmother, Maria. She meant the world to me. She took this wild animal of a man and tamed me. She accepted my many, many faults and loved me. When her life was stolen away by cancer, I was never the same. I was helpless. I reverted backwards, de-evolved in a way, to what you see now. I became cancer.

"Not just any kind of cancer. I became Schneider's Lymphoma, the cancer that robbed her of her beauty, of her elegance, of her soul. I couldn't get over the loss, my boy. I pray that you will never have to experience anything like it. I was broken. In my grief, I began to personally research a cure. Every moment I wasn't busy running the Company, I was in the lab working with cell cultures and drug candidates. As you can imagine, that didn't leave much time for your dad, your aunt Hannah, or your uncle Albert," Grandfather continued.

"Don't be so hard on yourself," I said.

"Well, I'm afraid the results are obvious," he said. I learned a long time ago there was no arguing with Grandfather once his mind was set, so I just let him continue. "The thing is, I'd lost so much. I knew what bitterness tasted like, and I was tired of having it for a steady diet. Schneider's Lymphoma is a very rare form of cancer. It attacks lymphocytes, which are a type of healthy white blood cells, and makes it difficult for the body to remove waste and fight off infections. The first case was reported in 1947 in Palestine. There are fewer than five new cases of Schneider's diagnosed each year. So, there isn't a whole lot of research being done out there since there isn't a building full of money to be made on a cure."

"What do you mean, Grandfather?" I asked.

"Pharmaceutical companies, even my company—your company— can't afford to be in the business of niche diseases. They have to market to the masses to survive. That is basic economics. A disease with fewer than one hundred living occurrences is a major loser from their perspective."

"What about academia?"

"Researchers at the major colleges and universities of the world are still dependent on grants from the government. Governments want to spend their dollars in a manner that affects the most people," Grandfather said.

"At least that is what they want you to believe," I suggested.

"Very true, Andrew, but no one was interested in studying this obscure form of cancer. And if they were, they were unable to find funding. I did my research, of course."

"You are always thorough."

"Some call me obsessive."

"I'm learning that it's a defining family trait," I said.

"About ten years ago, something peculiar happened in the lab. I discovered a drug that could kill the cancer cells, but unfortunately, it killed healthy red blood cells, too. Now, this isn't a terribly uncommon problem in oncology and hematology, but with Schneider's Lymphoma, not many chemicals would kill it—period."

"Where did you find the drug?" I asked.

"It is actually a natural product. It has a chemical name with fifty-seven syllables, so I just call it 'crown jewelium'. It is a metabolite found in very small concentrations in a creature called *acanthaster planci*, more commonly known as the *Crown of Thorns Starfish*. The species is indigenous to the warm waters in the Pacific Ocean and is actually considered a pest since it eats coral. Greenies organize snorkel parties where folks go diving and spear the creatures in order to protect the reef. They retrieve the bodies in plastic bags so that any young contained inside aren't left in the ecosystem. Kind of puts a new spin on survival of the fittest, huh?"

"It seems kind of barbaric," I admitted. I reached into my pocket for my iPhone in order to google the subject, but remembered I was in 1972.

"Even though the starfish is available in large quantities, it was not practical to produce crown jewelium in the natural way," Grandfather continued.

"What do you mean?"

"Well, I actually tried to extract it, but I found grinding thousands of the creatures in a blender in order to produce just a few milligrams of the crown jewelium distasteful."

"But you're a scientist."

"Yes, but I'm a chemist, not a biologist. I don't like dealing with bodies," Grandfather said. "Besides, having the large quantities of the creatures delivered to the lab raised too many questions; the blasted things reek. So, I devised a total synthesis strategy for crown jewelium, and after a few years, I produced a couple of grams."

"That's it?"

"That's it. Well, the synthesis scheme involved seventy-seven reaction steps and less than a one percent yield."

"Ouch! That sounds terrible."

"Well, that is pretty standard for that type of work. I've done this sort of thing a hundred times. I love solving a puzzle, so I enjoyed it, actually," he said swollen with pride. "That was only the first step. Am I boring you?" he asked and paused.

"No, Grandfather, I enjoy listening to you. After all this time, I'd listen to you read the dictionary," I said. It was true; it was almost like we were back on his porch. "What does the crown jewelium do in the cell?"

"Good question. It affects the mitochondria. The mitochondria are the energy factories in the cells, remember? The jewelium works kind of like a monkey wrench. Throw it in factory's gears and the cell cannot produce energy. Instead of the uncontrolled growth that's characteristic of cancer, the cancer cells die. It is a thing of beauty. Does this make sense?" Grandfather asked.

I nodded.

"After the discovery of the jewelium, what I needed next was targeted delivery," he continued. "What you may not know is that this is one of the Holy Grails of pharmaceutical science. If you discover a way to deliver your drug to only the unhealthy cells and kill only those unhealthy cells, then the Nobel Prize committee calls. Anyway, after many years of research, I managed to achieve it. But of course, there were side effects."

"With great effort, I designed a polymeric dendritic delivery system from scratch. It's quite elegant. This tree-like molecule allowed for the specific targeted delivery to the Schneider's Lymphoma cancer cells and nothing else," Grandfather said.

"Like a tactical nuke?"

"Yes, exactly. The dendrimer acts like a key and opens the cancer cells' membranes like a door. It's perfect. I believed I achieved a miracle, but I was wrong. In science, one breakthrough often gives birth to more problems to solve, like a complex puzzle," Grandfather said.

He was a natural at instruction. I wondered why he didn't enjoy formal teaching.

"The cell studies were a tremendous success. The dendrimers delivered the crown jewelium straight to the cancer cells leaving the healthy cells alone. Perfect apoptosis. Only the healthy cells remained. I began the live animal studies. But, something was different *in vivo*. Everything is different in real life," Grandfather said.

"I was doing a series of rat studies. I gave the rats Schneider's Lymphoma, and I was testing the system I'd created. The dendrimers delivered, but crown jewelium did not pay the price of admission. I was frustrated. But after many tests, I figured out that in the living system, the crown jewelium requires more energy to achieve the proper geometry within the cancer cells. Essentially, the monkey wrench was too small and kept falling through the gears."

"So, what'd you do?" I asked.

"Well, I had to draw deep to figure out an answer. I needed an activator."

"An activator?"

"In this case, Andrew, it's a concomitant chemical to initiate a desired reaction."

"Sort of like a catalyst then?"

"Yes, exactly. You must have paid attention in your general chemistry class in college. I'm proud of you," Grandfather said.

I laughed. I didn't learn too terribly much in my science classes, just enough to pretend to understand what was going on in my conversations with Grandfather.

"So, I needed targeted delivery of the activator to the Schneider's Lymphoma cells. The easiest way to achieve this was to use the same dendrimer system that I had synthesized. I tested a lot of fancy chemicals without success. Then I started testing more traditional compounds. One day, I was beginning a series utilizing Activator 42, and a most peculiar thing happened: All of my rats infected with the cancer disappeared right before my eyes when I gave them the shots of the two dendrimers. They just melted away. It was the most ghastly thing I had ever seen in my life. I couldn't believe it. I thought I was vaporizing them, like spontaneous combustion. Over the course of several weeks, I kept rerunning the experiments with different animals, from rats to rabbits to monkeys, just to be sure I wasn't crazy. Always the same result. I didn't tell anyone, though. It was just too crazy, and I didn't want some animal rights group to get wind of the experiments, throwing paint around, telling the world that I was disintegrating animals."

"That's kind of funny," I said. I laughed and imagined how wrong everyone would have been.

"Yeah, you keep laughing, kid. It wasn't funny to me. There was an accident. Sometimes, that's how the best discoveries are made. I started a study on beagles. Right as I was injecting one of the dogs with the dendrimers, it reached up and took a bite out of the Hershey's bar that I had hanging out of my lab coat pocket. I should've never had any food in the lab in the first place. The three dogs I injected disappeared in the same way, but the one that had taken a bite of my candy bar quickly returned. You know what they say: A lost dog always finds his way home."

"It didn't take long for me to realize that I had made a crazy and unexpected discovery. I tested every animal that I could think of, varying the amounts of dendrimer and chocolate. I always got the same result: Animals with the Schneider's Lymphoma that were injected with the dendrimer and the chocolate always immediately returned. Those without chocolate never returned," Grandfather said.

"This is all very interesting," I said, glued to his incredible story. I could never be a part of anything this important. I just didn't have the same make up as Grandfather, the perseverance, or the propensity for luck necessary for a discovery of this magnitude.

"Thanks, my boy. I'm glad you think so. I completed my animal studies by testing the drug system on healthy animals and animals with different forms of cancer. The phenomenon works on animals that receive my treatment and have Schneider's Lymphoma."

"Okay. This is very crazy. Well, it sounds like you cured the disease, Grandfather."

"Well, there's more. I couldn't be sure I had a viable cure until I did human testing. Of course you understand that this is all against FDA regulations, so it was off the books. So I did what any scientist in my position would have done: I tested it on myself."

"That would mean you gave yourself Schneider's Lymphoma, too, right?"

"Yes, that's right. I've given us both cancer. I've put us both in the same predicament."

"I hope you know what you're doing," I said. He didn't respond. The glow of his sterling confidence disappeared. "What else do I need to know?"

"A lot. There's so much, Andrew. So, so much," Grandfather said. I saw his exhaustion. "Let me try and fill in a few more gaps before we take a break. The more crown jewelium you take, the farther back in time you go. The phenomenon works on a mass-to-drug ratio."

"Is that why I had to be a certain weight?"

"Yes, I left you a premeasured pill that would take you back here to this very specific time if you followed my directions. You did great making weight, by the way."

"Thanks."

"It appears that when the Activator 42 is added to the cancer cells, the energy cascades across all your cells since it is in your blood. It permeates all of your matter, in fact. There's a quantum effect. The best we can tell is that a wormhole is opened and your individual molecules move faster than the speed of light though this wormhole. That is how time travel is achieved."

"You lost me there."

"I know it is hard to comprehend. You almost have to be Einstein to appreciate what is going on," Grandfather suggested. "The bottom line is, the more drugs in your system, the higher the excited quantum state on the molecules in your body and the farther back in time you go."

"Okay. I think I follow you."

"When you eat the chocolate, a chemical present in the cocoa facilitates the relaxation of the excited quantum state back to the ground state."

"All right, you lost me again."

"What I mean is this. If you eat the chocolate, the time travel phenomenon is reversed, and you go back to the time that you came from. I haven't nailed down the mechanism yet, but I believe it is a combination of the flavanols present in cocoa that facilitates the reversal of the quantum effect.

"You need to know something else, too. The entire project is, to this point, basically a failure. I haven't been able to synthesize a human cure for the Schneider's Lymphoma. Unfortunately, the energy from the Activator-42 initiates the quantum effect in the cancer itself, but it doesn't translate the energy to the crown jewelium when introduced in the human body. The addition of the activator unfortunately doesn't kill the cancer in the way that I had hoped. The result is that this time travel phenomenon is limited to those who suffer from Schneider's Lymphoma, and to date there isn't a cure for human patients."

"So, you are saying you gave me a disease that you knew has no cure, Grandfather?" I asked.

"Yes, that's correct," Grandfather replied. I sensed the weight of failure on him, but this recklessness felt like murder and suicide.

"This is crazy. I don't understand why you would do this. How do I even have this disease?"

"You have a right to be upset. You do. I know that. But right now, I need to get some rest. I'm an old man, and I need to take my nap. Rose." She stood up from her lab work.

"Yes, David?" Rose replied.

"It is time for Andrew's physical evaluation, and it is time for my pills. Do you mind taking over?"

"Of course not." Rose gathered several pills from bottles into a plastic cup, filled another plastic cup with water from a pitcher, and brought them over to him. He swallowed them and forced a smile.

"Let's have a team dinner when I wake up, ok?" Grandfather said after a minute.

"All right, no problem," Rose said. Her smile seemed to soothe him. Grandfather stood and left the room, but not before giving my shoulder a boney squeeze. All of this was having a negative impact on his health. I needed to help him, but what could I do?

"Well, chief, you heard your grandfather's orders. Follow me," Rose said as she led me into one of the bedrooms. It was full of exercise equipment and more scientific instruments.

"This is a pretty impressive set up that you have," I said, shocked and confused. *Maybe she will be able give me the answers I need?*

"Thanks. I haven't left this hotel suite very often over the last year. I'm beginning to feel like a sardine. I don't like to look at myself in the mirror anymore. I've put on about twenty-five pounds in the last twelve months," Rose said to me. From the look of it, she probably could lose five or ten pounds, but *only* *if she really wanted to*; she looked healthy to me. "There're some exercise clothes over in the closet. Why don't you go to the bathroom to change while I prep some of the equipment?"

"All right, no problem." I found a pair of shorts, a t-shirt, and some sneakers in the closet and entered the bathroom. The clothes were much tighter than I would have preferred, but it was the 70s. What could I do? I went back to the converted bedroom and found Rose perched by one of the larger machines. She handed me a couple of pills and a cup of water.

"Take these please," she said.

"What are they again?" I asked as I swallowed them, always compliant.

"They are keeping you alive." She stood up and cleaned my arm with a cotton ball and some rubbing alcohol. "I need another blood sample."

"Be my guest," I said. I was used to needles. When she finished, she prepared the sample and placed it into a machine for analysis. She seemed to move without much thought like she had done this a million times. I wondered if Grandfather went through all of this, too?

"Now I need to hook these electrodes to your heart." She picked up a pile of the wires and motioned to them.

"No problem. I do this for a living." She fumbled with the wires for a moment, clearly frustrated.

"I'm sorry, I'm not real good at this. I need you to take your shirt off," she said without quite making eye contact. She blushed. *How could I intimidate her? I'm no one of concern.*

I took off my shirt, and it became clear that she liked what she saw. She didn't have to shave my chest since I keep it bare; my job as a lab rat required this sort of thing. She couldn't quite get a handle on her nervousness. After she placed the devices, her hand grazed my pec like a butterfly kissing a lily. I did the only thing I could think to do: I flexed my chest. Her reaction was priceless. She jumped back in shock. My laugh didn't help, but it seemed to arrest her free fall from the gravity well she found herself in. I wished I had my iPhone to record her reaction.

"Sorry about that, Andrew. I just kind of zoned out there. I've, uh, I've never been next to such a nice body before. You look spectacular, if you don't mind me saying." I just laughed some more. "I need to just stop talking. I'm so weird. I'm sorry," Rose said as she looked away. Her embarrassment made me feel remorse for creating her discomfort.

"I'm sorry I scared you, Rose. I shouldn't have done that to you. That was mean."

"It's ok. It's done now. No more unprofessionalism from either of us. Time to get on the treadmill," she said, snapping her mind back into nerd gear.

"What do you need me to do?" I asked.

"Well, just start jogging. You're going to do ninety minutes of intervals." The heart monitor started beeping across the room as I began to pump my legs. The shorts were too, too tight. She wasn't going to be able to keep her mind on her work if I didn't find a pair of loose sweat pants or something, especially if this was going to become a routine.

"Ok." I felt energized on the treadmill, like my feet were lighter somehow. I hadn't noticed it before.

"So what is in those pills, by the way?" I asked her, wondering if the contents had something to do with this airy feeling.

"Well, since you have cancer, we need to do our best to keep you among the living. It is a cocktail of state of the art anti-cancer drugs. You need to take them every day."

"Did you and Grandfather make them?"

"Well, it's combination of what is available on the market plus a lot of new compounds that your Grandfather suggested. I don't know if he invented them or has just brought information back in time with him."

"Does it work? I'm not keen on dying here. The 70s are great and all, but I have a life I want to get back to." I wanted to get back to what was familiar at least.

"Well, they're working so far. Your Grandfather's still alive, but it's not a permanent solution," Rose said. "It is one of the projects David has me working on. We're close to a cure for Schneider's Lymphoma, but there's a lot of work to do still."

"But if you cure his cancer, won't he be stuck here in 1972? Why would he want to stay here?"

"Yes, I suppose that's true. I'm not sure what all he has told you so far, but you will understand once you get the big picture."

"Well, I'm ready to go back. I don't care what's going on; you two'll have to get along without me. Sounds like all I have to do is eat a bit of chocolate and I'll head straight back to where I came from," I said. The situation made me hot, and the exercise didn't help.

"Look, you are welcome to do that, of course, but if you go back, you'll die. There isn't a cure yet for Schneider's Lymphoma, and to my knowledge, the only two people working on a cure are in 1972." She had me. I began to understand. A prisoner, no doubt, but for my own good.

"Ok, that's enough talking for now. It's time for the first interval. I need you to sprint as hard as you can for the next two minutes," she said.

What could I do other than follow the doctor's orders? It sounded like my life depended on it.

I woke Grandfather up from his nap after my workout so he could prepare for our "team dinner." He had aged so much. *What had happened to the stalwart man from my youth?*

In the shower, I reviewed my situation. What didn't I know? *Lots.* Could I trust Grandfather? *I wanted to, but he gave me cancer.* Could I trust Rose? *Unknown.* A simple bar of chocolate would take me home, but I couldn't test the veracity of the solution without risking my own death. *There is no cure yet.* With Grandfather's condition, that much had to be true. *How long had he been managing the disease? Is he dying? More directly to the point, how long have I had I have Schneider's? Under the circumstances, what was my prognosis?* I was pretty sure I knew how I had contracted the disease, and I needed to confront Grandfather on the issue, but how hard could I push?

I was stronger now for some reason. After the treadmill session, Rose put me through an incredible circuit of free weight training. Not only could I lift about fifteen percent more weight than I was accustomed to, but I also seemed to recover much faster than normal. *Was it just the pills?* I couldn't risk not taking them under the circumstances, but I wanted to know more.

The three of us walked a few blocks to a small Italian joint off of Fifth Avenue. We were the only patrons for dinner. Grandfather seemed to have a knack for picking empty restaurants. We sat in silence until our food arrived.

I decided to break the ice. "What do Marty McFly, Dr. Who, and John Conner have in common?"

"Who are Marty McFly and John Conner?" Rose asked.

"They're all time travelers," I said, answering my own riddle after a long pause.

"I don't follow you," Grandfather said.

"Don't you ever watch TV or go to the movies?"

"No. Not too often. I generally find that sort of thing to be unproductive," Grandfather said.

"Sorry, Rose. It'll make more sense in 1985," I said with a chuckle. *Who laughs at his own stupid joke?*

"So how does this all work? Is there a space-time continuum? Will the universe collapse in on itself if I go and meet a younger version of myself?" I asked with genuine curiosity.

"Don't be so asinine," Grandfather said. "That's the stuff of science fiction. We're in a serious predicament here."

"All right. Go on," I asked. He could get in these moods. Science was almost a religion to him. Just like power and control.

"All this mumbo jumbo about multiple dimensions, Nabokov's time consistency principle, and predestination paradox is just not relevant," Grandfather lectured.

"Grandfather, you aren't speaking my language."

"Rose, can you help me out?" Grandfather asked.

"Sure. I'll try," Rose answered. She seemed honored to be asked to help. Grandfather loved the spotlight, even when in the company of just his own family. "Understand, though, that for me, this is all conjecture. I'm not a time traveler like y'all. I can only communicate and extrapolate information based on what I've been told." Why are scientists and lawyers compelled to give full disclosure and apologize for the shortcomings of their beliefs, I wondered?

"I understand. Just remember to dumb everything down for me."

"I'll try my best not to insult your intelligence."

"Well, when it comes to science, think of me as a kindergartener," I joked. Rose smiled a bit. It seemed like she had gotten past our awkward encounter in the exercise room, and I felt grateful for that.

"Let me educate you then. Remember, the principal is here at the table with us, so you better behave," Rose said.

"I'll try."

"Sounds like you're familiar at least with some concepts from entertainment. There's a movie that came out a few months back called *The Godfather*. Have you seen it?

"Have I seen *The Godfather*?" I repeated incredulously. "It is considered an American classic."

"Your grandfather forced me out of the lab to see it opening weekend. Frankly, I don't see what the fuss is all about, but David shares your sentiments."

"Just wait until you see the second one, Rose. It's just as good. You have to see them back-to-back because they are really more like one really long movie. I think you'll appreciate it more then," I said.

"I don't think I can sit through a six-hour movie, but I'll take your word on it."

"There's a third part, but I refuse to watch it on principle. Everyone says it's terrible, and I don't want it to tarnish the image that I have in my mind."

"Why don't you watch it for yourself? If you're a big fan, then you should have your own opinion, don't you think?" Rose asked. She's right. Maybe I should sit down and watch it, since there are rumors of a fourth movie floating around.

"I'll add it to my growing to-do list when I get back."

"I'll never understand men and their fascination with guns," she said. "But I'll use it to illustrate the concepts for you," Rose said.

"Ok, I'm with you."

"Imagine Michael Corleone at the end of *The Godfather* has a change of heart about how his life turned out as a mobster. He takes all of his ill-gotten riches and invests in technology, which results in the invention of a time machine. What if Michael goes back in time? What if the older version of Michael beat the younger version of Michael to the bathroom and takes the pistol hidden behind the water closet and deprives the younger version of himself of the murder weapon? Well, the younger Michael would either find another way to kill his enemies that night at the restaurant, or he would merely kill them later. The end result would be the same. Michael would still avenge his father and become the Don. The Nabokov Principle would prevent him from effectively changing history. The older and wiser Michael's actions in the past may very well be the reason the younger Michael ends up committing the murders in the first place. Under this theory, Michael was destined to take his father's place and become the Godfather, and nothing could prevent the inevitable event in his history."

"Hmm. I see," I said. "So in essence, if this theory is true, then when we time travel, we do not have free will."

"That's right," Rose said. "Consider this variation: The older Michael Corleone goes back in time, finds a way to change his decision to become the head of the family, and lives a life of peace and prosperity in Sicily with his sweet Sicilian wife. It doesn't matter how he achieves this; he just changes the course of his life."

"Sounds like free will."

"Yes, you're right. But if we are talking about creating a brand new timeline where there are multiple Michael Corleones who make different decisions, then we are talking about multiple dimensions, multiple timelines, or parallel universes, whatever you prefer to call it," she said.

"Right, I am familiar with that concept. It always seemed far-fetched to me. An infinite number of Andrew Acheson's making an infinite number of different decisions whenever one is required," I said.

"Good, Andrew," Grandfather chimed in. "But it doesn't take into consideration general thermodynamics. Each change to the timeline would create a brand new universe with mass and energy. You can't create something from nothing."

"Unless all the infinite universes already existed simultaneously because time isn't really a variable," Rose suggested playfully.

"You are both blowing my mind up. This is too existential for me," I said. "Teach me what really matters. Is it possible for me, an older version of me, to come to the past and for me to become my dad?" I became nauseated at the thought of romancing my mother in 1972.

"Actually, what you have described is the predestination paradox. You would be required, fated even, to go back in time to play your role in your own history," Rose said with a laugh, reading what was on my mind.

"Sick."

"But everything we have just discussed is not reality, Andrew, at least as far as I can tell at this point," Grandfather said as he looked up from his pasta. "This is what I think happens, but it is impossible to know for sure. It's possible to come to the past and make changes— major changes. There's no supernatural force that stops this from occurring. When a change is made in the past, all of the possibilities collapse into one present. There are no parallel universes."

"What else do you know?" I asked.

"Well, you do look a lot like your father did at your age, so I guess it is possible that you are your own father," he said.

"Or your own grandfather," Rose said. They proceeded to laugh at my discomfort. I needed to change the subject.

"Is there anything else?"

"Have you noticed how strong you have become, Andrew?" Grandfather said.

"Yes, actually, I was surprised during the workout."

"It's a side effect of the phenomenon. Interesting, huh?"

"So it has nothing to do with the cocktails that you are giving me?" I wanted to believe everything they told me. I just needed reassurance.

"The pills are for maintenance. Did Rose explain this to you?"

"Some." I nodded.

"Listen, it's very important that you stick to the exercise program. It helps stimulate your immune system."

"Is that how you gave me the lymphoma? You gave it to me when you gave me the job in the lab, didn't you?" I asked.

"Yes. Yes, that's right."

"Why didn't you tell me then? How could you do this to me without even asking me what I thought, Grandfather? Is my life inconsequential to you? What am I, a slave to you?"

"At the time, I convinced myself it didn't matter. I told myself that if you knew everything that was going on, you'd want to help me in any way that you could. I hope that I'm right about that," Grandfather explained. "I saved your life, Andrew."

It sounded crazy, but it's true that he'd helped me get past my heroin addiction, but did I owe him this? *Is he insane?* I loved him. I loved him with all my heart, but how could *this* be right?

"Besides, it's not like you aren't getting anything out of this. You get to go on a trip of a lifetime. You own my Company now. And, you get to see me again. You sound like an ingrate, like your aunt and uncle. I know I can get us out of this," Grandfather said. He started to choke on a bit of ravioli. Rose handed him his glass of water and persuaded him to take a sip.

"I'm sorry, Grandfather," I said. "I love you, and I'm glad to see you again. I'll do whatever it takes to help you get healthy." We ate the rest of the meal in silence.

We made the journey home in zigzag fashion in order to satisfy Grandfather's paranoia. I understood why they ordered room service most of the time. Dining out wasn't worth the extra effort.

Or maybe it was.

I opened the door to our suite and everything was in disarray. All of the furniture was turned over with the cushions cut open, the contents of the drawers spilled onto the floor, and the mattresses split. Ransacked. Nothing was spared.

From the far corner, a lone intruder bull-rushed Grandfather and me and knocked the three of us to the floor with his bulk. The intruder was quick and landed a couple of punches on my chin, which disoriented me, but when he kneed Grandfather's stomach, as he lay helpless on the floor, adrenaline flowed into my veins. I wrestled the intruder back to the floor before he could escape through the open doorway. In the commotion, Grandfather found his feet while the intruder and I traded desperate punches. A massive elbow knocked the wind out of me. Like a tag team wrestler, Grandfather cracked our unwanted guest on the back of the head with a dislodged desk drawer, sending the behemoth to the ground. The move worked, leaving him incapacitated.

"Rose," Grandfather said. I heard her crying across the hall.

As we raced across the hall to Rose's suite, we watched a second intruder disappear down the stairwell, backpack in hand. Grandfather fell to his knees in horror as the lab mirrored the situation in our rooms. Rose huddled hopelessly in a corner, her lip bloodied. *What was going on?*

"It's gone, everything is gone. They've taken everything," she said. "I couldn't stop him."

"They know we're here," Grandfather responded. "Did they take our medicine, too?"

Rose went to the refrigerator where all the meds were stored. It was open, its contents missing.

"Come on, there's no time to waste. We have to get moving. Now." Grandfather said. Grandfather's normal demeanor returned. "Rose, check our backup next door. Andrew, come with me." I obeyed and followed him across the hall where the sizable intruder was conscious, but moaned on the floor. "Give me a hand," he said to me and grabbed one of the man's arms. I took his other limb, and we dragged the man into the hallway and into the stairwell.

"What're we doing?" I asked.

"We've got to make sure we aren't followed," Grandfather said. "Get him to his feet." I complied and hoisted the intruder into a standing position. As soon as I had achieved this task, Grandfather shoved him down the staircase, where he landed a few flights below with a loud crack. I looked, and to my horror, the giant convulsed, gripped by a seizure.

"That's not good," I said.

"It's a lucky break. I was hoping to give him a severe concussion," Grandfather said. We met Rose in the hallway as she exited one of the adjacent suites.

"It's gone. The medicine in the back up fridge is gone, David," she said. Panic invaded her voice.

"Time to leave," Grandfather barked. I grabbed Rose by the arm when she hesitated—a bit rougher than I intended—and the three of us ran to the elevator. "They found us. I don't know how, but they found us," Grandfather said to himself.

"Who found us?" My demand went ignored. "Grandfather, who found us?" I wanted to shake him.

"Not now, Andrew. We've got to get out of here as fast as we can," he responded. Rose clung to my arm in tears, and it irritated Grandfather. "Get her to shut up. We can't draw attention to ourselves."

"Rose, calm down. You have to stop crying," I said to her. *How do you soothe a crying woman? We're going to be on the ground floor of the hotel any second.*

"We have to stop at the lobby desk and pick something up. Shut her up," Grandfather said.

We left the protective confines of the elevator. Grandfather scanned the lobby for trouble before we shifted to the service counter. No one was there except the hostess. I held Rose close to me and positioned our backs to the counter so I could watch the lobby while Grandfather conducted his business.

"I need the packages you're holding in the safe for me, please," he said to the hostess.

"Which room was that, sir?" the hostess asked. I thought Grandfather was going to go behind the counter in anger and retrieve his packages on his own, but he collected himself in time.

"Room 1807. Please hurry, we're in a rush," he said. She vanished behind the counter with a sense of urgency. *At least the service is good in the hotel.* She returned and handed him two large briefcases.

"Will you be checking out of all of your rooms today, sir?"

"No, it's not necessary." With that, we raced across the lobby and towards the unknown dangers that lay ahead.

"Hail a cab, Andrew, and make it quick," Grandfather said. "I don't want to put down these cases: They're our only lifeline now."

With one hand around Rose and one hand in the air, I hailed the first cab I saw. We loaded into the back seat.

"Where to, pal?" The cabbie asked Grandfather, with one hand on the steering wheel and the other on the radio's volume knob.

"Penn Station, please," Grandfather told the eager cabbie. He pulled into the heavy traffic and turned his radio back up. Clapton was busy playing a solo.

"Listen," Grandfather whispered to me. "Take one of these cases. It'll help you figure out what to do next if we get separated or something happens to me."

"Grandfather," I started to say. I searched for words to gain clarity but found none.

"Everything is going to be fine. Just keep up once we get to the train station," he said. I popped open the case for a peek. Inside, were three things: a large brown envelope, a Colt .45, and cash—lots of it.

Within a few minutes, we were inside one of the largest and busiest train stations in the world. Rose emerged from her shock a bit, but I couldn't risk losing her in the crowd, so I clamped onto her hand, and we navigated our way through the crowds by staying in Grandfather's wake. Again, I kept watch with my back to the counter as Grandfather purchased our tickets from the agent.

"Platform nine," Grandfather said to me. After a quick scan of the signage, we found our bearings and set off down a lengthy set of stairs. Grandfather labored ahead of us.

"How much time do we have?" I asked him. No response. His heavy breathing wouldn't allow it.

"All aboard," the conductor announced as we burst through the doors. Our Amtrak train waited in the station, but not for much longer.

"Just get on," Grandfather managed to order. As we passed him, he made me take the second briefcase from him. I wasn't sure he was going to make it on the train.

"Where?" I asked him.

"Anywhere." The first open door was thirty yards ahead. As Rose and I stepped onto the train, I looked back and saw Grandfather struggling. *He's not going to make it.* I jammed one of the briefcases into the door to keep it from closing and ran back towards him. When I reached him, I had no choice but to carry him over my shoulder like a fireman. The train started to pull out. I watched Rose wave her arm from the gap in the jammed door. I closed the distance as fast as I could with the old man weighing me down. I grabbed the door with my left hand and forced it open. Out of the corner of my eye, I saw that we were approaching a concrete support pillar. The train accelerated. *We won't be able to go around it and still get onto the train. It's now or never. We need those cases.*

I held Grandfather's legs tight, closed my eyes, and leaped.

We landed inside the train, and Rose steadied us before our momentum carried us into the angry conductor.

"Find your seats, please," the conductor barked. I set Grandfather on his feet. The relief washed over us for an instant.

"Grandfather, do you have our tickets?" I asked.

"Yes, of course." He pulled them out of his jacket pocket and handed them to the conductor.

"The sleeper compartments are three cars ahead." He punched our tickets and handed them back to me. I scanned them for our compartment assignment and noticed our destination: Chicago, Illinois. I had no idea why we were going there.

We stumbled through the train cars until we found our three sleeper compartments. Rose and I got Grandfather settled in his car and tucked into bed. It was clear that she loved him in some manner just as I did. *Why did he let all this happen to him? He wasn't the strong man I remembered from my childhood or even a year ago.*

"I'll come and check on you soon, Grandfather," I whispered into his ear, but I was pretty sure that he didn't hear me. He was already asleep.

Rose and I relocated outside his room and lingered. I had so many questions. *Did she have any answers? What was I being sucked into?*

"I see on our tickets that we're going to Chicago. Do you know anything about it?" Rose asked me.

"Listen, I don't know what's going on. I was hoping you would have some answers," I said.

"You don't have to talk to me like that. I'll tell you everything I know, which isn't much. He's a very private person, you know." She held her ground.

"Okay. I'm sorry."

"Let's meet up in a few hours to check up on David. You need to sleep as much as possible. Things are going to get really rough," Rose said.

"What do you mean?"

"We don't have any of the maintenance medication, and he needs some heavy painkillers," she said.

"He's not in good shape. What's going on?"

"The cancer is taking its toll. If we don't get him some medicine soon, he'll be in excruciating pain."

"Can't we just get off of the train and get him some?"

"I wish we could. Some of the components are available commercially, but I need to synthesize the majority of it. Whoever broke into our rooms took what we had. They took everything."

"I don't know who broke in. I don't know who would be after Grandfather, but I understand if you want to get off the train at the next stop and disappear, Rose," I said.

"No. I don't think I could do that. No."

"Ok. Let me know if you change your mind."

"Andrew. If we don't get the maintenance meds soon, you're going to get very sick, too. The best thing you can do is to rest as much as possible and hope your Grandfather has a plan," Rose said.

"Ok. If you don't hear from me in a couple of hours, come in and wake me so we can talk," I said.

"Ok. I will."

She went to her compartment, and I went to mine. The world whizzed by outside. *How did I get into this mess, and how was I going to get out of it?* I opened one of the briefcases and counted the cash. $150,000. That's a small fortune. I could disappear for a while if I had to. Upon examination, the second case had the exact same contents. I opened one of the envelopes and looked at the papers. They where what appeared to be various synthesis schemes and other text-heavy documents. Grandfather's research. All was not lost.

Rose. *It's a good thing I didn't leave the second case in Grandfather's room.* Grandfather said to trust no one. *Could she be involved in the ransacking somehow? Could she have engineered all of this? Who was after us in the first place and what was Grandfather's role? I could leave.* But these were the only two people I knew, and I didn't want to be alone in 1972, not in my condition. I could buy a chocolate bar and return to the present, but who could help me there? *Maybe Dad could help me?* But if he couldn't, then I would die from Schneider's Lymphoma.

I promised myself I'd have a closer look after I rested for a few hours so I could concentrate. *I'll decide what to share with Rose then.*

"Andrew. Andrew. Wake up." Pounding on the door. My head throbbed in a thick fog. *How long had I been asleep?*

"Andrew." It was Rose. The train wasn't moving. *Something must be wrong.* I jumped to my feet and opened the door. Rose stood there with Grandfather. She supported his weight.

"We're in Chicago," she said. "We have to leave now." I couldn't believe it. I must have been asleep for twenty hours.

"Get us to the ticket counter," Grandfather said, "and buy tickets to Flagstaff, Arizona, on the next available train."

"Can't we just take a plane? It'd be faster," I said.

"No. It's too dangerous. Too easy to track," he said. "And we don't have any travel documents for you yet. We were going to have a driver's license and passport prepared for you next week."

We had one option. I grabbed the two briefcases. Rose helped Grandfather disembark while I searched for familiar faces. It didn't appear that we were being followed. The ticket kiosk was positioned across the lobby, and I purchased three tickets on a train leaving in ten minutes. It was going to be a forty-hour trip. *Forty hours. Could Grandfather survive that long? Could we survive that long from whoever was out there?*

We settled on the train. I went to the dining car and used some of the money from the briefcases to purchase as much food and beverages as I could carry. Back in Grandfather's sleeper compartment, I presented the sandwiches, chips, and drinks to my companions who were crammed into the tiny space. They were happy to receive it.

I chomped on a burger. I had a migraine again. Grandfather labored on an Italian sub while Rose ate a hotdog.

"Why didn't you wake me up, Rose? You shouldn't have let me sleep so long," I said.

"I tried to wake you up several times, but you locked your door. I didn't want to draw attention to us by yelling at you through it. Sorry."

"The long deep sleeps are a side effect of the time travel, Andrew. It will stabilize in time," Grandfather said. "As will your increased appetite."

"How are you feeling, Grandfather?"

"Not too good. I'm going to make it, though. I've come too far to fail," he said. I wanted to believe him. I wanted to believe *in* him. Rose reached down and touched his leg. Grandfather squeezed her hand in what seemed like an action of gratitude. "Things are going to get worse before they get better. You should pack some food into your compartment and just try and sleep and survive this second leg."

"How many legs are on this dog?" I asked.

"Thankfully, just two. Flagstaff will hopefully be our terminus," Grandfather said.

"What's in Flagstaff anyways?"

"Patience, my boy. Patience. Let me rest. There will be plenty of time to talk."

"I'll stay with him until he goes to sleep," Rose said. I appreciated her offer. Most people aren't built to take care of sick people.

"Thanks." I gathered some food and stood to leave. "Hey, Rose."
"Yes?"

"Come by my room later so we can discuss things."

About an hour later, Rose knocked on my door, and I let her in.

"He's asleep."

"Has he ever been like this before?" I asked.

"No. Well, not since he first came back about a year ago."

"What happened?"

"He recruited me two years ago while I was still doing my post-doc. My research wasn't going well. I'd been stuck there for three years because I didn't have any publishable results. I would still be there if it wasn't for him. He promised that he had a fully funded project for me that would make my career. David gave me a $25,000 bonus on the spot, in cash, and we set up the lab at the hotel together. Money was no obstacle. He emphasized secrecy, but he's open to discussing all the scientific aspects of what we were dealing with, even the time travel. It's unbelievable, but not too far of a leap for a scientist like me."

"Where did things go wrong?"

"He told me I had two years to get the anti-cancer cocktail perfected and to find a cure. I wasn't ready when he showed up again twelve months ago, but I won't let him down."

"I'm sure you're doing your best," I said. My head pounded, and I couldn't hide it any longer.

"Take these pills."

"What are they?"

"Aspirin. I managed to get a few pills from an old lady a few compartments down."

"Save them for Grandfather."

"No, we can get some more when we need to. You'd better take them. I can't carry both of you off the train." I took them.

"How long will it take to make the cocktail when we get to Arizona?"

"If I have all the equipment and supplies I need, I can have a crude product in just a few days. What do you think we'll find there?"

"A safe house, I think," I said. I was guessing, though. Grandfather always did his best to be prepared.

"Is there anything helpful in the briefcase?" Rose asked.

"I haven't read anything in detail yet. Wake me up in a couple of hours, and we will go through it together."

"Ok." I could tell she wanted me to trust her and let her have access to the cases on her own, but I wasn't ready to give in yet. I made sure that she left before I allowed myself to pass out.

━━━

I didn't sleep for long before the pain returned and toyed with my soul, a pain I had not experienced since my tortured nights in rehab. The crushing feeling was inescapable, like a shadow fractured across a dimly lit compartment. I forced myself to vomit in the small sink in my room. *Why can respite be found by exchanging forms of pain in the marketplace of Life?* A Coca Cola afforded a spike of energy. *Another addiction from my past.*

Out in the corridor, I rapped on Rose's door. No answer. I knocked on Grandfather's door and entered, setting the two brief-cases on the floor. To my surprise, he was awake and staring out of the window.

"Grandfather, are you all right?" I asked. My voice seemed to snap him out of a trance.

"Oh, Andrew. How long have you been standing there?" Grand-father replied.

"Not too long. I just came in."

"You look terrible, grandson."

"Yeah, well, you don't look too sharp yourself." He met my reply with an inspired smile.

"Yes, the Acheson men have seen better days. Come sit down," he said. I fell into the seat next to him. These compartments were not designed for maximum comfort, but for survival. "It's too bad the medicine cocktail had to be refrigerated. I hadn't really planned for that contingency yet."

"This is all so crazy for me," I said.

"For me, too." He trailed off for a moment, lost in his thoughts. "I've never liked trains. To me, they are always filled with the ghosts of my early childhood. The last time I was a passenger on a train was as a boy in Europe with my mother."

"I'm sorry, Grandfather. You've been through so much. I wish I could take away your pain. All of it."

"Having you here with me goes a long way. Believe that."

"I'm glad to be here with you." I wasn't sure if my statement was true, but I wanted it to be.

"Your Grandmother Maria was so good to me. Before her, I don't think I was even human. I was an animal, concerned only with survival. I was like a rat in a wasteland collecting whatever I could get my hands on in order to make my existence more palatable. She created me. God gave me life, but she sculpted my humanity. She showed me what it means to be alive. Did you know that starting the Company was her idea?" he asked.

I shook my head.

"Well, she always thought that I was too talented, too creative, and too wild to have a master. She knew I needed to be free to explore and fashion my own way of life. Maria thought that need was born during my formative years in Germany. Because of what happened to my family, the price we had to pay, I needed to live life for all of them. It's up to me to live for everyone who never had a chance."

"Sounds like a burden."

"To some it could be interpreted that way. But it's an honor to me. Life is both a gift and an expectation." In that moment, I realized that I might never understand him. My life could never hold such promise. Only one in a million people could forge the success that Grandfather has produced. That sort of hope would crush me.

"Sounds like you were happy," I commented.

"Happiness has always been a difficult concept to me. I figured if I accomplished enough with my life, someday I would tip the scale from grief to contentment," he said.

"Did you ever achieve that pivot point?" I asked. I regretted the question under our dire circumstances.

"If I can find a cure for this blasted Schneider's Lymphoma, then I will have done something to honor my family's legacy," he said.

"Grandfather, you have done so much for your family already."

"Yes, but it is not enough." I let a minute pass to calm the tension of expectations.

"Have you ever thought about going back in time to heal her? Couldn't you save her from her cancer once you figure out the cure?" I asked.

"Yes, the thought has crossed my mind, but the ethics are troubling. I think about ethics a lot these days. I'm not sure what is right anymore. Right isn't always black and white," Grandfather said.

"I thought there was always a bright line?" I asked.

"That's what they tell you in school, but academia isn't the real world. They want you to believe that if an action feels wrong, then it probably is wrong. But that doesn't take into account the guilt complex that has been forced down our throats. We've been taught to be soft, that pain and suffering are the same as evil. But they aren't always. Pain can motivate."

"Is that why you have done this to me?"

"In some ways, yes. Don't get me wrong. Part of me harbors guilt for the situation I have subjected you to, but I have given you an opportunity. Andrew, I have given you a chance of a lifetime. You get a chance to have a pivotal role in a defining moment in humanity's existence."

"But I didn't ask for it."

"No, but it is what you need. I believe in you. You won't let me down," he said. I wished he could transfer his confidence to me.

"Grandfather, what is your plan? Obviously, someone is after us," I said.

"Yes, that is why you are here. Many entities are 'after us.' You and I are going to lead the battle against them. I thought we would have the element of surprise. We still may."

"Who is after us?"

"Just about everyone you can think of, Andrew. Militaries, governments, terrorist cells, and rival corporations. You can imagine all the possibilities for time travel," he said.

"It's the ultimate power play." It seemed ironic that Grandfather, who valued power and control, discovered time travel. I wasn't comfortable with the notion.

"My first thought was it might be used for research purposes. We could take academia back in time for first-degree historical observation. Wouldn't that be amazing? Can you imagine hearing Abraham Lincoln give the Gettysburg Address live? Or silently observe the Titanic from a distance? Cheer on Jackie Robinson during his first game as a Brooklyn Dodger? Or perhaps take in the first live performance of Pearl Jam? You'd like that. Or being able to solve the mysteries behind the deaths of JFK and Princess Diana, simply by being present and having open eyes?"

"It would be cool, in a way. I'd love to see Ali versus Foreman for their Rumble in the Jungle," I said.

"Exactly. I then realized there's more at stake. Tourism. For example, folks would pay millions of dollars to be able to experience the death of Jesus Christ each Easter or hear Moses deliver the Ten Commandments, or Muhammad deliver a sermon in Mecca. It would redefine the word 'pilgrimage,'" Grandfather said. I had to admit to myself that it also sounded a bit morbid, too. Many of the most captivating events in world history are focused on death or controversy. Why are we so fascinated with death? Could death be turned into a theme park ride experience? *Should it?* Would we rob people of faith of their admiration for those who had become larger-than-life symbols? "Time tourism" could spark a war if mishandled. No, war would be inevitable.

"Grandfather. I'm not so sure tourism would be a good idea."

"Why not? As long as you only observe and don't change anything, you are only sharing the experience of truth. But there's another benign development, a new tool we could offer. We could offer immortality."

"How?"

"That is a good question, but it's simple. A young man could go back in time say sixty years and live his days in comfort. Before his death, he could eat a bit of cocoa and find himself back in the present, all shiny and new," he said.

"It works like that?"

"Yes, it does. If I ate a Snickers bar right now, I'd immediately find myself in the present about one year younger physically, but with all my experiences intact. When the phenomenon is initiated and the matter reaches the level of excitation that is necessary for time-travel, the energy acts as a marker of sorts for the reversion process. It's fantastic."

"If a person were rich enough to afford the technology, he could live a lifetime over and over again," I said.

"Yes, exactly. Imagine living your life with the chance to reboot it once the experience had run its course."

"Doesn't that cheapen things? Isn't life meaningful because of the impending death we all stare down from the time we are born?" I asked.

"Maybe so. I can't be sure, though," he said. "But I think it sounds fantastic." I wondered if he had tried this in some fashion. All of this was said by a man currently dying of self-inflicted cancer to his grandson who was not too many steps behind him, by his own hand. The irony wasn't lost on me.

"Of course, we can't help but meddle in things. That's human nature," he said. "I've done my best to keep knowledge of the discovery in as few hands as possible."

"Does Dad know about it?"

He didn't answer. An unmistakable scream outside interrupted us.

"Rose," Grandfather said. He moved towards the briefcases. I was already at the exit.

I pushed the door to her room open with a kick. A man on top of her attempted to subdue her. I lowered my shoulder and knocked him off balance, which allowed Rose to get out from underneath him. A quick elbow to his face busted his nose open and stunned him. I grabbed him by the collar and pulled him up to his feet. Grandfather entered the room with one of the guns in his hand. *Good. Time for answers.*

"Who are you?" I asked.

"Screw you," he said.

"Fine," Grandfather said. He put the barrel of the gun into the intruder's mouth and backed him up to the window.

Bang.

Grandfather blew the man's brains out into the night air.

"What are you doing?" I asked. Rose started crying and fell down to the floor in shock. I wanted to join her. *My life can't get any crazier, can it?* He used the barrel of the gun to remove the remaining shards of glass from the window frame.

"Give me a hand. We need to get rid of his body," Grandfather said. I stood there frozen in place. "Hurry." I grabbed the man's shoulders and Grandfather hoisted his feet. Grandfather struggled with the weight, but in a moment we had the body out the window. I paused to watch it tumble in the darkness.

"What have you done?" I asked.

"What I had to do. Now get Rose up on her feet and into my cabin. There isn't time to waste," he barked back at me. "He may not be the only person following us."

I complied. I waited a few minutes before I broke the silence in Grandfather's room. Grandfather had removed his ear from the door and fallen into a seat. His body was covered in sweat. *How much longer could he hold it together?*

"Anything?" I asked.

"The conductor walked down the hallway, but he didn't knock on any of the doors. It's too late at night for that. This train's too noisy; I'm not sure if anyone heard us. The intruder must have been alone."

"What now?"

"I was afraid something like this would happen. We're getting off at the next stop. We can't take a chance," Grandfather said.

Within an hour, the sun began to paint the desert our train traversed, and the train started to slow down.

"Next stop, Albuquerque, New Mexico," the Conductor announced over the intercom system.

"This is us. Grab the briefcases," Grandfather said. Rose had gathered herself by then. We left the compartment and departed the train as soon as it stopped in the station. We watched everyone who disembarked with us onto the platform. Only a family with three small children and an elderly couple joined us on the empty platform before the train continued to blaze its trail westward. This made me feel safe. I wanted to let my guard down.

"What now?" Rose asked. "I can't take this anymore."

"You're free to leave whenever you want if this is too much for you," Grandfather answered.

"I don't want to watch the two of you die slow deaths anymore, but I can't leave you two in this condition. You've taken the choice out of my hands," she said.

"We'll be okay if you leave," Grandfather responded.

"Besides, how do I know you won't shoot me in the back if I try to walk away?"

"I wouldn't do that to you. I'm no monster," Grandfather said, ignoring the fact that he had shot a man in cold blood.

"Let's stop messing around," I said. "Rose, make a decision. In or out. Grandfather. Focus. We are dying. We need to figure out how to live." I was desperate to get healthy. I needed Rose and Grandfather to find a cure for the cancer I was afflicted with in order to get home with any chance of survival.

"We need transportation. Get a cab," he said.

"Pick out a car, Andrew," Grandfather said. "I'm going to go sit down inside the business office with Rose."

The cab dropped us at a used car dealership, and I scanned the lot. This could be a trap to an ordinary consumer, but we weren't in pedestrian circumstances. Our situation demanded haste. I saw the quick and obvious answer over in the corner, a dream come true, a silver 1966 G.T. 350 Shelby Mustang. I walked over to it, confirmed that it had the optional back seat and a manual transmission, and then I joined the party inside.

Grandfather paid cash, with a little bit extra, to make sure his real name didn't end up on the paperwork. You can count on a used car salesman to be down with shady dealings for a little extra to grease the wheels. We were on the road a few minutes later. Grandfather relegated himself to the backseat so he could lie down to relieve his pain while Rose joined me in the front seat as the navigator, map in hand.

"Make sure you don't get pulled over. We don't need any more trouble, Andrew," he said before he drifted off. I swallowed a handful of aspirin we had purchased at a gas station. I didn't know how long I could focus on the road.

"You sure you don't want me to drive?" Rose asked. My condition must have been obvious.

"No, I don't want to pass up the opportunity to drive this classic. It may be my only chance."

"Okay, but if you start to swerve, then I'm going to make you pull over," she said.

"Fair enough. Can you drive a stick?"

"Of course, I grew up on a farm."

For the next few hours, I made a point of talking as little as possible and keeping the Mustang on the road at just above the speed limit. It took a surprising amount of energy to accomplish this simple task, but the endorphins from driving a car from my fantasies helped to buoy my deteriorating state. The picturesque deserts and mountains along Interstate 40 reminded me of my solitude. Even though I was reunited with Grandfather, and Rose had decided to stay with us, I felt alone on this journey. The road to death can only be traveled in your own boots. I longed for my guitar and the familiar surroundings of my apartment. *I could sort this out if only I could filter my emotions through a distorted amplifier.*

When I started seeing road signs for Flagstaff, I reached behind me and woke Grandfather.

"Hey, we're close to the Flagstaff city limits. What exit should I take?" I asked.

"None."

"What? I thought that was where we're going?" I responded.

"No. Continue on to San Bernardino, California," he whispered. Rose looked as surprised as I felt.

"Grandfather, why did we buy train tickets to Flagstaff?"

"I didn't know if we were being followed or not. I wanted to keep our destination a mystery from watchful eyes, if possible." I had been keeping an eye on the rearview mirror. I didn't think we were being followed.

"David, is San Bernardino our final destination? I am getting extremely worried about your condition. It's been three days without your maintenance cocktail. You and Andrew can't survive much longer like this. I need to get started on the synthesis," Rose said.

"Yes, San Bernardino will be the end," he said.

Several hours later, when we reached the San Bernardino city limits, Grandfather wasn't able to sit up, but he managed to give me directions that led us to a large, nondescript warehouse in the industrial district. The parking lot was half full, and I found a space near the entrance. I turned off the engine and a familiar face emerged from the complex.

An authoritative woman strode over to us with urgency. She looked older than she appeared in the few family photos I had dug up in Grandfather's things when he disappeared, but she was most definitely my Great Aunt Eva, Grandfather's younger sister. By my quick mental estimation, she must have been in her mid to late twenties. It's funny how a guy's mind does such maneuvers even in great pain. Her beauty struck me and made me feel awkward. I wanted to take control of the situation, so I opened the car door. With great effort, I placed my feet onto the ground. When I tried to stand, I discovered that I didn't have the energy, and I tumbled to the concrete. Hard. *How did things get so bad? Was death creeping up on me this quickly?* Yes, without a doubt. *How could I not fully sense it before?* Because I am a fool.

From this prone position, I heard Rose's frantic pleas for help, what must have been Aunt Eva's response, and many footsteps advancing towards us. I tried to hold on, but the blackness engulfed me.

Consciousness was elusive. I spent hours in oscillation between distorted images of my hands reaching for the boundaries of Light's sanctuary of hope and Darkness's prison of confusion. When I awoke, I was lying on a stretcher. After my eyes adjusted, I could see that Grandfather was lying motionless on another stretcher a short distance away.

"You're awake," I heard a female voice say. I turned my head towards the sound. It was Rose. Her edginess transformed into relief, and she came over and hugged me.

"What's going on?" I asked.

"I thought you were going to die," Rose said. "They told me to keep an eye on you."

"Wait, is Grandfather dead?" I felt my blood pressure rise with the sense of fear.

"No, he is fine. He woke up about twenty minutes ago, but he fell back asleep. He's just taking a nap. He insisted on waiting for you to recover before we relocate," Rose responded.

"Where are we? Are we in a hospital?"

"No, not exactly. We're still at the warehouse you pulled up to, but I don't feel safe here. No one's talking to me."

"I saw a woman come out of the building before I passed out. Did you meet her?"

"Very briefly. She's busy with something. I didn't catch her name. Why?"

"I think she is my Great Aunt Eva, Grandfather's younger sister," I spit out.

"You think so?"

"Well, I've never met her before, but I'm pretty certain," I said. I was positive, but I didn't want to give Rose the impression that I was a know-it-all in my current diminished condition. It seemed too arrogant. "What time is it?"

"It is about three a.m. local, I think. I'm going to get the security guard. He's supposed take us someplace where we can rest," Rose said. She left the room and returned a few minutes later with the security guard, who looked middle aged and very tough. I was surprised to see that he was carrying a revolver. I didn't expect to see that. Where I come from, security guards carry a Maglite for protection.

"Ready to go?" he asked me, his voice rough like sandpaper.

"Yup," I said.

"All right. I've got the keys to your Mustang. I'll drive you there myself," he said.

"I think I can manage on my own," I said, as I placed my feet on the ground, surprised that they didn't betray me this time. Rose woke Grandfather with a gentle touch. "Can you help the old man, though? He's had a rough time."

"Sure, of course. I'm paid to help." He helped Grandfather stand. It looked like between him and Rose, Grandfather would be just fine.

"What's your name, by the way?" I asked the guard.

"David. I'm fine, you don't have to worry about me," Grandfather said in a soft voice. "My body may be weak, but my mind is as strong as ever."

"Not you, Grandfather," I suppressed a laugh because I feared it would cause me to fall apart. Rose snickered a bit, though. I'm glad someone could enjoy the moment at least. "I'm trying to find out what your male escort's name is, Grandfather."

"Oh, sorry. I must admit that I feel, I feel messed up. I may need a bit of time," Grandfather said.

"You can have all the time you need. Hopefully, you will feel like yourself tomorrow," Rose said.

"Bud," the security guard said.

"Bud?" I asked.

"Yeah, Bud's my name. Cut out the escort talk, though. I'm a man that happens to be paid to accompany you somewhere, but I ain't no male escort or anything funny like that," he said. I realized my *faux pas.*

"I like him," Rose said. "He's got a sense of humor."

"That's a bonus. It doesn't cost anything extra," Bud added.

"Thanks for the clarification on the job description. I'm sure Rose appreciates it," I said. Rose hit me on the arm. It hurt. I let Rose sit up front with Bud when we loaded into our car.

Bud transported us across town. The desert city was silent this time of night. We stopped at a large nondescript house on the far edge of the inland wasteland. We could see for miles in any direction.

"This is it. The Boss said to keep you here at my house for the time being," Bud said. He got out of the car and we followed. I think we were all too tired to do anything but be compliant.

"I want to go back to the warehouse first thing in the morning," Grandfather said.

"Of course you do, Pops, but I'll have to clear it first," Bud said. He walked back to the trunk. "Kid, don't forget your luggage." I met him at the trunk. Bud pulled out a shotgun and pumped a cartridge into the chamber.

"You are such a boy scout," I said.

"I've got a lot a merit badges. Pray you don't have to experience my skill first hand. I'm your host and your bodyguard for the time being."

I grabbed our two briefcases and followed Bud and the group inside the house. We could use this place like Russia used its vast lands during the Napoleonic Wars, I thought. Isolation can be a great weapon when you have nothing else.

Upstairs inside the house, we found three bedrooms. Rose helped Grandfather into bed—he was very weak—and then chose the room across from his for herself.

"I'll take this room if you don't mind," she said.

"Of course not," I said. "I'm going to check on Bud and make sure he's okay." I took one of the handguns out of the briefcases and put it in my waistband along the small of my back.

"Do you mind if I take the other gun?" she asked. "I'll feel better if I'm in a position where I can take care of myself instead of relying on someone else."

"So you don't trust me?" I asked.

"Your Grandfather trusts you. I know he does, but there's no reason not to give me a weapon, is there? Unless *you* don't trust me."

"Touché." I reached into the second briefcase and handed her the other gun. Truth is, I didn't know yet if I should trust her or not. "Do you know how to use this thing?"

"Yes. I just saw *The Godfather*, remember? I'm prepared to take this to the mattresses if I have to," she said.

"I'll take the bedroom down the hall. Come get me if anything goes wrong with Grandfather or if you need help with anything," I said. She giggled at me. *Did she think I was flirting with her?* Maybe I was. "You know what I mean."

I retreated down the stairs and found Bud in the living room staring out into the night from behind the closed curtains. If he ran on batteries, they were Energizers.

"Anything out there we should be worried about?" I asked.

"I don't see anything," Bud said, "but if someone comes after you, I'll be able to see them from at least a mile away. That'll give us a bit of time to be prepared."

"That's not much."

"No, but if someone comes, I'll be able to hold them off long enough for you to get a start towards that rig of yours. You'd be able to outrun most folks around here in it."

"We wouldn't leave you behind, Bud."

"That's not your decision," he said. He was so authoritative.

"I'm human, at least the last time I checked," I said.

"You sure?" A hint of a smile cracked the corner of his lips.

"Well, I'm not one to let anyone die. At least I hope I'm not."

"Listen, kid, the Boss told me to protect you at all costs. I don't know everything that's going on inside that warehouse, but the Boss pays me very well. More than what I was paid by the Army to protect the U.S. of A. in Vietnam. So, I'll do what it takes to keep you alive."

"If it makes you feel any better, I don't know what is going on either."

"Fair enough, but if you do figure anything out, do me a favor and keep it to yourself. I don't want to grow a conscience and be forced to pick sides. I'm strictly a soldier of fortune now." I stood next to Bud for a few minutes of silent contemplation by the window. *There's nothing out there.*

"The world is messed up," I said.

"You've got that right, kid," Bud responded.

"Nothing ever makes sense for me. I don't know what I'm supposed to do, and I'm afraid that I never will."

"You've got to accept something: Nobody has any idea what they're doing in this life. If you're lucky, you will make peace with this truth before you're old and too stinking tired to do anything about it. But if you keep your wits sharp and keep your eyes on your loved ones, you may find a way to do some good in this world, even if it's just a small amount. That's the only way you can measure the usefulness of your life," Bud said.

"Thanks, Bud. I'll think about that as I'm trying to fall asleep."

"You're welcome. Try and get some sleep. You're safe for now."

Grandfather startled me when I found him waiting for me upstairs outside his room, dressed in his underwear and looking serious. "We need to talk," he whispered.

"Are you okay?" I asked.

"Quickly, come in the room," he said. I obeyed as always. He closed the door behind me.

"Listen," he started.

"Maybe you should try and get some rest." I took him by the arm and led him towards the bed.

"You're right. I know you know that, but we still need to talk. I can't predict the future."

"Or the past," I added.

"Stop clowning around. What I need to tell you is important. So, sit down, shut up, and pay attention."

"Sorry."

"I'm sorry, too. I'm sorry I've messed everything up, but here we are, and now we have to find our way out of this mess together," Grandfather said.

I protested.

"Look. I know you want to go home. My sister Eva has stitched us up okay with an infusion of the anti-cancer cocktail, but I'm not certain of our long-term condition, to be honest. Just so you know, Eva and I aren't on the best of terms."

"Why is that?"

"That's up to her to tell you if she wants. It's her business. But that isn't why I pulled you in here. We need to talk about contingencies," he said. "You and I are the rulers of the Kingdom of Davidistan."

"Are you okay Grandfather? I've never heard of this place before."

"That is because I made it up. I invented it."

"So you pulled me in here to tell me stories? Goodnight, I'm going to go to bed now so you can get some rest," I said and stood up.

"Sit down and pay attention," Grandfather said and pulled me back with surprising force. "This is no children's game that I'm describing to you: This is life and death."

"I'm sorry. You have my attention now. I thought you were delirious from your drugs."

"Coming to the past with the knowledge of the future provides a lot of opportunities to make money."

"Okay, I've seen *Back to the Future.* I get it," I said.

"Well, I borrowed some money from myself. While I have bank accounts and assets spread out all over the world, I've kept my first bank account open, the one I opened at Beneficial Bank when I was a teenager. Since I've been coming back to the past, I've used the money in that account to buy and sell stocks, place sports bets, and buy and sell real estate. I have a few rules: I never hold onto anything for very long, I work with straw men or shell corporations whenever possible, I never buy or sell stock in large enough quantities to draw attention of regulators or outsiders, and I always make sure the account at Beneficial Bank is balanced at the end of each day. By dealing in small to medium transactions and never losing, you don't have to hit homeruns: You just have to have a positive return. I've been back and forth to the past and future many times now, and I always bring a transaction game plan with me in my mind so I can make the most of my time while I'm back here taking care of business."

"I'm sorry if I'm a bit slow, but why do you have to balance your own account at Beneficial Bank every day? It's your money after all," I asked.

"Right, good question. Well, I can never be certain of who my enemies are. I don't think they can access the balance sheets of my personal bank accounts, but I can't be certain. I cash out at the end of every day that I make a transaction, like a day trader, so I don't leave a trail."

"Where do you put your money then?"

"Very good. You're with me on the forensics. I can't have the account in my name, so I got creative. I invented a country," he said.

"Davidistan?"

"Yes, exactly."

"Why did you have to invent a country?"

"Gold. Kings are made with gold, they say. I convert everything I make with this process to gold."

"You are the world's first successful alchemist then, Grandfather."

"I suppose you're right, my boy. I convert the money to gold so I can store it at the New York Federal Reserve. Not only is it the most secure banking institution in the world, but it has the largest deposit of gold in the world."

"More than Fort Knox?" I asked.

"Yes, and it's not even close. But more important than the fact that gold's real value has increased by twenty fold over the last thirty years is that it provides anonymity. The gold accounts at the New York Fed are completely anonymous, and the deposits are static. No one can mess with them because it is hard currency. It can't be messed with by internet hackers and what not."

"But why Davidistan?"

"I wanted an extra layer of security and the Fed only deals with national banks and governments. There's nothing directly in our names there. It's in the name of the National Bank of Davidistan. That way no one knows it's our money."

"That's genius, Grandfather," I said. I was impressed.

"Thank you. I'm a scientist, not a financial mind. It's the best I could come up with."

"But why did the Fed let you invent a country?"

"Well, they don't make interest on our deposit, but they stand to make a large transaction fee when we liquidate our assets there. So, for the right amount of money, they're willing to tolerate a fabrication. Let's just say, I made it worth their while."

"You're a definitive king maker."

"You have no idea, my boy," he said, with a bit of a frown. "But before I forget, there're two other features that make it possible for only you and me to access it. First, you have to make weight. You have to weigh in at precisely 187.0 pounds. Second, if you want to make a withdrawal before 1985, you have to provide a blood sample, and it needs to match the data for your blood that I provided to them. If it's after 1985, you have to provide a matching DNA sample. Of course they have matching data points for me as well."

"Sounds complicated," I said.

"It is." He leaned in closer. "You can't tell anyone about this. No one knows except you and me. Make sure you keep it that way. This is your inheritance I'm talking about, Andrew. It's worth much more than the Company in the present. Much, much more. You just need to live long enough to take advantage of it."

I just need to kick this cancer habit and not be murdered and I will be a sure-fire multi-billionaire when I return to the present. But what good is all of that cash if I'm dead? What good is it if I don't have anyone to share it with? I wished Jennifer was with me. She could help me sort through details. She could help me make good decisions. That's all I could think about as we rode back to the warehouse with Bud in the morning. At least he let me drive this time, but he insisted on riding shotgun. If someone had offered me a taste of heroin, I would have taken it without question and retreated into its cocoon of detached safety regardless of the consequences.

Every bit of information confused me, but a decision had to be made, and I didn't know who I could trust. Rose? Grandfather? I wasn't even sure if I could trust myself. So, I decided that as soon as a proper cure presented itself, I would return home to the present. This is all too much for me. I would do my best to convince Grandfather to join me, but he would have to make his own decision. I don't fully know what Grandfather has gotten involved in, but he has survived without me and his chances of continuing down that path will increase without my involvement.

We entered the warehouse and were led into a conference room where a buffet was spread for us. While we filled our plates, Great Aunt Eva arrived and greeted us. I couldn't ignore the noble air to her presence.

"David, you're looking much better," Eva said, giving Grandfather a hug. "I'm still not used to seeing you looking this old." She played a bit with his grey hair. I found her playfulness amusing.

"And you must be Andrew," she said to me. Her embrace was full of sentiment. "David, your Grandfather, has talked about you so much. I feel like I already know you. It's kind of strange seeing you for the first time." A tear developed in her eye. "It's just that I've never even seen a picture of you and now I've seen you in person, yesterday and today." She trailed off and fought to hold her composure.

"It's okay," I said. It was weird actually. At this juncture in time, I was chronologically older than my great aunt.

"I guess I just miss my family, and it is hitting me now after all this time," Eva said. Grandfather walked over and hugged her. "Has anyone told you how much you look like David when he was your age?" she asked me.

"No, but I'll take that as a compliment," I said.

"When this is all over, I guess I may have to head back East for a reunion. It's been too long," Eva said.

"I think I'd like that, the younger version of me, I mean. You may not like me as much as you like this version of me, though," Grandfather said.

"So you've met Bud," Eva said.

"Good morning, Boss," Bud said, and set down his coffee in order to shake her hand. In his own way, it seemed to be his best effort at intimacy and comfort. The gesture was not lost on Eva.

"Yes, he is both an outstanding bodyguard and philosopher," I said with sincerity. Bud gave me an appreciative head nod.

"Really?" Eva said. "You'll have to share some of your wisdom with me in the near future, Bud."

"I'm at your disposal, Boss."

Eva went to the buffet and poured herself some coffee. It was obvious that she wasn't used to losing control. It dawned on me that in the 1970s women were still battling for respect in a world dominated by men. She took her time and then joined us at the table. I'd never met Aunt Eva before, but I was developing a fondness for her. *If I survive, I'm going to go and find her out West and get to know her in the present.*

"Rose, I've heard a lot about you, too," Eva said. "I've actually been receiving reports on your progress for the cure for Schneider's Lymphoma for some time."

"Really?" Rose said. "I didn't know anything about you until yesterday."

"Your work is very progressive and outside of the box. With some luck, I think you will have a cure for these boys in the next calendar year, don't you think, David?"

"Yes, I think that's possible," Grandfather said.

"So, there isn't a cure here with you then, Eva?" I asked.

"No, I'm afraid not. But we will be able to prepare a lab for Rose to continue her work. It should be ready in a few days."

"Thanks, that sounds great, Eva," Rose said.

"I have some ideas I'll share with you later in private. No need to bore Andrew with the details," Eva added.

"Can we back up for a minute? I'm sorry, I don't mean to sound rude. Eva, what exactly do you do in this warehouse?" I asked.

"Well, we do a lot of things. Of first importance, we synthesize your anti-cancer cocktail here. We make it as a backup to the operation in New York," she said.

"You always need a contingency for these sorts of things," Grandfather added.

"David contacted me some time ago. It was out of the blue; we hadn't talked in years. He said he needed my help and that there wasn't anyone else he could trust," Eva said. This sounded very familiar. *Was there anyone else that he had drawn into this mess with the same play?* "I was even more surprised when he showed up in

California one day in a very old version of himself. It was unbelievable."

"How did he convince you?" I asked.

"He knew some things about me that only *he* could've known."

"Can you fill in the blanks a bit? I'm very curious," Rose said.

"Eva, you don't have to talk about the details if you don't want to," Grandfather said.

Before she could respond, I said, "Well, I think we all have a right to know what's going on. We've all been dragged into this, whatever *this* is. I want to know why I've never met you in my entire life, Eva. Why did I have to come to the past to meet you? From what I can tell, you're a tremendous person."

"Andrew," Grandfather started.

"No, Grandfather. Our family sucks. For every achievement realized, we're driven another mile apart. You're the only person I feel close to, Grandfather, and over the last few days, everything has come into question for me. Here's Aunt Eva, who seems like a great woman, someone I'd like to have in my life, and I've never met her. I'm scheduled to meet her next week at your funeral, Grandfather, and you're not even dead!"

"Andrew, stop it now," Grandfather said.

"Why isn't Aunt Eva a part of our lives?" I repeated. "It's like she's been withheld."

"David, it's okay. Let's get everything on the table," Eva said.

"Are you sure you want to talk about the past?" Grandfather asked Eva.

"Yes." She took a moment and prepared herself. In the gathered silence, I hoped that my outburst wouldn't do more damage, but who was I kidding? *I probably won't be around long enough to regret it.*

"Okay, here it goes. Time for a family history lesson," Eva said. She had everyone's attention, even the loyal Bud. "David and I are half siblings. He and our mother came to America following World War Two because David's father didn't survive the war. To be honest, I don't really know much about your father, David."

"That's a story for another time," he said.

"Our mother married my father, and I was born shortly thereafter in 1947. David is thirteen years older than I am. When my father died, David became a father figure to me, especially after Momma took her own life. I was just a kid." Tears formed, but she remained stoic.

Bud brought her some napkins to wipe her eyes.

"I don't really have any memories of either of them," she said. "For years, I thought it was my fault that Momma was gone, that I must have reminded her of Daddy and that memory was too painful for her. I'm sorry; I'm still trying to make peace with everything." She paused again. "So, we were in a Catholic orphanage together for some time, until David started college at Princeton. The Nuns let David take me, and he was able to get us an apartment near the Princeton campus. He raised me despite his classes and labs. It was a struggle for us, but we made it work. I felt loved. We were a family, the only family we had. Until Maria."

"I married her in 1957," Grandfather said.

"That's right," Eva agreed, "the year before you completed your Ph.D. and took the professorship at Harvard."

"She changed my life."

"Mine, too. For the first time in my life, I had a mother figure," Eva continued.

"And none too soon. You needed a woman's influence in your life. You were ten years old on our wedding day," Grandfather said.

"It was hard to leave my friends in Princeton, but your father, Peter, was born very soon afterwards. It was like having a little brother. I loved babying him, and we were just about inseparable," Eva continued.

"He loved you, too," Grandfather said.

"We were in Cambridge for only about two years because David started the Company in 1960, and we moved back to Philadelphia, the city of our broken childhood. Your Aunt Hannah was born shortly after the move." Grandfather nodded his head in agreement.

"The family was growing and everything seemed normal from what I could tell. I graduated from high school a year early and was accepted at Princeton in 1964. I was thrilled to go back to the place where I had made real friends for the first time," Eva said. "Your Uncle Albert was born in 1965 and it was nothing but cheerful times, the pinnacle of happiness. But 1966 was different. It brought suffering."

She looked me in the eyes.

"I began seeing a young man in 1965," Eva said. "He was from a prominent family and the younger brother of a close friend and colleague of David's at Harvard. I began dating him after an intro- duction and recommendation from David. He was my first love, and I was sure that my life would have a happy ending. But he began to drink too much and to experiment with drugs. One night he had too much to drink, got violent, and forced himself on me. I became preg- nant. I was distraught because it meant my career was over. I wouldn't be able to finish my degree because I wouldn't be able to be in the lab anymore. Popular convention for a couple in our situation would be to get married, but I couldn't marry that monster after what he did to me. I wasn't ready to be a single mother."

"What did you do?" Rose asked.

"I took the train home to Philadelphia one weekend and talked to Maria about it. She was so angry. She wanted to get David and the police involved, but I was afraid of what David might do. You know his temper. I didn't want him to blame me for all of this, so Maria used some of her connections and found a doctor who was willing to help. The procedure was quick and physically painless, but not a day goes by where my heart doesn't bleed. Even after all these years, I'm not sure that was the right decision."

"Eva, I'm sorry. I've been insensitive. I should have--," I said. I didn't know what to say.

"It's okay, Andrew, you couldn't have known," Eva said.

"Eva, you might as well finish the story," Grandfather said.

"A few months later, Maria became ill with the Schneider's

Lymphoma. She died that summer; I couldn't take it. With every-thing that happened, I thought I was going to end up in a mental hospital. I thought everyone was being punished because of me."

"Eva finally told me everything that had happened," Grandfather said. "I was in a state of grief and didn't know what to do. I pulled some strings and helped her transfer to Stanford University for the fall semester. I thought she needed a fresh start."

"With the distance, I ended up losing my family with the move. I threw myself into my studies. When I graduated, I quickly started an M.D./Ph.D. program that I completed last year. It was a family reunion of sorts for me when David-from-the-future arrived. And now you're here. I'll be honest, though; I didn't agree with David bringing you. But now that you're here, I'm glad to see you, Andrew," Eva said.

"And why am I here, exactly? It's still not clear to me," I said.

"David, you haven't told him yet?" Eva asked.

"I haven't found the right way," Grandfather said composing his thoughts. "Andrew, your father is the one who is trying to kill us."

"What are you talking about? You're saying that Dad is trying to kill us? To kill me? That's ridiculous. I just saw him a few days ago. We had a talk about you, Grandfather. And we talked about the future of the Company," I said.

"I'm not surprised, Andrew. He can't make a play until he knows where I am. He'a using you to find me," Grandfather said.

"How can you say that? He's your son, your oldest child. Dad's your right hand at the Company."

"I know it sounds bizarre. If you bear with me, I'll do my best to explain the remaining details to you, once and for all."

"Am I the only person in the dark here? Rose, do you know what is going on?" I asked.

"I'm in the dark too, Andrew. I know about the time travel discovery and the link to cancer, but that's it. David, is my life at stake, too?" Rose asked.

"I am afraid so. Everyone close to me or even just associated with me is at risk. I'm very sorry for that. But to be clear, there is more at stake than our lives or the health of our dysfunctional family," Grandfather said.

"He's right, Andrew," Eva added. "But maybe a solution will present itself. I believe in miracles."

"Okay, I will do whatever you're asking of me because our family is involved. I'll do whatever it takes to try and bring us some peace," I said.

"I hope that's possible," Eva said.

"Me, too, but I'm not holding onto too much hope for our family. I'm afraid it's very complicated," Grandfather said. "But if you can find a way to live outside yourself, you may find a way to save the lives of millions of innocent people." Maybe Grandfather was right. The key for me in all of this could be to look past my own insecurities and incurable defects, and maybe for once, I could find a way to love myself.

"I'm ready. Enlighten me."

"Forget everything you know about world history following the end of World War Two. It is all a lie," he said.

"Bud, do you mind getting the documentary ready?" Grandfather asked.

"Not at all," Bud replied. Within a handful of minutes, Bud had a movie screen and 16mm projector set up in the conference room.

"You may not believe me under these circumstances, Andrew and Rose, but I'm a man of precaution. Over the last year, I've worked to assemble a record, which right now functions as an internal memorandum, but it could be a gift to the world if unwrapped under the right conditions. We can talk about that more later, but you should know what you're going to see is completely true."

"Okay, I'm ready," I said.

"Hit it, Bud," Grandfather said. Bud started the first reel, and for the next ninety minutes, Grandfather's recorded voice narrated post World War Two history, complete with stock footage and interviews with scholars from the 1960s and 1970s. "I am Dr. David Acheson, a chemist, and more recently, a historian," he began.

The first third of the film dealt with subject matter that was familiar to me. Grandfather recounted how Adolf Hitler and the Nazis murdered six million Jews in the 1930s and 1940s, leaving a permanent scar on human history. After winning the war, the United States, Great Britain, and the rest of the Allies wanted to help the Jewish survivors recover from the Holocaust. Many of the Jews that were lucky enough to survive the Nazis did not feel welcome in Europe any more, but the Jews didn't have a nation to call their own. They had nowhere to go because they had left Israel during the first century, after the conquering Romans destroyed their Temple, which deprived them of their spiritual connection to their homeland. In the Jews' absence, Palestinians took control and loved the land. Israel became known as Palestine or "The Holy Lands" because it holds tremendous religious meaning to Jews, Christians, and Muslims. With the discovery of oil in the region, around the turn of the 20th century, new conquers took control: the British and Americans. So, after World War Two, the United States and Great Britain were in a position to give the Holy Lands back to the Jews, which they wanted to do as a way of easing their suffering from the Holocaust. Of course, doing this required taking it away from the Palestinians who still lived there, but they were very poor and thus lacked significant international political power.

The transfer of power occurred in 1947. Immediately, the Jews went from surviving the Holocaust to fighting for their independence. They fought fiercely, beating back the Palestinians and the Arabs who supported them. The Jews refused to lose, even in the face of overwhelming odds. Other wars followed because the Palestinians and Arabs have resolve, too. But the Jews always won. Grandfather made the point that it's hard to blame any man who raises a hand to protect himself, but all the parties involved feel threatened. The longest lasting result is maybe the permanent unhappiness among the aggrieved, with peace talks and mediation perpetually failing. The U.S. has been involved since 1947, as Israel has been one of the largest beneficiaries of American foreign aid. Many international entities believe that American involvement is duplicitous because it tolerates Israel's possession of nuclear weapons—one of the world's worst kept secrets—while sanctioning other regional nations that attempt to develop the technology. Many believe the Jews will only use the technology if their neighbors invade and overrun them, and to date, the U.S. is the only country in the world to use nuclear weapons on their enemies.

The second portion of the film shifted in tone. "The preceding 'historical' account that I have relayed to you is a fabrication. It should have never happened," Grandfather narrated. "In the twentieth century, I invented time travel. How that happened is complicated and for another documentary. What's important to know is that my technology found its way into the hands of people willing to change history for their own advantage. For this, I am sorry. What follows is what really happened. I know, because I lived through it."

Grandfather described how in 1946, the United States and Great Britain did indeed talk about giving Palestine back to the Jews. However, at the last minute, an alternative plan was presented and accepted by Jewish and world leaders. Prominent Jewish-American leaders presented their unconventional plan to world leaders during their final decision-making summit in London at what was known as the Anglo-American Committee of Inquiry. The plan proposed that instead of removing the Palestinians from the Holy Lands, the State of Florida would be given to the displaced Jews to create a new nation. The plan had the support of many Jewish-Americans, and preliminary surveys of those most aggrieved supported this move over the return to the Holy Lands.

As news poured in regarding the liberations from the concentration camps, Americans, regardless of ethnicity, had great concern. The war had become a Holy War for Americans, so when President Truman presented the Florida plan to Congress, it was met with overwhelming approval because it felt like the only proper conclusion to the war. Jewish-Americans wanted it, the majority of displaced Jews wanted it, the non-Jewish Americans wanted it, and so it was approved by the newly established United Nations. America got to play the hero in a story once again.

Establishing a new nation was complicated for the two and a half million people living in Florida in the mid-1940s, but the Federal government took steps to make the transition as smooth as possible. First, the nation of New Israel was created on May 14, 1948, which took over the territory of Florida, but there were six months of lead-time before the exchange, which allowed for a smooth transition. The New Israel government agreed to respect the property rights of anyone who decided to stay or keep their holdings in Florida. For those who wanted to leave, the Federal government agreed to exercise its constitutional eminent domain power over any land, business, or property they weren't able to liquidate in advance of the turnover. Many people who wanted to leave were able to sell the lands and businesses in advance to incoming Jews. Others decided they would prefer to relocate elsewhere in the United States, and the Feds, by eminent domain, paid a fair purchase price for their property. Displaced former residents from Florida were given hiring preference within the federal employment program on par with returning veterans. During this time period, the Feds also helped Florida settle all of its state debts. Many Floridians elected to stay; it was their home after all. By international agreement, those who stayed received dual citizenship with New Israel and the United States. Thousands poured into Florida beforehand. Many were Jews from around the world that wanted the opportunity to be a part of the new Jewish-Democratic nation. It was a very exciting time in world history. Of course, others were smart businessmen who saw an opportunity and bought property and businesses at good prices, Grandfather pointed out. When the transition occurred, New Israel agreed to purchase all of the government property, including lands and business assumed under the eminent domain provision. This was all tied into a debenture, a bond of sorts, that was worth several hundred billion dollars, a large sum, no doubt, but the Feds tied it to a reasonable interest rate and allowed for repayment over one hundred years. By all accounts, it was an extraordinarily smooth transition considering everything that had to be pulled off in that six-month window.

"The miraculous creation of New Israel pales in comparison to the glory of what happened in Palestine," Grandfather continued. Based on a proposal from the same American diplomats, Britain and the U.S., through the Anglo-American Committee of Inquiry, implemented a new policy for how Palestine was governed. In essence, it required world cooperation from the outset. In real history, Palestine operates on a three-year cycle. It's an elegant creation because the Holy Land is too important to too many different religions to be controlled outright by any one of those groups. To establish impartiality, the Brits and Americans involved the Swiss because, for centuries, they've been able to avoid involvement in most world conflicts.

The rotation works like this: The Jews control Palestine for a year, followed by the Muslims for a year, and then the Christians take their turn for a year. The three groups made massive contributions to a pool of money managed by the Swiss called the Palestine Fund. Many foreign governments also supplemented the Fund with donations or long-term loans. This money was used to construct living quarters, restaurants, and modern infrastructure to rebuild and maintain all of the designated Holy sites. The cooperation on this last issue was tremendous. The management of the Palestine Fund allows for constant improvements. The Swiss manage everything: The money, the government, and pilgrimage.

The Palestine Lottery was implemented at the same time as the means to select pilgrims each year. During each rotation, more people want to visit Palestine than space allows. There are limited places for them to stay. So every year, two thirds of the space is available by pure lottery. For example, if the Christians' year for possession is coming up, people belonging to the Christian faith who want to spend the next year in Palestine file paperwork with the Swiss, making themselves eligible for the Palestine Lottery. Lottery Day has become a holiday worldwide, with many people taking off work in order to wait for the mail to arrive. Anyone who enters the Lottery gets a written notice, whether they are selected or not. It can be tumultuous. The Swiss, with their moneymaking genius, created a system wherein winners of the Palestine Lottery—no matter who they are or where they're located—go to the Holy Lands free of charge. The Swiss take care of everyone. They fly everyone in. They feed everyone. They provide entertainment options. All of the doctors are Swiss, but they hire and screen the remaining workforce from an international pool of candidates. The Swiss even arrange and regulate the tours of the religious sites and for proper observance of any religious holidays. The remaining one-third of the tickets are disposed of on the Supplemental Palestine Market, wherein those tickets are sold by auction to the highest bidder from the pool of people not chosen during the Palestine Lottery. It is by most accounts a fair process because those who pay the large sums to ensure their pilgrimage are not given any better treatment than the rest of the population. Everyone has the same accommodations. Everyone has access to the same food and health care. The large sums paid by the people utilizing the Supplemental Palestine Market are deposited into the Palestine Fund managed by the Swiss, ensuring a positive income every year.

"The Swiss have been perfect partners. Not only have they been able to expand the number of pilgrims that can be accommodated every year, but also their peacekeeping forces have a nearly flawless record," Grandfather narrated. Some police units wear the same colorful, clown-like suits designed by Michelangelo for the Swiss Guard at Vatican City. The Swiss Palestine Police do not generally carry any weapons, but they are trained in the latest martial arts and peacekeeping techniques. All of the religious groups seem to be happy with the arrangement. They all get complete control of the region; they just wait their turn. The presence of the Swiss ensures that all of the religious sites are properly maintained and respected, with a policy of no tolerance, as stipulated by the Palestine Civil Code. The Swiss require compliance with the Code as a condition of immigration. Deportations are swift and difficult to challenge in international courts. At the end of the day, peace and harmony are the end goals. The Swiss were able to begin the three-year cycle in

1949 and accommodated 50,000 Jewish pilgrims. With their management of the Palestine Fund, they were able to accommodate nearly three million pilgrims in 2010. Because of its remarkable efficiency, the management of Palestine is studied in business schools worldwide.

The creation of New Israel and the management of Palestine are not without their critics, Grandfather noted. The agreement required the displacement of the Palestinians that lived in Palestine in 1946. The Palestinians were given several options: If they wanted to stay in the region, Egypt and Jordan agreed to accept them as refugees. The Allies agreed to open their borders to immigration, too. While many in the region relocated to Great Britain and France, the majority ended up in the United States. The U.S. government helped the refugees find jobs and homes. No matter where they went, by most accounts, they had a better life.

However, there weren't just Arabs in Palestine. A large population of Jews and Christians were residing there at the time of the agreement. While most of the Jews elected to immigrate to New Israel, roughly 100,000 people had to be removed with force. Led by the Swiss Army and the United Nations, every effort was made to peacefully relocate this remnant.

In the last third of the documentary, Grandfather explored the larger global political ramifications. With the creation of New Israel via ceding the state of Florida, the United States had detractors within its own population. After the Cuban Missile Crisis in 1962, New Israel solidified its position as America's strongest ally in the western hemisphere. When Khrushchev and the Russians deployed their nuclear weapons to Cuba, it became public knowledge after President Kennedy addressed the nation and put the American people on high alert. The U.S. Navy initiated their "quarantine" of Cuba to prevent any more offensive missiles from entering Cuba, but of course, Cuba is just ninety-nine miles from New Israel.

From day one, the Israelis had been building their military. Even though the United States felt threatened by the Russians, for many

Israelis, their treatment by the Russians during the last century was still fresh in their collective memory; therefore, the Israelis didn't attempt a diplomatic solution. They could not tolerate a nuclear threat in their backyard. So, without consulting President Kennedy and his cabinet, the Israelis sent in their Air Force, Navy, and Marines to Cuba. Within ten hours, the Cuban Communists were crushed. Within twenty-four hours, Fidel Castro was hanging from the gallows. New Israel's Prime Minister had vowed never to stand by idly again in matters of national security after President Kennedy's attempted coup during the Bay of Pigs Invasion failed. The Israelis, with quick decisive action, accomplished the feat, which had been embarrassingly elusive for the U.S. military and the CIA just eighteen months before during the fiasco of the Bay of Pigs invasion.

The free world applauded the outcome, and in the aftermath, New Israel annexed Cuba. Generously, property that had been expropriated or nationalized by the Cuban Communists was returned to their owners. Under the control of New Israel, Cuba turned into a first world entity that thrives on its sugar exports, tourism, and dedication to the arts. The appropriation of Cuba made both the Cubans and Israelis wealthy, but the real prize for the Israelis was the confiscation of several dozen Russian nuclear weapons that had been deployed on the island, which the Israelis refused to return.

Israeli action also shifted the balance in the Cold War. Khrushchev's loss was so devastating to his reputation that his own people assassinated him less than a week later. The Russians could not retaliate against the Americans with a nuclear response because it had been an Israeli initiative. Even if the Russians wanted to retaliate, they couldn't. During all this chaos, the U.S. intelligence community determined that a position like Cuba was necessary for Russia to reach the U.S. with nuclear weapons because they had not developed a reliable long-range intercontinental ballistic missile system. All of their posturing was a well-constructed farce.

President Kennedy was emboldened by the turn of events. He sent more troops to Germany, and the Berlin Wall was torn down. With Khrushchev's assassination, Russia did not have the leadership to respond, and they lost control of East Germany. With that, like dominos, the rest of the Eastern Block Communist countries fell because Russia was not economically prepared to fight a land war with the United States. President Kennedy was not assassinated under ambiguous circumstances in 1963, but rather retired from office as one of the most respected American Presidents of all time.

Grandfather concluded his film with the following statement: "Citizens of the world: If you are seeing this film, I am dead and have not been able to prevent a great atrocity. Some things should never be forgotten, and some things should never be experienced. So that you know I am not a liar, I give you the following as proof of my veracity." The documentary concluded with a series of historical footage. The first clip showed Grandfather touring the construction of the World Trade Center Twin Towers in Manhattan in 1970; the second was footage of Grandfather attending the Beatles debut performance on the Ed Sullivan show in 1964; the final offering, most disturbing of all, was of Grandfather taping John F. Kennedy's assassination in 1963 in a manner that revealed shots from a second gunman, hidden on the Grassy Knoll.

"This is propaganda," I said. Grandfather's documentary was both disturbing and beautiful, disturbing in that it painted mankind, even the narrator at times, in a soulless hue, beautiful in that Grandfather's passion combined with the productions values of the film to create a moving product that could win an *Academy Award*, but for its controversial subject matter.

"No, it's all true. I promise, every effort has been made to be objective, Andrew," Grandfather said. It wasn't easy getting the self-proving footage at the end. I had to go back in time and film in a discreet manner, and then leave the reels for myself where they wouldn't deteriorate and where only I would find them."

"David, you promised me that you would stop time traveling without my consent because of your health," Rose said.

"Yes, I did, Rose. It wasn't easy sneaking around your watchful eyes, but it couldn't be helped. I'm sorry," Grandfather said.

"Grandfather, what went wrong? Why would anyone want to alter this course of history?" I asked. These were no small changes, and from what Grandfather said, they seemed mostly positive. *Why would anyone want to erase them?*

"It's thorny. People want peace, but they are not sure what it looks like anymore. I'm actually quite embarrassed about it. For the only time in my life, I was fooled," Grandfather said, his eyes smoldering with hatred. He was hot: I thought his face might melt off.

"This is all complicated," I reminded him.

"You're right, Andrew. You see, your father tricked me. After I made the time travel discovery and established a protocol for going back in time, I brought Peter up to speed. Obviously, the discovery is potentially lucrative, but I was conflicted on how it should be used, if at all. I turned to your father because I trusted him. He's my second-in-command at the Company, you know. At first, he was skeptical. It was too much for him to believe, I think."

"It's a sensational discovery, David," Eva said.

"Right. So, I ended up taking him back in time," Grandfather said.

"Did he let you give him cancer or did you have to trick him?" I asked.

"It was voluntary," he said after a pause.

"Where did you take him?" Rose asked.

"I needed to take him to witness something that was indisputable. I decided on Washington, D.C., August 28, 1963. I wasn't there myself, but I always wished I had been. It was hot and muggy, marching to the steps of the Lincoln Memorial, but hearing Dr. King's speech was like a breath of fresh air," Grandfather said. "And after the speech, Peter had his own dream."

Grandfather scratched his forehead.

"We became tourists. Peter and I went back and forth in time probably one hundred times together. We made a list of events to see, and we just checked them off, one every night. He enforced the limit because he wanted to savor the experiences. We were connecting in a meaningful way for the first time since he was a kid."

"What all did you see?" Rose asked.

"Just about everything you can think of. But we were reckless. We got so caught up in the excitement of the breakthrough that we nearly forgot that we needed to address the fact that we did not have a cure yet for the Schneider's Lymphoma. I doubled my efforts on the research, and I designed the cocktail that we take every day and made steady improvements to the formulation. It slows the progress of the disease, but it's not a cure.

"We needed to keep the technology secret, but at the same time we needed more than just me working on the project. Peter and I debated the issue at some length. Our trips back in time together ended when our relationship couldn't handle the emotional strain caused by the disease anymore. I wanted to increase the research on Schneider's Lymphoma and time travel in-house at the Company, but Peter feared that one of the employees would leak the information to the public, and we would lose control over what was rightfully ours, either by espionage or from the government taking over on the grounds of the national security risk.

"Eventually, I was forced to accept Peter's point of view. If I died unexpectedly, no one would be in place to immediately continue the research. We decided that we would bring in the Feds as a preemptive action. About two years ago, we went straight to the top, to the President of the United States. He, in turn, brought in the Vice President. They were extremely skeptical at first, but they came around with Peter handling the negotiations. The Feds agreed to provide a top-secret government laboratory dedicated to providing a cure for the Schneider's Lymphoma, and it was agreed that these scientists would not know the complete picture of the technology. That knowledge would remain with the four of us and select high-level officials in the government. In exchange for this laboratory, I agreed to leave twenty percent of the Company to the United States General Fund in my Will with the President acting as a Trustee," Grandfather said. "Your father didn't know about that requirement, however."

"That solves one odd mystery," I said.

"Yes, I suppose it does," he answered. "Things went sideways very quickly. I was right not to want the government involved. They wanted to use the technology as a tool for the intelligence community. I was against this, but I tried to have an open mind because we need a cure for the disease. I agreed to participate in a proof of concept with Peter and a small Federal team. The plan was to go and observe the final hearing of Anglo-American Committee of Inquiry in 1946, before the Committee sought world approval. Gathering information while not interfering was our mission. If we could gather intelligence without drawing attention or altering history, then the Feds would initiate a small covert program. Unfortunately, Peter betrayed me. He had made a side agreement with the Vice President where the federal team prevented the Jewish-American delegation from making their Florida relocation presentation to the Committee, and, instead Palestine was given to the displaced Jews. I was forced to run for my life when I made it clear that I disagreed with the technology being used in this manner. This allowed Peter to seize control of the Company. He always wanted power over me.

"I eventually ended up in exile here in the past. Peter has been trying to find me and kill me since. This was the only place to hide from his vast resources now that he has control of the Company. I quickly found Rose and got her working on a cure. Even though your father and I have only had brief periods of perfect synergy, I never expected his betrayal. But I never should have trusted Vice President Hamilton Sherman. He is the man that raped Eva at Princeton all of those years ago, her first love."

"I still cannot fully believe that someone as vile as Hamilton Sherman could rise to the office of Vice President. I would kill him myself if I could get away with it," Eva said.

"My mind is blowing up," Rose said.

"Why, Grandfather? Why would the U.S. government want to make such a drastic change to the world?" I said.

"It's complicated, my boy. Hamilton Sherman always had anti-Semitic leanings, and he had placed the United States and New Israel on the verge of war. After New Israel took over Cuba, the rest of Latin America noticed how it prospered. The U.S. didn't mind when the island nations of the Caribbean, one by one, asked New Israel to annex them. New Israel obliged, and from most perspectives, the locals are better off for it. Back in the present, New Israel has entered into negotiations to take over Mexico and Central America. It looks like several nations in South America are interested in becoming part of New Israel, too. They're amassing large amounts of natural resources through this process. After New Israel 'went rogue' during the Cuban Missile Crisis, politicians like Sherman don't trust New Israel. They consider all the annexations to be a land grab that weakens the United States. 'His America' can't tolerate the situation. He believes the United States made a drastic mistake in giving

Florida to the Israelis after World War Two because he believes it will lead to America's demise. He's willing to wage war over his beliefs. If there is no New Israel, then there is no threat of war. You see, Sherman is very popular and poised to win the next Presidential election, and the discovery of time travel merely gave him the means to cut the Israelis out of the equation."

"So history really collapses into a single timeline like we were talking about earlier? There aren't parallel universes?" Rose asked. Everything started to make sense now. *At least the theory.*

"Yes, that's correct, Rose," Grandfather said. "If a time traveler goes back in time and changes history, he can remember things they way they were, and the altered history is very foreign to him. A quantum event occurs in the cells where the memories are stored and are retained upon reversion back to the present. The memory cells revert to their original state, even if the memories are no longer accurate in the modified timeline. This is why my I'm able to remember the way things should be."

"I have a headache," Rose said.

"Let's take a break and let everyone ruminate over all of this information," Eva said. She stood up. "I've heard all of this before, and I still find it overwhelming. I'll get you some aspirin, Rose."

"Thanks, I'd appreciate that," Rose replied.

"Why don't you walk with me down to my office, Rose? David, why don't you join us? The three of us can talk a little chemistry and cell biology," Eva suggested.

"A meeting of the minds. Of course, I'm always up for talking about a cure to my life-threatening disease," Grandfather said.

"I hate to impose on you, Rose, if you are feeling bad. We can wait until tomorrow if you need to lie down or take a break," Eva said.

"No, it's okay. Time waits for no one. At least it didn't used to," Rose said.

"Good. Time is of the essence after the attack on the New York lab," Eva said. "Bud, do you think you can keep Andrew busy for the next couple hours?"

"Sure, I have some ideas," Bud said with a hint of a smile.

We all left the conference room. "Have a good time," Rose said. I felt a twinge of abandonment over being left alone with Bud. Eva, Rose, and Grandfather went in one direction, while Bud took me through a series of corridors in the warehouse until we stopped at an unmarked door. From a peg rack, he pulled two sets of sound-suppressing headphones and goggles and handed me one of each. I put them on.

"Welcome to my office," Bud said as he inserted a key into the lock and opened the door. He switched on a series of lights, and as they powered on, I realized that we were in a gun range.

"Cool."

"Thanks. I do all of my best thinking in here. The Boss built this especially for me because she insists that I be in combat-ready condition at all times. I didn't argue with her much."

"I imagine not."

"Do you still have the pistol that you were carrying last night?" Bud asked.

"Yes." I produced the Colt .45 from my waistband. I fumbled around with it before letting my arm drop down to my side.

"What are you trying to be, some kind of gangster? We need to get you a holster so you don't accidentally blow an extra hole in your butt." Bud walked over to a large cabinet, inserted a key, and opened it, revealing about two-dozen assorted handguns, rifles, and semi-automatic weapons.

He handed me a tray and forcefully placed a brick of .45 rounds and some extra magazines onto it. He grabbed a brick of .44 magnum shells and put them on his own tray. "Okay, let's see what you can do."

He led me over to the range where he put a human-shaped target on each of our sleds and sent them back halfway towards the far wall that was lined with several rows of sandbags about fifty feet away. I loaded my extra magazines with ammo. I was nervous. I had shot guns once before in college for a friend's bachelor party. I wasn't the best shot in our group, but I didn't embarrass myself either. The hand-eye coordination I had developed in sports saved me from embarrassment, but most of my experience with guns came from watching action movies and playing video games.

"Ready?" Bud asked. I nodded my head. "Okay, take your time. Take aim and fire."

I managed to get a magazine into my pistol, turn the safety off, and put a round into the chamber. As I took aim, Bud fired his own weapon. It was loud even with the sound-suppressing headphones on. I didn't remember it being so loud before; it startled me. Before I fired a single shot, Bud had finished his first set.

"What are you waiting for?" he asked. "Relax. This isn't a pissing contest. I'm trying to give you some therapy."

I took aim and fired. I felt the endorphins releasing into my blood stream. I felt powerful. *Maybe everything would be okay?*

"Thanks, Dr. Bud. I'm starting to feel better already."

"Good. Think of this *country boy* more as a teacher, not a doctor," Bud said. He grabbed the sled controls and brought our targets forward. I had hit the target with all of my shots, with half of them even hitting the target's body. Bud had hit the head and body with all of his. "Don't get discouraged. I'm going to make a crack shot out of you before long."

He sent our targets back down the lanes and then he watched me fire a few shots. "Lock your right arm and use your left hand to steady the gun. Squeeze the trigger; don't jerk it." His advice worked: I hit the target's body consistently. We worked at our targets until we both finished our bricks. Not much was left of either paper bodies at that point.

"This is fun. I could get used to this," I said.

"Can you feel your blood pressure lowering?" Bud asked.

"Yeah, I'm pretty calm now."

"Can I give you some advice, kid?"

"Sure. Of course," I said.

"Look, I don't really understand everything that is happening with the Boss and your family. I could spend a lifetime trying to understand and still wouldn't be able to. After Vietnam, I lost my way. I needed something to believe in. God, fate, luck, whatever you call it or believe in, brought me to the Boss. During my job interview, she saw something in me and took a chance. I believe in her because I need to believe in something larger than myself. I certainly can't believe in the ideal of the United States after the war. We've lost our way somehow. Truthfully, we may never have been on the right path. All of these revelations or whatnot from the Boss and your Grandfather confirm it for me. Given the chance, mankind will do unspeakable evil if he thinks he can get away with it. But I believe in Eva's goodness. I don't trust everyone else. Your Grandfather, I just don't know about him. I don't even know if I trust you yet, kid, but you are growing on me. I see a younger version of myself in you," Bud said. "The only thing I know is that if I spend enough time here in my 'office,' I think I will figure things out."

"I've spent my whole life trusting my grandfather, Bud. But now everything seems turned around, and I don't have a compass," I said, surprised by my admission to a near stranger. *Bud was right about his "shooting therapy."*

"Have you considered that maybe your Grandfather brought you here because you are his compass?"

I hadn't. Grandfather had said he needed me, but I hadn't let myself believe it. I didn't want to be counted on.

"I don't know what skill, strength, or courage I can bring to this chaos, but I'm going to do everything I can to save my Grandfather and my Dad and set things right," I said.

"That's the spirit. You want to try a heavier tool?"

"What do you mean?"

"How about a shotgun?"

"Sure," I answered. He handed the weapon to me.

"Maybe if you're lucky, the grey you see in your family's quest for *righteousness* will fade and leave only black and white."

Bud and I fired weapons in his office for the next few hours without spoliation from conversation. It was cathartic in way I didn't expect, and my thoughts drifted to Jennifer. History defined her world; she lived in the past. She was an expert at all of this; Jennifer didn't love me: I knew that. I'd probably never be able to win her back: I realized that, too. But I knew that she'd want to see me make honorable choices regarding my involvement in this historical predicament. *She would know what to do though I doubted my ability to do so.* I wished she were here with me. *Maybe I could impress her, by Grandfather's faith in me?*

We rejoined the others for a quick meal in the conference room. Afterwards, Grandfather took a dose of heavy-duty painkillers, and then Bud drove us all back to his house on the outskirts of San Bernardino. When we arrived, Bud went to the trunk and motioned for me to follow.

"I've got something for you," Bud said. He pulled two shotguns from the trunk and handed one to me. "Always be prepared for war. You never know when it will come to your doorstep. I can't stay awake every night. I need your help keeping watch."

"Okay. I'm glad to help," I said.

"Good. We'll do three-hour shifts. I'll take the first one."

"You know, I think I can handle guard duty here if you want to watch the Boss's house."

"I have two guards with her every night and at least one at the factory at all times. She wants her best with you all at all times. She's fearless, but I'm cautious," Bud said.

Grandfather was getting better, but he was still weak. Rose and I helped him get into bed, and I was in bed quickly myself. A knock on the door startled me awake, but it was just Bud letting me know that it was my shift.

"Don't worry, kid. I'm going to sleep on the couch just in case you need me," he said.

I grabbed my two guns and followed him downstairs like a cowboy, exhilaration juxtaposed with intense fear. I liked it. In the next room, I heard Bud hit the soft fabric on the couch. Alone again with my thoughts, I stared out into the desert, longing for some music. *Rock music would be a great companion.*

Moments later, I heard footsteps behind me. I turned to see Rose.

"It's just me. I can't sleep. I saw that your door was open, and I figured I'd find you down here," she said.

"Need a teddy bear?" I offered, pointing at Bud who was snoring.

"Very funny."

"This is all screwed up, isn't it?" I said.

"Yeah, it is. I've had a head start on the craziness, but today was just too far out there."

"I know. I can't stop going over all of the scenarios in my head," I said. "I'm having a hard time keeping all the details and nuances straight. I always knew that my family was dysfunctional, but this takes it to a new level. Your family can't be this bad."

"Well, you'd be surprised," she said.

"What do you mean?"

"I don't have any family. Not anymore. Not really. When I was seven, my momma and daddy died. One night, I was in the kitchen helping Momma fry up some hamburgers for dinner. Daddy was on his way home, and Momma was worried that she wouldn't have it ready in time. He always got angry when that happened. When he got home, he was fuming about something, and Momma left me in the kitchen to finish cooking the food. They went up to their bedroom to argue. She didn't want me to get upset, but I could hear them yelling through the walls. I thought if I could get the burgers cooked faster, maybe they would stop fighting and Momma and Daddy wouldn't hurt each other. I turned up the flame—too high. I quickly had a grease fire in the kitchen. They never heard my screams for help, not even when I ran upstairs to pound on the door. I didn't know what to do, so I ran next door to the neighbor's house for help. We lived on a farm so that was a half-mile away. By the time I got back, the house was engulfed in flames. My aunt Erma, Momma's younger sister, raised me after that. She resented having me around because I stole her freedom. I left for college as soon as I could, and I haven't seen that old town since. Too many bad memories," Rose said.

"I'm sorry," I said, realizing how cheap my words sounded.

"It's okay. It's not your fault," she said. In the relative darkness, I could still see that her cheeks were flushed.

"I've spent most of my life feeling like I killed them."

"No, it's not your fault. You were seven." I put my shotgun down and hugged her.

"I know that intellectually. Emotionally, it's hard to get there," Rose said. She leaned into me. "Thanks for the hug. I haven't received too many of those in my lifetime." I hadn't either, of course.

"Is that why you are so attached to him, to Grandfather, because he is a father figure to you?"

"Yes, I think so. I don't think I could stand to lose him."

"Even when your mind tells you to run for the hills?" I asked.

"I would be devastated. He's the only person I've felt close to my whole life. I have his complete attention when he is here, and he is dependent on me. I sort of like it," she said.

"A psychiatrist would have a field day with the two of us," I said.

"What do you mean?"

"He's been my anchor my whole life. He has helped me survive some pretty dreadful situations. Now, though, I'm not so sure I will survive my relationship with him. But he's my family. I love him— and my dad—so I'll do my best to be a remedy." I released her from the embrace and reached down to pick up the shotgun.

"You've got a new toy, I see," Rose said.

"Yeah, Bud has me in training. He calls it 'gun therapy.' If you can slip away from your nerd meetings sometime, you can join us," I said.

"Perhaps," she said. We sat in silence for a while and let the night wash over us.

"Rose, I still have so many questions," I said.

"Me, too."

"How was your meeting with Eva? Did she offer any insight?"

"Not really, Andrew. We just talked science," Rose said, but she sensed that I wasn't satisfied. "We went over the progress on the cure for the lymphoma. She has lots of good ideas we'll start implementing tomorrow. There's more, but I'm just not sure I am the right person to tell you," Rose said. She was having a hard time meeting my eyes.

"What is it? Please don't hide anything from me. I can't take any more cloak and dagger."

"You have a right to know, and I don't think they want to hide anything from you. I think David is just looking for the right moment."

"What is it?"

"He is Stage Four."

"What does that mean?"

"He doesn't have much longer before the disease claims him, Andrew."

"How long?"

"I don't know. Maybe a few months," she said. She started to cry a little. "It's sad. All of this started because of his love for his wife, Maria. He just wanted to find a cure to honor her memory."

"This isn't your fault, either. Don't forget he's been reckless. He gave himself the lymphoma believing he had discovered a cure for his late wife's disease. He's been cavalier at best," I said. Grandfather has never thought he was wrong about anything.

"Yes."

"How far along am I? Do you know?"

"You are still Stage One. Don't worry, you still have quite a long time," Rose said. I was sorry for being so forceful. *I need more shooting therapy.*

"Listen. You must be under a crazy amount of pressure, but you can't let yourself take emotional responsibility for any of this. It's not your fault," I said.

"Sometimes I think about what it would be like to go back in time," she said. "I want to grab that little girl in the kitchen and prevent her from starting the fire. I want to kick down her momma and daddy's door and save them. I want to make her life better. But I'm not sure that would make *me* any better. Our scars can make us stronger people, Andrew. I have to believe that."

Our family of four—Bud, Grandfather, Rose and I—made it to the warehouse in the morning, and we ate breakfast in the conference room with Eva. Grandfather and I shared our special cocktail of life-extending drugs. Afterwards, I gave him a squeeze on the shoulder.

"Rose, I came in a bit early and started the assays we discussed yesterday," Eva said. "But they won't be ready for a few hours. I was thinking that Bud could take the three of you out shopping. I bet you could use some clothes and toiletries."

"That's not a bad idea," I said.

"I could use a few things, too," Rose said.

"What about you, Grandfather? Do you want to take a trip to the shop?"

"No, I think I'll stay here and rest. If you want to pick up several changes of clothes for me, though, I'd appreciate that," Grandfather said. He was pretty frail. I remembered what Rose said last night. *Maybe she was being optimistic about his prognosis?*

"All right," I said. "But there's no need for Bud to join us. I'm sure he could use a break."

"Okay. But if you are not back in two hours, I'm going to send the whole security team after you two," Eva said.

"Keep sharp, kid, and stay close. There's a shop ten blocks west of here," Bud said.

"Which way is west?"

"Take a left out of the parking lot. You've got so much to learn."

We found the store without a lot of effort. I parked the Mustang, and Rose and I got out and went inside. I walked around to get a feel for the offerings. I've never been a big fan of clothes shopping, but at least this was a full-fledged department store. Still, I wasn't pleased with what I found at first inspection.

"I hope this isn't the only place around here selling clothes," I whispered to Rose.

"Why?" Rose asked.

"I'm not sure I can find anything here that I'll like."

"Look around and find something. We shouldn't waste too much time here."

"I feel like I am stuck in a vintage clothes store," I said.

"What, you didn't like the running shorts that I picked out for you in New York?"

"Well, they were pretty tight. I usually wear shorts that have more breathing room. You know, less form fitting."

"Well, that's the style right now," Rose said. "If anything, you should be more worried about trying to fit in and less about impressing me with your modern tastes." She was funny. I was starting to appreciate her sense of humor.

"Maybe we can start by getting Grandfather some clothes," I said. I pulled a card from my pocket and doubled checked the sizes he had given to me. I located several racks of men's suits, and searched for three-piece suits in Grandfather's size. I held up a wool and a polyester model. "What do you think about these?" I asked Rose.

"Those will work, Andrew."

"Good. That was easiest thing I've done in quite a while." I took them to the sales counter and set them down. "Where can I get socks and underwear?" I asked the salesman.

"Back and to the left," the salesman said. Even though the shop wasn't too busy, I was glad he wasn't interested in following us around in order to increase sales.

Rose and I traveled to the back, and I grabbed some socks for Grandfather and me. Rose chose some for herself, and then we meandered to the underwear department.

I picked up a pair of white briefs and modeled them.

"For yourself?" Rose asked.

"No, these are too small for me. I noticed that Grandfather is a fan of briefs. I'm actually more of a boxer fan," I said. I enjoyed teasing her and seeing her uncomfortable. "What is the contemporary style for men?"

"Uh, I wouldn't know."

"I need room to breathe. What do you think about these?" I modeled a pair of sixty-inch waist boxers for her.

"We could both fit in there," she said.

"Good, then we can share," I said with a smile. Rose appeared to enjoy the flirting, but she seemed to be in uncharted territory, not wanting to get hopelessly lost. *But that is when it becomes fun.*

"I'm going to go over there," she said, pointing to the far wall. "I'm going to pick out some women's unmentionables for myself. Feel free *not* to follow me."

Her smile was growing on me. While I selected boxers for myself, I found that my eyes were magnetically drawn to her across the store. I decided I needed to give her some privacy; all women should be treated like queens. I delivered my new choices to our growing pile on the counter.

Outside, I saw a few young men walking around in jeans and t-shirts. Unfortunately, the jeans were flared just like the pair I was wearing. *Ugh.* I found a bright tracksuit in my size. It was a start at least. I resigned myself to the options and found a few pairs of jeans that fit reasonably well and some cool t-shirts to go with them. A sports jacket and two dress shirts for each of us rounded out my pile on the counter. Rose still hadn't come to the front of the store, so I went to the back to locate her. She had about a dozen items in her hands.

"All done?" she asked.

"Yup. I'm a standard dude. We don't shop: We hunt and conquer."

"Good. I'm glad you're done. I have too much stuff," she said.

"What do you mean? We have plenty of money; get whatever you want."

"Thanks. But I still need to try on everything and see if anything fits."

"I saw a dressing room in the back," I said.

"Okay. Do you mind helping me? I could use an opinion on some of these things, on whether they are professional or not," Rose said. It was clear she had debated asking me for help. "I haven't shopped for clothes in a while; there's never time with the research going on. And when there is, I'd rather sleep."

"Sure. I'll give you my opinion. Just know in advance that I'm a harsh critic."

"Then go wait at the counter. I already have a complex about clothes."

"Don't worry. My best friend is a girl. I know how to be constructive," I said.

"Never mind. I can see this was a bad idea," she said. Rose was playful, but serious.

"Too late. I've already accepted your invitation. Besides, my life literally depends on getting you out of this store as fast as possible and back to the lab."

"Just remember, I have a gun in my purse, and I'm prepared to shoot any critic that's too harsh."

"Here, let me carry some of those for you," I said and took the clothes out of her arms. I tried to take her purse, too.

"Oh, no, you don't," Rose said. "That stays with me." Her smile was securing a firm hold on me because everything about her was genuine.

Over the next hour, I watched her model skirts, jeans, and wrap-dresses, which seemed to be the latest thing in fashion. It was kind of fun. She had said earlier that she had put on a lot of weight, but I didn't see it. She was cute, maybe even perfect. She's one of those girls who didn't know she's attractive. I chose some clothes around the store for her to try on that I thought she might enjoy. It felt like we were on a date, and I hadn't been on one of those in years.

"We can't forget shoes," Rose said when she was finished selecting her garments. "I need something to go with the slacks you picked out for me." I couldn't argue with her. I picked up a new pair of Nike's for myself, which to my surprise was a brand new company, according to the salesman.

Like a child holding onto the last rays of light at sunset, I didn't want the experience to end.

As we pulled into the warehouse parking lot, one of the security guards exited the building. He flagged us down, so I drove up next to him and rolled down my window.

"Hey, I'm Michael. We haven't met yet. Bud just asked me to pick up the lunch order for you all. Since you're already in your car, do you mind going?"

"No problem," I said.

"It's a little Mexican restaurant about three miles from here. It's one of Bud's favorites." He scribbled some directions onto a slip of paper with the order on it and handed me some cash. "I love your car, by the way," Michael said.

"Thanks, me, too. You can take it for a spin sometime if you like," I said.

"Cool, man. See you in a few minutes."

"Are you up for a quick drive or do you need to get back?" I asked Rose.

"It's your life that's on the line, remember? Can my return to the lab be delayed a few more minutes?" Rose answered.

"Let's go." I was glad she wanted to spend more time with me one-on-one. As quickly as we had pulled into parking lot, we were back on the road.

"Do you think your dad has found a cure for the cancer?" Rose asked.

"I don't know. I hadn't really considered it."

"It's just something that crossed my mind last night."

"Why do you ask?"

"It's something you should consider. If he has it or if you think the government lab that your company is working with may have it, you should really think about going back," she said. "You need to consider all of the possibilities available to you."

"How do I know that my father won't kill me?"

"Well, you don't, but from what you said yesterday, you just saw him."

"That's true. I did say that," I said. "But to be honest, it wasn't the most positive conversation."

"What did he say?"

"He wants me to take a bigger role in running the Company with him."

"Did you sense any hostility or urgency in him?" she asked.

"Yeah, he was interested in getting me out of the experimental program Grandfather had me in and upstairs into the executive suite."

"So he can keep you close?"

"Maybe. Maybe so. I don't know. It's hard to believe that he would want to hurt me. We've had our major issues over the years, but I don't think he has it in him to kill. I don't think he could kill me."

"I didn't think David could kill either, but he shot that man on the train without hesitation," she said.

"Yeah, I haven't mentally dealt with that yet."

"Everything that is happening is bigger than me, Andrew. I feel caught up in the wave," Rose commented.

"Me, too."

"I'm just thinking out loud, but if there were a cure for the cancer, could we go back in time and heal your grandmother Maria and put a stop to all of this? Could we prevent David's discovery of time travel?" she mused.

"I don't know. If Grandfather's right about memories being retained after regression to the present, Dad and the other Feds would remember the existence of time travel. Even in the most altering timeline change, they may still find a way to reinvent it. Closing the loop would require preventing the impetus for the discovery of time travel and the death of everyone that knows about the discovery, even us," I said.

"Maybe you're right."

"Listen, Rose. I believe in your ability to find a cure for this disease, and a cure will give us more options. I think Grandfather chose you for this project because he has faith in your ability to solve that part of the equation."

"I wish you could just jump forward in time a few years to see if his trust is well placed."

"Yeah, it's too bad it's just a one-way ride back to where I came from," I said. "It's too bad we can't make some other stops along the way. At the end of the day, my faith is in you, too. Rose, I don't know how to say this, but I can't regret this whole experience anymore. I may be dead from a disease that was forced upon me by my own grandfather, or killed by the government or even my father. It could happen tomorrow, next week, or next year. I don't know. What I do know is today, I feel alive. Spending the morning with you makes the danger seem inconsequential."

"Andrew, I don't know what to say."

"Say you will work as hard as you can to save us. When all of this is done, I'll find a way for us to be together."

"Wow. That's a forward statement," Rose said.

"Maybe it's all the drugs in me talking," I said.

"I hope not. I like it."

We arrived at the restaurant, and I went inside and picked up our order. It smelled great. I couldn't wait to eat. *It was too bad we have to rejoin the others.*

As swiftly as we were back on the road, we were stopped at a traffic light. I thought about kissing Rose, but I lost the nerve like I always do. I looked out the window at the pickup truck stopped next to me and saw a ghost. Geoff Henderson, my best friend Jennifer's boyfriend, sat in the passenger seat. *It can't be him. It can't.* I noticed the mole under his eye—the one that robs him of Ken doll status—just as he turned and looked at me. For an instant, we locked eyes, and he seemed just as surprised as me. *Something is wrong.*

"Hey, what are you doing here, Andrew?" Geoff asked. He alerted the truck driver and exited the vehicle. He approached the Mustang and attempted to conceal a pistol in his waistband. *Why does he have a gun?* I floored the accelerator, sending our car down the street. In the rearview mirror, I saw Geoff dive into the bed of his truck as it began its pursuit.

"What's going on?" Rose asked.

"Someone from the future. They've found us again," I answered. We wove through the lazy afternoon traffic at a frantic pace. I knew we'd have a chance to escape if we left the city streets because the Mustang could outrun the pickup, but there were few options. After a series of turns, we were on a less populated street, and Geoff began to shoot at us from his perch in the back of the truck. He emptied his gun and banged his hand onto the roof of his vehicle. The truck moved in closer to try and ram us. I made a hard right and ahead lay a stretch of open road, but the only problem was that a set of railroad crossing safety arms had begun to descend: A train was approaching. For an instant, I considered punching the gas and breaking through to the other side of the road, a risky proposition. The alternative was to stop and fight. I didn't get to decide: The pickup plowed into the Mustang's back quarter panel. I slammed on the breaks and jerked the steering wheel, sending us spinning. The truck's momentum carried it forward through the railroad crossing arms. The Mustang came to a complete stop in the middle of the road as the truck came to rest on the railroad tracks. Geoff rose to his knees in the bed of the truck, and we locked eyes for a second time as he pushed another magazine into his pistol and took aim at me. I realized we were sitting ducks just as a freight train plowed into the helpless vehicle. Geoff went airborne as the train crushed the truck, causing an explosion. The train swept away the wreckage while it decelerated. I knew it would take several minutes for the train to stop because it had at least fifty cars. *No one could have survived that.*

For the next thirty minutes, I zigzagged the Mustang across town. I was certain that we hadn't been followed, but as an extra precaution, I parked in an alley three blocks away from the warehouse. Rose and I grabbed the food and ran inside. I held her hand to make sure she didn't fall behind.

The others were waiting for us in the conference room.

"What took so long? I'm famished," Grandfather said.

"I saw someone," I said.

"What? Who?" Grandfather asked.

"Do you know Geoff Henderson?"

"Jennifer's boyfriend?"

"Yes."

"Are you certain that it was him?"

"Absolutely."

"Did he see you?" Grandfather asked.

"Yes, but he is dead. A train hit him."

"A train?"

"Yes, a freight train. There wasn't anyone else following us, but we parked several blocks away in case witnesses noticed us in the car," I said.

"What was he doing back here? What do you know about him?" Grandfather asked. Eva and Bud stared in silence.

"He's a professor at the University of Pennsylvania. My understanding is that he's an expert on international relations and terrorism."

"Yes, I'm aware of all of that. Anything else? Did Jennifer ever mention him?"

"She said that he had started consulting with a company called the The Philosopher's Cave. Have you heard of it?"

"Yes, of course," Grandfather said.

"Well, Jennifer said they had been after him to consult for a long time but he had been resistant. After the terrorist attack on the cruise ship in the Mediterranean, he couldn't say no to a more formal commitment anymore," I said.

"Why is this important?" Eva asked.

"I can't be certain, but my guess is that the President and Vice President have brought The Philosopher's Cave in on the project. Doctor Henderson is one of the preeminent experts in his field," Grandfather said.

"But why is he back in 1972?" I asked.

"Because the federal government now considers me a terrorist," Grandfather said.

"This won't look good on our résumés," Rose said.

"What are we going to do to make this right?" I asked.

"First, I think we need to take extra precautions," Eva said.

"Agreed," Grandfather said. "Your father is getting closer to finding us, but with some luck, the trail will grow cold in a few days, and Peter will move onto the next town. My guess is that his team is basing their search on the train schedule. They probably have figured out that we bought tickets with a terminus in Flagstaff. Protocol dictates that they would have started there and gradually fanned out. They don't have much to go on, so with some luck, they will move on quickly."

"Let's go on lockdown," Eva said. "Bud, I want you to go to my apartment and your house to pick up our things. Then open up the warehouse dorms, and make sure they're ready for use. Then let the rest of the staff know what's going on because we are all going to stay here for the time being."

"I'll bring the Mustang inside the cargo bay, too," Bud said. "Kid, throw me the keys." I tossed them across the room to Bud and he left without hesitation.

"Won't Peter and the others eventually think to check on Eva to see if she knows anything?" Rose said.

"Yes, but we thought of that. According to the trail of records we left behind at her condo in San Francisco, she's working for the next two years as a physician on a cruise ship that's circumnavigating the globe," Grandfather said.

"I was careful in prepping my friends and colleagues, too," Eva added. "Most of them think I'm crazy to take such a long break from my career. But those that are close to me know that I'm coming off a long romance that ended badly last year. Needing a break is the perfect cover story. Even if they follow up and try to find me on the ship, they won't know where to look next. I reported to the ship and quietly cancelled my contract once we reached the first port in Mexico. It was easy crossing the border back into the States. I just showed my driver's license. Mexico doesn't keep very good records. David and I set up the operation here together shortly after that," Eva said.

"What's the plan? I didn't ask for all of this, but I'm ready to do whatever it takes to survive and restore history to what it should have been. That's what you have in mind, right?" I said.

"Yes, Andrew, more or less," Grandfather said. "For what it's worth, I'm sorry. If I had been a better brother, father, and friend, none of you would be in this situation."

"Let's just get through this and deal with the regret if we survive," I said.

"Everyone sit down and calm down," Eva said. It was clear that the pressure of our situation redlined our stress gauge. "Our chances of success and survival depend on our ability to trust each other and continued hard work. Let's be honest: We're not in an ideal situation. But here we are, nonetheless, with thousands of innocent lives hanging in the balance. I hope and pray that we are worthy of the burden Fate has asked us to bear."

"Sorry. This is at lot to process," I said.

"It's okay. You've haven't had as much time as the rest of us," Grandfather said.

"Let's bring Andrew and Rose up to date on the plan, David," Eva said. "They have enough background now to handle it, don't you think?"

"Eva and I have spent a lot of time discussing the best course of action," Grandfather said. "Every idea we come up with has its advantages and disadvantages. Our main consideration is a solution that prevents the Feds from changing history for their own self-interest. The situation is complicated because our enemies have the same technology we have. Any action we take has to ensure that New Israel's creation isn't disturbed. If we fail, we condemn the world to a future of violence and terrorism."

"We cannot accept a plan that could easily be undone with time travel," Eva added. "But we know that no plan is perfect. David and I believe that if we present a strong enough response, our enemies will be wary of testing our resolve."

"We've been preparing to go back to 1942. Once there, we'll poison the Palestine water supply. The region is dependent on the Sea of Galilee. If the lake is compromised, it will not be a viable option to the Anglo-American Committee of Inquiry in 1946 for the displaced Jews to relocate to. The only viable option will be to accept the New Israel-Florida proposal," David said.

"This is crazy," Rose said.

"I agree," I said.

"Well, Eva and I are scientists. Our goal is just to create disruption, not destruction. We've been conducting research here in the warehouse, and we're close to completing the design of a simple system that would deliver a series of chemicals to the lake that would render the water undrinkable."

"That's severe. Isn't there a better way?" I asked. "How are we not terrorists if we do something like this?"

"Well, for a time, we considered setting off a nuclear device or a dirty bomb in the region in 1945. This would have a permanent effect and would be the maximal deterrent," Grandfather said.

"I can't believe you would even consider that. Do you hear yourself?" I said.

"Listen, the Sea of Galilee has a residence time of about five years," Eva said.

"What does that even mean?" I asked.

"Well, Andrew, it means that the water in the lake cycles out every five years. So, if we introduce the chemicals in 1945, the lake will be clean and drinkable again in five years," Eva said. "So, it would be severe enough to force the Committee to consider Florida as the only viable option when that plan is finally suggested. This would prevent the violence and destruction we're experiencing and will experience in this unfortunate new reality. That's a good thing, don't you agree?"

"We have to get our hands dirty in order to make things right. The end will justify the means," Grandfather said. I was at loss for words. I couldn't put a response together that articulated my feelings of disappointment.

"What about all of the people already living in the region? What about the ecosystem?" Rose asked.

"Yes, those are considerations. We will time the introduction of our chemical system to minimize human collateral damage. If we're able to achieve our vision, it'll actually aid in the peaceful removal of the remnant that resisted relocation in the first place," Grandfather said. "The five-year residence time still allows for the Swiss to implement the Palestine Trust and lottery program."

"And the plants and animals?" Rose asked.

"Our plan is to introduce a level of contaminants that will be just high enough to warrant evacuation and second thoughts, not irreversible consequences. Remember, the Florida plan was met with an overwhelmingly positive response. If the proposal is heard by the committee, it will be approved, especially if there's no other viable option," Grandfather said.

"So you will just be turning the tables on your son and his co-conspirators then, David," Rose said.

"Yes, that's exactly right. They removed Florida from the equation. We'll countermove and remove Palestine as a variable," he said.

"Couldn't they just get water from the ocean via desalination or ship water in?" I asked.

"Well, shipping water is not a viable option. Not on that scale. It would be too expensive. Desalination is possible, but it requires a lot of energy. A massive power plant would have to be constructed and that couldn't be done overnight. Remember, an ample hurdle is enough to achieve our goal," Grandfather said.

"What chemicals are you going to introduce, David?" Rose asked. Eva scribbled onto a piece of paper.

"This is a partial list," Eva said and passed the paper to Rose. Rose studied it for a minute.

"These are all nitrogen-based compounds. They're pretty common actually," Rose said.

"Exactly," Eva replied.

"I think I follow you now," Rose said.

"I'm the only non-scientist in the room. Feel free to shed some light," I said.

"Fertilizer. They're all commonly found in fertilizer," Rose said.

"We're going to introduce fertilizer into the lake," Grandfather said.

"And how exactly are we going to do that, Grandfather?"

"Actually, Andrew, we're not going to do it. You are," he answered.

"The nitrogenous materials in fertilizer are full of energy. In the wrong hands, it makes a powerful bomb," Grandfather said. "So, introduction into the water table must be done with great care. I'm afraid I'm much too frail for this sort of adventure anymore, so it will fall to you, my boy."

"Grandfather," I said, "There's nothing you can't do."

"Well, I have, unfortunately, hit the limits of what I can physically handle," Grandfather continued. We have selected seven underground springs and caverns close to the northern portion of the Jordan River and lake. There were countless possibilities, so these were chosen because they are hidden in area that is generally not well traveled.

"You will go to 1942. You will form a Welsh chemical fertilizer company and arrange for the sale of your product to the British entities that control Palestine. The region is in dire need of agricultural attention, so you'll be met with open arms. While you're dispersing your superior products around the farms and kibbutzim, you will take the opportunity to build and hide these seven devices," Grandfather said.

"Why seven?" I asked.

"Any one of these devices would be enough to sufficiently pollute the lake, but seven adequately hidden machines assures success if one of the devices is discovered or deactivated by our enemies," Grandfather said.

"David, maybe it would be helpful if we took a tour of the warehouse at this point? I think it would help complete the canvas we're attempting to paint," Eva said.

"You're right. Let's take a quick tour and then come back and eat," he said.

Eva led us out of the room and down some hallways.

"This is my office, Andrew, if you ever need to find me," she said, pointing at a door as we walked by. We stopped at another door a little further down. "And this is the anti-cancer lab." She opened the door and led us inside. Three scientists were working at lab benches and fume hoods around the space. I figured there were other people working in the warehouse, but I hadn't seen any of them.

"Team, this is Andrew, David's grandson. He'll be working with us," she said. I waved and felt sheepish. "And this is Rose. She's the scientist working directly with David and will be leading this task group. We'll do formal introductions in our weekly group meeting tomorrow."

"Hi. Nice to meet you," Rose said.

"We've had to shift some personnel recently to accommodate this new research focus area. Okay. Let's continue our tour," Eva said. The scientists waved and otherwise acknowledged us as we departed.

Eva continued the tour. Another lab was dedicated to preparing the anti-cancer cocktail that Grandfather and I required daily. "Graduate school level expertise" was all that was needed, according to Eva. Rose agreed. A single technician inhabited that workspace.

A third space housed various chemicals and supplies. The fourth area was quite large and indeed spectacular. It had the appearance of a large greenhouse, including skylights and rows of plant life.

"What's this?" I asked.

"We call this the Green Lab," Eva said. "Its objectives are twofold.

First, your designer fertilizer, in addition to being the perfect poison, must be remarkably advanced for Mideast conditions in order to attract the interest of the British rulers in Palestine. So, its utility must be tested against actual crops. Second, we need to control the concentration of the nitrates in the water so we don't kill the fish and wildlife. We're developing a model where corn can be introduced along the riverside and lakefront to remove the nitrates, but not too much water. What we've discovered is a hybrid of three corn varieties available in the 1940s that will meet this requirement. You'll be able to accomplish the hybridization and produce enough of these corn seeds within two years. The corn product isn't suitable for human consumption because of the low water content, but it is adequate animal feed and is cheaper than waiting five years for the water supply to self-regulate or to implement a reverse osmosis or electro dialysis solution."

"So while you're building up your stock of fertilizer and preparing to impress the British, you will also be secretly developing your corn," Grandfather added. "You'll be a savior twice. The fertilizer will boost crop yields, and your corn will purify the water supply on a two-year time frame."

"I'll also be a villain by poisoning the water supply in the first place," I said.

"No, that's actually the third way you're acting on their behalf. Believe me, this is the lesser of two evils," he said.

"At any rate, Andrew, you will be able to sell the corn technology to the Swiss when they take over control of the region," Eva said.

"Most importantly, the timeline of the Palestine Trust can stay on track because our biologist believes the long-term health effects will be negligible," he said.

The fifth research suite had two scientists working on electronic components.

"These two hardworking people are engineers, working on designing the delivery devices," Eva said. They greeted us more warmly than the last group. "This is especially sensitive because your personal safety's at stake. The fertilizer is both a poison and an explosive, so it's of utmost importance that you don't kill yourself while setting up the devices."

"How does this work?" I asked.

"Hi, I'm Doctor Amos Barnes," one of the engineers said. He shook our hands with exuberance. "We're finalizing two systems that are comprised of simple components that are readily available in the early 1940s. These two systems are essentially the same, with one minor variation. The first system is just a pump and dump. For example, five of the seven locations are underground caverns that lead to springs, which, in turn, feed the river and/or the lake. This system is simple: You just hook together your drums of fertilizer in a series then connect the system to a radio-controlled device. Once the radio is initiated, it activates a hydraulic pump that delivers the chemicals directly to the water source."

"Sounds pretty straightforward," I said.

"Yes, there is more. We've designed the drums and pumps out of organic materials. After the chemicals are pumped, a burn sequence is initiated which will incinerate most of the evidence. I'm pretty proud of the design," Amos said.

"What about the other system?" Rose asked.

"It's essentially the same, except it has an explosive component in case you need to move some rock in order to get the chemicals into the water system. It's pretty crude, but you shouldn't have any problems constructing it yourself," he said.

"Thanks, Amos. We'll get a schedule together for Andrew's study so you can be prepared to instruct him," Eva said.

"I didn't realize that I'd be going back to school," I said.

"I want you ready to go back in no more than two weeks. So treat this as final exams," Grandfather said.

"So there will be tests?"

"Yes. But there won't be any grades. Think of it as pass/fail. If you fail, you and many others will die."

"I'll get you a backpack and some notebook paper," Rose said, with a wink.

"What I need is a tutor."

I hoped a room full of heroin was waiting for me on this walking tour. Instead, our last stop was an advanced research lab that Grandfather and Eva would occupy. It looked pretty much like the other labs, with fume hoods and lab benches, except it was much larger. A lot of experiments appeared to be in progress. A set of empty animal cages in the back of the room caught my eye.

"This is where I do all my magic," Eva said. "With David's help, hopefully we can fully cultivate the fruits of this extraordinary discovery."

B ack in the conference room, I ate my cold Mexican takeout in silence. Rose chatted with Eva and Grandfather about science stuff, so I was left alone with my thoughts. Cold and dark, they circled me like dragons and threatened to eat me alive.

Being deposited at a crossroads is better than being stranded on the sidelines, but it was unfamiliar. I had spent my whole life mired in self-doubt. I didn't know if I would be up to the task, but Grandfather believed in me. Despite the cruelty of his machinations, I still loved him. I loved Dad, too, even if he preferred me out of the way or dead, but I wouldn't allow myself to think about that. I wished there were a way to speak to him, to get his side of the story, but that was impossible without eating some chocolate and risking certain death back in the present. But there was more, sitting right in front of me: Rose. The love of a woman is spectacular, the kind of love that makes a man feel invincible.

"What do you think about all of this?" Rose said as she descended into the seat next to me.

"Sorry. What?" I was still in a daze.

"What do you think about David and Eva's plan?"

"I don't know," I said.

"Well, I think it could work. They've put a lot of thought into it. If you can execute it, I think the region will have minimal long-term damage. And if they are correct, when things are set right, a lot of people will get their lives back," Rose said.

"I'm not a scientist. I have to rely on everyone else's opinion on the matter, and I'm not comfortable being in that position."

"That's why you have to trust your advisors," she said. I looked over at Eva and Grandfather. They were sharing a plate of nachos and talking nerd talk.

"Well."

"I know you trust me. Just ask me questions, and I'll always be honest with you," Rose said with such earnestness in her smile. Her smile could burn through my most stubborn insecurities. I wanted to ask her if she wanted to kiss me, but I struggled to form the words.

"The dorms are open and ready, Boss," Bud said, as he entered the room.

"Good work, Bud," Eva said.

"I've assigned rooms to all fifteen of us." He handed Eva a roster.

"Any questions or complaints from the scientists?" Eva asked.

"No, but I told them all that you'd be giving a more formal briefing later today."

"Thanks. Why don't you take our guests and show them where they'll be staying for the time being?" Eva asked.

"Ok," he said. Bud took us to the far side of the complex. Our rooms were better than the average dorm, styled more like a decent motel. We even had our own showers and mini-fridges. I was pleased to find my new clothes hanging in the makeshift closet, the Mustang's keys sitting on the desk, and the two briefcases in the closet. I opened the two briefcases, and everything seemed in order. I picked up the keys and put them in my pocket.

Grandfather's room was on the other side of mine. I picked up the clothes that we purchased for him and brought them over to his room. He was asleep on his bed, so I hung them up and closed the door behind me.

"Is he okay?" Rose asked from behind me. I must have jumped a bit.

"Yeah. I think he's fine. As good as can be expected, I think."

"Sorry, I didn't mean to scare you," she said.

"You're fine."

"Oh, thanks for the compliment."

"I meant-"

"I know what you meant," she said. I wanted to pull her in close to me, but Bud started toward us from down the hall.

"You want another shooting lesson, kid?" Bud said.

"Sure, I'm up for it," I said.

"All right."

"You want to come with us?" I asked Rose.

"Um, sure. Why not? I'm not supposed to take over leadership of my group until tomorrow," she said. But I could tell she felt a bit guilty.

"You don't have to stay too long if you don't want to," I said.

"Good, because I should check in at the lab this afternoon anyway," she said.

"I'm sure I'll get the study schedule Eva mentioned too at some point today," I said.

The three of us walked to Bud's office. As we arrived at the door, Michael, one of the other security guards, came running up.

"Bud, I'm glad I found you. Eva would like to see you in her office when you get a chance," Michael said.

"Okay, tell her I'll be right over," Bud said. Dutifully, Michael went back down the hall in the direction of Eva's office.

"Well, I was going to give this to you later. All of the security team has a copy, and I want you to have one, too," he said as he handed me a set of keys. "This will get you into my office and into the gun rack. Come whenever you want to, but keep it safe."

"Thanks, Bud," I said. He took his time walking down the hall to see Eva.

I handed Rose a set of earphones and shooting goggles and took a set for myself. I opened the door and we went inside the shooting range.

"Welcome to Bud's office," I said.

"This is great," she said. "But when are you going to get your own office?"

"Well, I think the janitorial supply closet we passed on the tour is my office. No one's told me yet, but I'm slowly piecing the evidence together."

"You're too silly," she said. I liked that our senses of humor clicked.

"Do you still have your pistol?" I asked her.

"Yes." To my amazement, she pulled it out from under her shirt.

"I totally didn't expect you to have it."

"I'm always prepared," Rose said.

For the next thirty minutes, I gave her basic shooting instructions not unlike the ones I'd received from Bud. It was fun, but I couldn't escape the feeling that this might be the only time I would be able to teach her how to do anything. I was okay with that.

We stopped and took a break after we had shot two bricks a piece. She hit the target consistently at that point, and I was proud teacher.

"Not bad. We'll make a Rambo out of you someday," I said.

"Rambo?"

"Oh, right. You'll have to wait until the 80s to find out, but I think you're going to like him."

"We'll see about that," Rose said.

"Andrew, there is a bit of a snag in the plan. We were talking it over at lunch," Rose said.

"What's that?"

"Well, someone has to travel back to 1942 with you," she said.

"Why?"

"Because someone has to keep you alive. You need to take the anti-cancer cocktail every day to slow the progression of the lymphoma. Either that or you need a cure. We've agreed that it would be too much for you to try and make it on your own with the technology that will be available," she said.

"I see. I hadn't really thought about it."

"Well, David wants to go with you."

"He said himself that he isn't physically up for it."

"Yes, that is true. He thinks he can go back and focus on making you a stockpile of the drug and then get back here to the warehouse as soon as possible."

"That sounds like a bad plan to me. What if he dies there?"

"Eva and I agree with you. So, one of the two of us has to go with you," she said.

"No. Absolutely not. That's not acceptable. I don't think it's fair for either of you to subject yourself to this disease. I'll just have to learn how to make the cocktail myself."

"You couldn't possibly master it on the two-week schedule your grandfather has us on."

"Why is he pushing it, then?"

"The destruction of the hotel lab in New York and the spotting of this Geoff guy on the way back from the Mexican restaurant has him scared. He's worried that it's just a matter of time before they find us," she said. Rose was right; his lack of confidence was telling.

"He knows better than anyone what we are up against," I said.

"I want to be the one to go with you, but Eva is insisting. I don't have much say on the matter. She got David to agree with us at lunch," Rose said.

"She's right, this is a family affair. If someone else has to risk death, then it should be family."

"Affair is right. Her plan is to pose as your wife," she said, half laughing.

"Well, that's weird. But I suppose it will make for a good cover story."

"It will help to have someone else there with you. This is a lot to handle."

"If you stay here, that means you can work on the cure," I said. "But if we are successful, then it will be like I was never gone, right?"

"I guess that's true," Rose said.

"But you're my backup. If I don't return—if time goes on and I haven't made things right—then it will be up to you to do it," I said.

"I know there are a lot of questions about what is going on," Eva said addressing the entire staff before dinner in the conference room. "It's my intention not to keep anyone in the dark, so I'm going to come right out and tell you. As most of you know, my brother David's laboratory in New York City was attacked a few days ago. Today, my nephew Andrew saw someone in San Bernardino that he believes may be looking for us, an individual from the future. As a precaution, for the next two weeks, I want everyone to stay here in the dorm facilities. I know they're not perfect, but they'll do until we're out of danger. I know you all work hard on a daily basis. David and I really appreciate that, and we hope you feel it, not only in your paychecks, but also from me personally. But I'm asking that you take advantage of the extra time you have here at the warehouse and put it to good use in your laboratories because we're ready to start Andrew's training phase. I don't have to remind you what's at stake because you all have been with me here from the beginning. Thank you for taking up this cause with my family and me. We know you didn't have to."

Grandfather didn't show up to dinner in the conference room. I mingled with the staff and tried to get a feel for their states of mind. Most weren't too shocked: They had signed up for this and knew that conflict was a possibility. After a while, I slipped away with a plate of lasagna and went to check on Grandfather. His door was unlocked, so I knocked and let myself in.

"Is that for me?" he asked, indicating the food in my hand.

"Yeah. You okay?" I brought it over to him on his bed. It looked like the nap had done him some good.

"Yes, I just need some rest. I'll be back to normal in a few days." I wanted to believe him. He started to eat the food while I brought him a glass of water from his sink. "It's still warm."

"Good. I'm glad. I haven't seen a microwave around," I said. Grandfather chuckled a bit.

"This whole thing is crazy, isn't it?" he asked.

"Crazy doesn't begin to describe all of this."

"I'm glad we've got some time together, just the two of us, my boy." I pulled up a chair to his bed so we would be close.

"Has your great aunt Eva cornered you yet about the change in plans?"

"Rose said that you wanted to go back with me, but she's worried about your health."

"Yes, she's right; I'm struggling here, but I think I'm up for it."

"Grandfather, I know you want to do it. But-"

"I can't let my sister down again. I've done that once, and I won't do it again. Let's not close the door on me yet. Can we agree to that at least?"

"Okay," I said. He had a hand in creating this mess. He had a right to remain the catalyst to its clean up.

"Good, now that we have that settled, we have a few things to discuss," Grandfather said. "We need to make some money in 1942 before you can open the fertilizer business. You'll have to get a job. I figure if you get a job in a factory in New York, we can save one hundred dollars in three months. That'll be enough to start my series of trades and bets to grow the money. In another three months, we'll have enough to move to the U.K. and start the fertilizer company in Wales."

"I didn't realize we'd have such a long lead time," I said.

"Well, I'm only eight years old in 1942. There's no money to borrow from my family or myself. During World War Two, my father was forced to fight for the German army. He did everything he could to avoid the war, but since he was young and able-bodied, it was impossible. He wrote to us often. He was first assigned to a war camp in Poland. His conscience forced him to find another post. He told us he requested a transfer to the front, which was granted by his commanding officer. His letters continued for a while then stopped. The best Mother and I could tell is that he probably died in the Battle of Stalingrad in Russia. His body was never found, so the Nazis assumed he abandoned his post, allowing them to refuse us any death benefits. We were left penniless and dependent on family and close friends for support. In the end, we were lucky to escape to America after the war. Mother was able to get us immigration papers through her mother who was a Hungarian Jew."

"Grandfather-"

"I'm sorry. I'm growing nostalgic these days. It's been a while since I've talked about my early childhood," he said.

"It's okay. I didn't know all of that," I said, glad he was confiding in me. I was shocked to learn that I have a Jewish heritage, but I was proud of it.

"I never enjoyed talking about my youth. I don't have too many happy memories," Grandfather said. "Now there's so much to share and so little time."

"How about starting with the most important stuff?" I said. I wanted to pick him up emotionally. It was heartbreaking to see him in this deteriorating condition.

"None of my personal history is important to anyone but you now."

"I count for something, though, right?"

"Of course, you do. Of course, my boy. You need to accept the fact that I'm old now. No matter what happens, cure or no cure, I won't live much longer," Grandfather said.

"But your note in the New York hotel said that if I took the pill and found you, I'd be able to save you."

"Yes, I did, and you have. Your coming here, loving me, and having faith in me has saved me. You've validated my life in ways that I do not deserve." I started to tear up. "But I hopefully have a few years left. I'd love to see you settle down and get married. I want to meet your children before I die."

"Love's so complicated. I don't think I'll ever understand it," I said.

"We never do, and that's what makes it beautiful. Sometimes the person we think is perfect for us doesn't see our real value, but the right person always drops right in front of your face."

"You're right," I said.

"Of course, I'm right. I'm right 99.9 percent of the time. I had a feeling you'd like Rose when you met her. You and I are so much alike, I knew she'd fall for you."

"But we're nothing alike, Grandfather. You're prodigious and sure of yourself all the time. Me, I'm always lost and insecure."

"Andrew, do you want to know my secret?" I nodded. "The secret is just being too afraid to fail. I see that in you now. You're desperate to save the ones you love. I hope in the end of this, that I'll have done all the right things, even for your father. Find a way to save him if you can."

"I will," I said.

"Good. Let's talk some more about contingency plans."

"Okay."

"You haven't told anyone about the gold, have you?" Grandfather asked.

"No, of course not. Part of me thought you were out of your mind."

"Never doubt me, my boy."

"Of course not," I said.

"Good. The secret gold's available to you any time from now

until the present. I wrote a clause into my Last Will and Testament. Perhaps you remember it?"

"Maybe, I'm not sure which one?"

"Remember the clause where you and your father lose control of the Company if you take it public? You don't lose control if one of you buys the other out."

"I don't understand," I said.

"If you buy your father's stake in the Company with the gold, it's not a public sale. You'd have a majority stake. You could keep the government and your father away from our technology."

"But they already have it."

"Yes, they have most of it, but there's more, and it's vital that they don't acquire the rest. I have some preliminary data encrypted on the hard drive in my office. It'll be only a matter of time before they break the cipher. In the meantime, I'm working with Eva to try to recreate the experiments here as a backup, but the data will take quite a while to reproduce."

"What is it?" I asked.

"Something that'll keep you alive, I hope."

"A cure?"

"Something like that. Not exactly what Rose's working on. It's the same issue but from a different angle."

"Ok, but what if Dad won't sell his stake?"

"He will, if you make him an offer he can't refuse."

"His life?"

"Yes, exactly. If we have a cure, he'll give up the Company in exchange for his life."

I spent the next week submerged in work. My sixteen-hour days consisted of working with Grandfather, attempting to memorize his trading scheme in the event that he wouldn't be able to join me on this leg of the mission. He had about three hundred transactions planned in succession to get us the seed capital we would need to get to Europe, start the fertilizer business, buy some land and begin to produce our hybrid corn. I was surprised how much progress I made in such a short time.

When I wasn't with Grandfather, I was learning how to make the chemical pump systems with Amos and Kenny, the engineers. I learned everything from constructing the pumps, the radio communication system, and the incinerator to procuring the parts I'd need for the device. Since they made the design simple, I could build their device in my sleep. The only thing that concerned me was whether I would be able to track down the seven locations chosen for the deployment of the devices. I only had maps and coordinates to go on, no GPS devices or Google Maps.

When I wasn't working with the engineers, I was with Diana, the biologist. She taught me first how to make the chemical fertilizer blend and where I could get what I needed for it in 1942. With some effort, I was able to memorize the compounds and the recipe. Subsequent to that, Diana trained me to make the hybrid corn that I would peddle to the Swiss to clean up the Sea of Galilee after I had temporarily poisoned it. It was very complicated because plant hybridization is just as much art as science. She did her best, and concentrated on the theory since we didn't have time to see if my lab technique was acceptable because the corn's growth cycle was longer than two weeks. But she suggested that if I got stuck, I could get help from the local farmers in Wales without drawing too much attention to myself. They would be glad to help a fellow farmer.

I saw Rose and Eva at meal times and only when their work in their labs allowed for them to leave. Rose and I made a point of sitting together for as long as we could. She was determined to discover a cure and save me. The thought of love, long elusive, escaping her grasp because of her own shortcomings became her motivation. Romance, she said, would have to wait.

In between, I spent time with Bud in his office. He let me graduate from pistols to rifles, and his brand of therapy allowed me to clear my mind.

The team that Grandfather and Eva put together was remarkable. It was dedicated to the cause, and through our open discussions, I determined that they were all paid handsomely: They had to be for this sort of secret project and the inconvenience that came with it. Some of team members had families at home across the country. But it was more than the money. They also had a real camaraderie. Over the time they had spent together in the warehouse, they'd become a patchwork family. Eva was like their mother, providing for them even though she was much younger than many of them. Most had been down on their luck and needed a hand up. Their prior situations had nothing to do with their competence, just bad choices for most. Amos's career had derailed when he couldn't stop drinking. He was a talented engineer, but he had survived D-Day while the rest of his platoon had been slaughtered. He had been sober for ten years now, but the destruction to his reputation was sealed when he assaulted his boss one day in a drunken rage. Diana's story was tragic, too. She lost the family apple orchard when her husband died of a heart attack. On her own, she couldn't pay the mortgage they had taken out on the property to pay for their children's college tuition. She planned to take the money she saved on this project to start over with a new farm. Kenny, who was young like me, loved football, and he loved to bet on college games. The problem was that he was terrible at picking winners and owed several sports books a pile of cash. This was the payday he needed to clear his debts and get a fresh start, even more so since he had four young kids at home.

Over the course of a week, I realized that despite the diverse reasons that brought us all together, we were bound by purpose although I didn't know if they believed everything that Eva and Grandfather told them. I wondered what would happen to them if I achieved everything in Grandfather's plan. What I did know was that everyone was giving his or her best effort; everyone was pulling for me to succeed, and I didn't want to let anyone down. But one week was not enough preparation. Unfortunately, that was all I was given.

It had been a normal day, as normal as any of the previous dozen in the warehouse, rotating through the different projects I was responsible for, and I was gaining confidence. It was nearly ten p.m. Bud and I were in his office when we heard it: A crash followed by gunshots.

Bud went to the gun cabinet and handed me a shotgun and a bunch of shells. I grabbed the magazines I had already loaded for my pistol. He picked up his radio.

"All units, report in," he said.

Crackling static and amplified shots were the only response.

"All units, status," he repeated.

Nothing.

"What's going on?" I asked.

"This is it, kid. Be ready for anything."

We went for the door. I stayed behind him as he opened it a crack. I shoved the pistol into my pants and rammed extra shells into my shotgun. In the hallway, there were screams and chaos.

"He we go. Shoot anyone that looks unfamiliar," Bud said. I pumped a shell into the chamber and followed him out. The adrenaline flowed, but I still felt fear's grip on my shoulder.

A masked commando with an assault rifle came around the corner. Before he could fire, Bud blew his chest open with a blast from his shotgun.

"Move, "Bud said. I ran behind Bud to the hallway's intersection. He peeked around the corner. "Listen. I'm going to go and try to secure the entrance. You go to the labs and do what you can."

Before I could say anything in acknowledgement, Bud ran in the direction of the warehouse entrance. I moved in the direction of the labs and reached the Green Lab first. A masked intruder had Diana backed into a corner with her hands up. He had a shotgun pointed at her face. I was too far away for a shot, so I did my best to get closer.

"What do you want?" she pleaded.

"Nothing," he replied. He pulled the trigger on his weapon, and it tore open her stomach.

I took a shot, still too far away to be effective. I hit the back of his knee, and he fell to the ground. He whipped around and sent a volley in my direction. He was too disoriented to hit me. Closer and under control, I put a shot into his chest and kicked his weapon out of his reach.

I rushed to Diana. She hunched up against the wall; blood spilled everywhere. I grabbed her hand.

"Go help the others," Diana said before she lost consciousness. The tears and anger stung my eyes. I put extra shells into my shotgun and ran for the door. I had to find Grandfather, Rose, and Eva.

In the hallway again, I heard an unfamiliar voice speaking on a radio. "There's trouble up here at the entrance. Be careful as you fall back," he said. *Bud must be giving them hell.*

I came around the corner with my shotgun firing. I sent two shots into the soldier, and he fell to the ground outside the engineering lab. One of Bud's security guards was dead inside the doorway. Inside the lab, I found that both Amos and Kenny were dead, too. The fury welled inside me. This wasn't fair. *I have to find the others.*

I was horrified when I reached Rose's lab; her entire team had been executed. Shotgun shells were all over the floor, but Rose's body was not among the dead. No one was in Grandfather and Eva's advanced lab, but it had been torn apart, too. Eva's office was empty as well. I heard a lot of shooting in the direction of the entrance as I slipped over to the dorm wing.

I kicked Grandfather's door open: Nothing. Next, I smashed open Rose's door. She sat on her haunches in the far corner, staring at a dead intruder in a pool of blood in the middle of the floor. She dropped her empty gun when she saw me and began to sob.

"Where are the others?" I asked as I bent over and helped her to her feet.

"They took David. I was helping him get ready for bed. If we hurry, we can catch them," she said.

I reached down and picked up her pistol. I slammed one of my extra magazines into it and handed it to her.

"Let's go," I said to her.

"Wait." She ran over to her mini-fridge and pulled out a package. "We need those briefcases for insurance." She tucked her package under her arm, and we ran out the door. I crashed through my door and found the room was undisturbed. I collected the two briefcases and put them into Rose's hands. She opened one, put her package inside it, shoved her gun back into her waistband, and took the cases, one in each hand.

Off again, we wove through the corridors. Ahead at an intersection we saw Michael, one of Bud's security guards. Michael traded fire with an unseen assailant around the corner. As we arrived, he took a bullet to his shoulder and chest in succession.

I gritted my teeth as he crumpled onto the floor. Rose stopped to check his pulse while I peeked around the corner and caught a glimpse of Grandfather being dragged away by two intruders. Neither of them saw me, but Grandfather and I locked eyes for an instant. His eyes screamed of fear.

I grabbed Rose by the shoulder, and we began our pursuit. Up ahead, I saw that the two intruders and Grandfather had joined four more members of their crew on the ramp leading to the loading dock.

They were shooting at the rest of our group, which was pinned behind some barrels and freight close to the far entrance. The soldiers had crashed a big rig tractor truck though the garage doors and knocked it off its hinges, narrowly missing the Mustang. Outside, their escape vehicle, a cargo van, waited as they advanced towards it, protected by a volley of suppressing fire from two more intruders inside the van. I sensed that it was our only chance: I had to be a cowboy. I had to be Clint Eastwood.

I took Rose's gun from her waistband and put it next to the other pistol in my pants.

"Stay down," I whispered to her. She obeyed.

I began to walk towards the unsuspecting commandos: Their attention was focused on the bullets coming from the far side of the warehouse loading dock. My only chance was to get them caught in crossfire.

"Hey," I yelled, when I was twenty feet away from the door leading to the ramp. I drilled the trailing man in the stomach twice as he swirled around to meet me. My presence was enough for Bud and Eva, at the far side of the room, to come out from behind their tenuous shelter and take out another assailant during the confusion. I dropped my empty shotgun and pulled out the pistols and released a torrent of death, dropping the third member of their party and hitting a fourth. But it was no use. The last two were able to get Grandfather into the van and out of the warehouse.

"Rose," I yelled. "Let's go." Police sirens wailed in the distance.

I did a sight check of the others. Bud had been hit in the leg, but Eva appeared unscathed. On the ground next to me, one of the assailants writhed in pain.

"Help," he said. "*Andrew*, help me." I went over to him and pulled his mask off: It was my cousin, Eduardo, who had—in the present—recently visited me at my apartment with his sisters, demanding a "fair share" of our grandfather's estate. He struggled to reach for something in his chest pocket, a bloody Hershey's Chocolate bar. I knocked it away from his hand before he could put a piece into his mouth. He expired seconds later.

"Diana, Amos, Michael, and Kenny are dead," I said to Bud and Eva.

"So are the others," Eva said. "We've got to get David back."

Rose came rushing down the ramp with the two briefcases as I threw the shotgun from the Mustang's trunk to Bud.

"You've got 'shotgun,'" I said. I climbed into the driver's seat while Bud claimed the passenger seat, and Rose and Eva jumped into the back. With a turn of the key, the engine roared to life. Without hesitation we busted out into the night.

We rocketed out of the complex. I saw the commando's van just ahead on a side street, heading towards a residential area. Bud rolled down his window, aiming at the van's tires with the shotgun as I closed the gap. I maneuvered through the traffic and into position for Bud to take the shot, but a second cargo van pulled up behind us and rammed us. The surprise of the jolt caused Bud to drop the shotgun onto the road.

Bud cussed.

"We've got company behind us," I said.

"I'm on it," Eva said. She took her gun and pierced the back windshield until it spider-webbed. Rose helped her kick it out of the frame and onto the highway.

Bud took out his pistol and began to shoot at the lead van's back tires while Eva opened fire on the van behind us. A thug from the passenger seat in the second van returned fire just as the first van's rear door swung open. Inside, I saw two of the men were working hard to subdue Grandfather, who was resisting. The third was driving. The fourth took aim at us with his pistol and sent bullets in our direction. We were trapped in a kill box.

I cut side to side like a running back attempting to break a tackle, making us a hard target. When the shooter ahead of us stopped to reload, I put the accelerator to the floor and rammed the lead van. Grandfather and the two men fighting him fell to the floor, and the shooter was deposited onto our hood. The look of surprise on the commando's face was priceless and short-lived. Bud put a bullet into his skull and launched the commando onto the road.

The lead van made a sharp right turn down a side street. I didn't anticipate the move and couldn't follow. I took the next right and began to double back. The trailing van stayed on us. In the rearview mirror, I watched Eva put a bullet into the driver, and the van slammed into a street-parked car. The passenger flew through the bullet-ridden windshield and onto the pavement.

Up ahead, I saw the lead van pull into the parking lot of an old Catholic church. The three remaining assailants dragged Grandfather inside the building and fired some shots at us, shattering the driver's side window, before slamming the church door shut. I slid the Mustang along side the van for cover.

"Let's go," Bud said as he disembarked. I drew my two pistols and followed him to the door. He kicked it open, and I covered him.

Soft candlelight bathed the nave. I felt exposed in the wide-open space, but Bud motioned for me to advance up the far side aisle so he could take the near aisle. He had to drag his injured leg. Nothing stirred. Then, I saw it by the altar: Four piles of clothes, three hand-guns, and several pieces of partially eaten chocolate candy. I picked up Grandfather's empty suit and slammed it onto the ground in frustration. We were too late. They had taken him back to the present.

"Eva's been shot!" Rose yelled when we emerged from the church.

"Out of the way, kid," Bud said, as he pushed past me to the backseat of the Mustang. Eva had been hit in her right shoulder, which was covered in a lot of blood. She screamed. Bud ripped off his outer shirt, leaving only an undershirt, and applied pressure to the wound.

"We've got to get her to a hospital," Rose said and climbed into the passenger seat. I went around to the driver's seat and closed the door. Bud stayed in the back and tended to Eva.

"You're going to be okay, Boss," he said stroking her hair back. "Take a right out of here and head north. The VA hospital is nearby." I followed his orders.

"David?" Rose asked me quietly.

"Gone," I replied.

"Get some of the money out of your briefcase for me," Bud said. Rose reached behind the seat and retrieved one of the cases. She pulled out several bundles of cash and handed it to him. He inspected it before stuffing it in his pants pockets. For the next several minutes, Bud fed me directions, and my mind buzzed. *What are we going to do now?*

I looked at Rose. She had some cuts on her face.

"Hey, are you okay? Your face," I asked.

"Yeah, just some cuts from the glass. I'll be fine."

"Listen up," Bud said. "I don't know how else to say this. Every-thing has gone sideways. I have friends at this hospital from the war, and I hope that a combination of that friendship and this money will convince them not to report this gunshot wound to the police, but I can't guarantee it. If you stay with us at the VA, you'll most likely end up in jail. If that happens, it will only be a matter of time before you either die from the cancer inside of you, kid, or the folks that paid us a visit tonight turn up again. The Boss needs these doctors, and I'm going to take her in there, regardless of the personal conse-quences. I owe that to her. You owe it to her and everyone else that died tonight to go into hiding and to find another way. I believe in you."

We arrived at the VA emergency room. Bud placed his gun on the floor as I pulled up to the curb, and I opened the door so Bud could get out. He lifted Eva into his arms: She was alive, but losing consciousness.

"I hope our paths cross again someday, kid. Good luck," Bud said. With that, he carried Eva as fast as his damaged body could move towards the ER doors.

"Thanks for everything, Bud," I said. He was right. We couldn't stay, but I was worried for them. *There must be more that I can do?*

I got the car back to the highway as fast as possible and headed west. Luckily, it was getting late and our beat-up transportation didn't draw a whole lot of attention.

In downtown Los Angeles, we found refuge in a nondescript no-questions-asked hotel. I paid a month's rent up front for a suite on the top floor. I left Rose upstairs with our few belongings while I drove to the wastelands of east L.A. where I found an abandoned lot and used five gallons of gasoline and a lighter that I had picked up at a gas station to set the car ablaze. Fire and flame can be purifying. It can burn away the past and liberate regret, but as I walked the streets in search of a cab or bus, the pistol in my belt reminded me that I was a killer and there was no escaping the remorse.

The sun had crept over the horizon by the time I got back to the hotel. I opened the door quietly in case Rose was asleep, but she was wide-awake, sitting on the floor, gun in hand, staring at the door. She didn't shoot me.

"Are you okay?" I asked.

"No. Don't ever leave me like this again. You were gone so long, I thought you were dead," Rose replied.

"Sorry. I had a hard time finding a ride back here. I had to walk most of the way."

I locked the door behind me.

"Come on, let's get you cleaned up," I said. I took her gun, put it on the coffee table in the middle of the room, and pulled her to her feet. She hadn't tended to the cuts on her face, so I led her to the bathroom and removed several tiny bits of glass from the lacerations before washing the wounds with soap and water. She winced in pain.

"This will probably leave a scar," I said. "The bits of glass shredded the skin, but it doesn't look like you'll need stitches."

"This is all screwed up," Rose said.

"I know."

"What're we going to do now?"

"I'm not sure. We've got to figure out how to get some of the anti-cancer cocktail, or it will be over pretty quickly for me."

"I've got you covered there," she said. I was confused. Rose ran to the briefcases, and she pulled out the package from her warehouse mini-fridge.

"Your family's so paranoid. Eva gave me this and told me to keep it just in case we had to run. We have a two-week supply of the cocktail and a bunch of the time travel drug," she said.

"Excellent. That's awesome." I was so relieved that I hugged her. The tension of attraction was thick, so I released her.

"We still have the synthesis schemes in the briefcases from New York, so I can make some more if you can get me the equipment and supplies that I need." She placed the drugs in our new mini-fridge. "So you're not going to die just yet."

"You're my savior," I told her.

"What happened back there at the warehouse?"

"I don't know exactly. My cousin Eduardo was there, and I killed him right before we left. I didn't know it was him until I took his mask off, but I still can't believe it; I'm not sure how I'm going to explain this to my family."

"From the look of things, he would have killed you if you got in his way," she said.

"You're right. It looked like a snatch and grab. The commandos rifled through some of the labs, but I think they were just after Grandfather, probably for questioning and information. They could've easily killed him, so extraordinary rendition—the government term for this sort of operation—must have been their focus. Grandfather is the key to everything since the rest of us are just interchangeable parts."

"Maybe they think David has the cure for the lymphoma?"

"I hope not. They may come after you if that is the case, if they discover that you're alive. They must be onto his plan somehow," I said. *Grandfather's encrypted research on his office hard drive: That must be what they're after.*

"What're we going to do? Are we going to go after him?" she asked.

"I don't know. We'll figure something out when I can think straight." I fell down on the couch, and Rose joined me.

"Okay."

"I can't get Eduardo's bloody face out of my mind. It feels like a permanent nightmare tattooed to my corneas." I rubbed my eyes, haunted by the finality of the deaths I had dealt to Eduardo and the others. Even what had happened to Geoff on the train tracks didn't sit well with my conscience. What I had been asked to do, to use lethal force, didn't seem fair because there could be no resolution to such distorted images.

"Quit it," Rose said. She touched my hands, but it made no difference. "Come on." She tried to pry my hands free, but it was hopeless: I was locked in. She lightly kissed my forehead and then each of my hands repeating the kind gesture until she was able to remove my hands from my eyes. Rose wrapped her arms around my body and snuggled into me. Holding her was all I could think of for the next few hours, and I didn't dare move a single inch because she fell asleep like a baby in my arms.

After a while, the sun was up in full force. I laid Rose onto the couch, found a pad and pen, scribbled a note—"out for supplies"— and left the confines of our new situation. At a corner market, I purchased some food and newspapers then went back at the hotel where I found Rose still asleep. I drank a daily dose of the cocktail, ate a bagel, and tore into the newspapers. I found a reference to a warehouse fire in a San Bernardino paper and a report of gunfire in the area prior to the fire. Police were investigating, but they had no leads. Someone must have returned to the scene to destroy the evidence, I thought. *It couldn't have been Bud. He wouldn't have left Eva. It must have been our enemies.*

I couldn't find any references to an incident or arrests at the VA Hospital. *Maybe Eva and Bud were able to negotiate anonymity?* There was no way to know their situation, whether they were alive or dead, in prison or free, or if we'd see them again. My gut told me it was too dangerous to try and track them down. Bud was right; we were on our own now.

When Rose woke up, she ate a bagel and made a list of chemicals and equipment she needed to begin making the drug cocktail. It wasn't too much to my untrained eye. The hotel suite had two small bedrooms, but we agreed that the best place for her to set up a new lab would be in the main living area where we had slept the previous night. I moved the furniture to accommodate the changes while Rose finished getting ready. When I finished, I counted our remaining cash. We still had more than $250,000.

We got on a series of buses, and by mid-afternoon, we were on the gorgeous grounds of UCLA. Rose had a friend from graduate school that was on the faculty of the chemistry department there. With helpful answers from several students, we found the office of Dr. Semisi Alofa, quirky, dark, handsome, gentlemanly, and surprised to see Rose. It was obvious to me that he had a crush on her. I wondered why she had never pursued a relationship with him.

After a short conversation in his office, we treated him to lunch at his favorite café in the area. He and Rose caught up on old times and life since graduation. Dr. Alofa felt lucky to be at UCLA, but he didn't have tenure, and he didn't have any publishable research results yet. Rose told him she had been working at a start-up that had just folded, had moved to L.A., had found an investor, and was ready to go out on her own to develop a new idea. Dr. Alofa was eager to help his colleague.

Rose handed him a list of equipment and chemicals that she needed to get started. To him, it was innocuous; to me, it was life. After a short examination of the list, Dr. Alofa said he had 95% of contents already in his lab easily obtained from the departmental chemical storeroom. The rest, he agreed to order for us and would have everything ready in two days. I handed him fifteen thousand dollars, told him to bill me for his time and the supplies, and I'd pay the balance in two days. Now he knew I was the investor; he had thought I was just a boyfriend. I told Dr. Alofa our company valued confidentiality because we dealt with trade secrets. The message was well received, but he assured us he had no friends and worked like a slave in the lab. I told him we'd keep him in mind for a job or collaboration when the company got off the ground. The meeting couldn't have been better; even if Dr. Alofa talked, he'd never be able to find us once I picked up the supplies in two days.

On the way back to the hotel, Rose and I stopped and bought more clothes and toiletries. Despite the success the day had brought, we didn't allow ourselves to have quite as much fun as our earlier shopping spree in San Bernardino.

While Rose emptied our bags, I searched the newspaper, this time for used vehicles. We would need transportation for the supplies, and after a few minutes, I found a winner.

"Here's an ad for a 1959 F-100 for a good price," I said to her.

"Good, why don't you call and see if it is still available?" Rose responded.

"I'm too paranoid to be on the phone. I'll go down to the lobby and have the receptionist make the call."

"Okay."

I walked down to the lobby and found the receptionist.

"Do you mind calling this ad to see if the truck is still available?" I asked. I handed him the newspaper.

"Is the phone in your room broken?" The receptionist asked.

"No, I just don't like to talk on the phone." I slid a twenty-dollar bill across the counter.

"We are here to serve you, sir." He dialed the number and had a brief conversation.

"I'm not sure if I understood everything, but I think the truck's still available if you can get there in the next hour. Sounds like he has an offer that he's considering," the receptionist said.

"Thanks. Can you call a cab for me?"

"No problem, sir."

I walked back upstairs to get Rose.

"Hey, you ready to take a trip to Chinatown? A cab is on the way," I said.

"Yes. As long as we can get some dinner while we're out. Sweet and sour pork with fried noodles is my favorite. I'm starving now. Oh, and sizzling rice soup and egg rolls," Rose answered.

I chuckled.

"Don't laugh. You might have to roll me out of the restaurant."

The cab delivered us to the address in the newspaper without any problems. I rang the doorbell and an old shirtless Chinese man answered the door. Through the screen door, I could see five or six young children sitting in front of a TV.

"I'm here about the truck for sale," I said.

"Okay," he answered. "Test drive?"

"Sure. Yes," I said.

He grabbed his shirt and keys and came outside. He handed me the key to the truck and led us to the vehicle. It looked okay from the outside, so I climbed into the driver's seat. In an odd move, the old man insisted on sitting next to me in the middle, relegating Rose to the seat next to the door. She tried her best to contain her amusement as I drove a few short blocks before returning to his residence.

"You like?" He asked me.

"Yes, how much?" I asked.

"I have an offer for seven-fifty," he said. I handed him one thousand dollars.

"Does this work?" I asked him.

"Yes. Thank you. Thank you very much!" He gave me some papers to sign, and I wrote down "Clark Kent." After a long moment, I realized he was trapped between Rose and me, so I let him out of the truck on my side. The Chinese man bowed to me before going back inside to his family. I got back into the truck, and Rose released her laughter.

"What?" I asked.

"Nothing. I just like spending time with you. I don't want this to end."

I looked around the busy street.

"Looks like there are restaurants everywhere. Do you want to get out and walk?" I asked.

"Sure," she said. As we walked down the street, she took my hand into hers. "I feel like I'm traveling in a foreign country. I love it." We stopped at the first restaurant we came to and were shown to a window seat. I asked Rose order for both of us, and she selected ten or twelve dishes from the menu. Her enthusiasm was deliciously contagious. While the waitress told us it would be twenty minutes for our order to come out, out on the street, a familiar stylized animal symbol caught my eye like a rainbow in a monochrome dream world. My heart skipped a beat. I couldn't believe it.

"We'll be right back," I told the waitress and took Rose by the hand and dragged her across the street.

"Where are we going?" Rose asked. Nothing I could think to say would make much sense, I thought, so I said nothing. We got to the door where the symbol hung. To a foreign eye, it could be mistaken for a wild dog or a wolverine, but I knew this creature had an African heritage.

"What is *The Way of the Hyena?*" Rose asked, reading the sign. Below the Hyena was a handwritten note in English and Chinese: "New Student Sign Up and Demonstration." Without hesitation, I pushed the door open, and in front of us, to my delight was a real, live, superhero: Victory George.

A crowd of about twenty women filled the martial arts studio. Victory George—Vikki to her friends—early thirties, tall, Black, beautiful, and athletic, stood up front, regal before her subjects. She was one of Bruce Lee's first and best Kung Fu students. They were close, and he encouraged her to develop her own style of Kung Fu, and *The Way of the Hyena* was born. Vikki's style focused on urban self-defense and targeted women. From my love of *Wikipedia*, I knew that she was poised to become a movie star after signing up to co-star in Bruce Lee's film, *Enter the Dragon*, but she was killed during the filming of the movie. The few video clips of her fighting on YouTube are legendary and have an underground following. I've seen them many times and considered her a master. Her murder was just six months from now, and back in the present, her demise remains of one the world's greatest unsolved mysteries.

"For my first demonstration, I will call upon one of my students," Victory said.

A young woman came forward, placing a chair directly behind herself and held a heavy cushion to her chest. Vikki got into position and extended the fingers of her right hand until they touched her pupil's protective shield. Vikki then made a fist, and without drawing back, she struck the pad, propelling the student backwards into the chair, causing the chair to flip and sent the student to the ground. The student returned to her feet with a smile.

"I learned that technique from my friend and master," Vikki said. I looked over to see Rose's reaction, and she was as amazed as I was. I couldn't believe that I had just witnessed Bruce Lee's famous one-inch punch.

Three of Vikki's students then brought out a ladder and a heavy punching bag. It took all three of the women to lift and hook it to an anchor in the ceiling.

"Three hundred pounds," she said. It barely moved from side to side as she leaned into it to demonstrate its weight. For the next few moments she jumped around the room to warm up before she unleashed a furious side kick into the bag, launching it into the ceiling. The crowed recovered from the explosion with applause. I clapped so hard I feared I might bruise my palms.

"I need a volunteer," Vikki said, but no hands went up. "Don't worry. I won't hurt you." This time nearly every hand went up. I grabbed Rose's wrist and raised her hand high in the air and wiggled it around. To my delight, Vikki chose her, and Rose went forward in front of the rest of the crowd.

"How are you doing, sister?" Vikki asked.

"Nervous," Rose answered.

"What's your name?"

"Rose."

"You'll do fine, Rose. Don't worry," Vikki said. A student came over to Rose and placed a large basket of apples in front of her. Rose looked confused. "In The Way of the Hyena, we teach improvisation. In a street fight, you have to be ready for any challenge."

A student launched two knives at Vikki, but she was ready, and caught them both. The crowd released a collective sigh of relief. Vikki laughed. "See what I mean? Rose, pick up one of those apples and throw it at me," Vikki said. Rose tossed one underhanded towards Vikki, who used one of her new blades to slice it in half. "Not like a girl. Throw it overhand, and throw it hard, as hard as you can." Rose complied and once again, Vikki sliced the apple in mid air. "Good, keep the coming, sister, as fast and hard as you can." One by one, Rose launched the apples at Vikki, who used her blades to slice the fruit in midair. "But, in a fight," Vikki continued while slicing Rose's barrage of apples, "attacks rarely come from head on."

At once, three of Vikki's students began to fire apples at her, each using both hands in a two-handed attack. Vikki became a blur of energy spinning and swinging, slicing each projectile. It was quite a spectacle. The students exhausted their supply of apples and Rose was about to hurl her final apple when Vikki threw one of her knives at Rose, piercing the apple in her hand, and delivered it like a nail to the far wall. Rose's face went white with fear. She checked her hand and confirmed there was no damage. With the second knife, Vikki stabbed a half of an apple on the floor near her feet, lifted it to her mouth, and took a bite, her crunching breaking the silence. I thought Rose might lose her temper.

"Are you okay, sister?" Vikki asked her.

"Yeah, I've never been so impressed in my life," she replied with a smile.

"She's a Rose with no thorns, folks." The crowd erupted into applause once again. Vikki bowed to Rose in appreciation then raised her hands to the audience, seeking silence.

"She's so fast," Rose whispered to me when she rejoined me at the rear of the crowd, just as Vikki began addressing the assembly.

"In Africa, everyone respects the lion, the king of the jungle. But a man underestimates a hyena to his own peril. If you dedicate yourself to the teachings of The Way of the Hyena, you can become as nimble and devastating as the wind." Vikki bowed to the crowd signaling the end of the demonstration. With that, several audience members advanced, seeking autographs and signing up for training. Rose restrained me from going forward.

"Don't forget about our dinner," she said.

"Oh, yeah." For an instant, I was torn, but choosing Rose was the right thing to do.

Our delicious dinner was brought out to us when we returned to the restaurant, and it did not disappoint Rose. A kernel of hope budded inside me, and I knew if I tended to it, it would bloom and, in turn, nourish me.

"You've had a smile on face all night, Andrew," Rose said to me on the drive to the hotel. She was right. I had been smiling so much my face hurt.

"I just shared a perfect day with a perfect person." I kissed her on the cheek. "And I have a plan." I just needed to convince Victory George to train me in Kung Fu.

"Grandfather's plan is too violent," I told Rose as she watched me pace back and forth in front of her perch on the couch. "I'd have to be naïve to believe there wouldn't be serious collateral damage from poisoning the Sea of Galilee and the Jordan River. Worse, I'd be a terrorist. I can't live with that no matter what the circumstances are.

"For the first time in my life, I'm going to decide what happens. If it's going to fall to me to aid the citizens of the world, then I'm going to do it my way. Dad and Grandfather have always been there during my decision-making process. They can only see their own vision, and that handicaps them because they only know how to support their own plans. If I'm called on to fight and die, then I choose to do so with honor. I will not be the catalyst for needless violence," I said.

"What do you have in mind?" Rose asked.

"Well, Grandfather spoke of responding with such force and resolve that our enemies' will would be broken. There's a certain barbarism to that idea if you expand it too far. I believe a concise yet powerful statement is just as effective. If measured properly, it can open a dialogue of mutual respect. Am I making sense?"

"You don't want to lose your humanity in all of this," she said.

"Exactly. I'm not afraid of dying for something I believe in, but I'm afraid to kill for that same belief. Taking a life should be a last resort."

The next day I woke up early, ready to implement my plan. I drove to *The Way of the Hyena* studio; the door was open, so I went inside. Victory George pounded on a practice dummy, her speed and power impressive as she continued to punish the wooden imitation for thirty minutes while I watched in awe.

"Did you enjoy the show?" she asked, turning around to face me. *How long did she know I was there?*

"Umm, yes," I replied.

"I mean last night. I saw you in the audience; you came in late, right?"

"Yes, you're right. And yes, I enjoyed last night," I said, realizing that I must have a creepy grin on my face. *How old am I, five?*

"If you want to sign up for training you should come back in an hour. The Sifu will be here then, and he will be glad to take you on. He's good. I've trained him myself."

"Actually, I was hoping you'd train me."

"I don't have time to take on private students anymore," Vikki said.

"Not even for a worthy cause?"

"Don't tell me you have a bully problem," she said with a smile. I wanted to laugh; she was so charming.

"Yes, actually, but it's complicated." Vikki didn't seem interested, and this was my only chance. "I have a proposition for you," I said and handed her an envelope. She looked inside.

"That's fifty thousand dollars. Take me on for two weeks, and if you sense for one minute that I'm slacking off, then cut me and keep the fifty grand. If I make the cut, then train me for a year, and I'll give you a million dollars. No strings attached. You can make a movie, open more studios, or travel the world and disappear if you like," I said.

"No matter what I do, it sounds like I win." Vikki handed the envelope back to me.

"Come back tomorrow morning at seven a.m. sharp, and I'll give you my answer. I need to think about it because it will impact my family and other commitments."

I went back to the hotel. The anticipation made me grumpy, so I forced myself to go to bed early. It still took me three hours to fall asleep.

In the morning, like clockwork, I went back at *The Way of the Hyena* studio, early enough to show a positive attitude, but no one was there yet. At seven sharp, Victory George came around the corner.

"Ready to run?" she asked.

"What should I do with this?" I asked indicating the envelope.

"Carry it." And like that, we were off. By my estimate, we ran about five miles before returning to the studio. Vikki made us fresh carrot juice and protein shakes in a blender before we began a long series of flexibility exercises, followed by heavy weight training, twelve miles on a stationary bike, and jump rope work. After that, we ate a healthy Chinese lunch across the street. I was starving and consumed more than Vikki, but I was careful not to eat too much because I didn't want to throw up on my hero's feet.

After our meal, there was an hour of abdominal work, including hundreds of sit-ups and leg-raises. At one point, we were alternating beating a heavy medicine ball into each other's core.

"Are you still in?" she asked.

"Of course," I said.

"I'm impressed with your physical condition. You need a lot of flexibility work, but you're already very strong." Even though I hadn't realized it, I had kept up with Victory George during her training regimen. It must have been a combination of the training Grandfather had me on for my job the last few years and the strength enhancing effects of the time travel. But I couldn't discount my determination. I couldn't fail. "It will be like this every day except Sundays from seven to five, no exceptions," Vikki said. I swelled with pride. *I've shown enough promise.*

"I'm not going anywhere," I said, handing her the envelope of cash again.

"Okay. I just want you to know what the expectations are before I take your money." She was a class act. "What is your name, my friend?" the master said.

"Andrew."

"You have no problem being trained by a woman, Andrew? There're plenty of male Kung Fu masters that would be happy to train you, especially for this stack of cash."

"I want to be trained by the best. Your gender doesn't matter to me," I said. She seemed to like my answer.

"Andrew, are you ready for part two?"

"Yes, absolutely."

For the next few hours, Vikki lectured me on key concepts of her martial arts philosophy: The importance of being nebulous and unpredictable, but forgiving; adaptable to any situation, but ferocious and opportunistic like the African hyena; immersed in the pursuit of collective knowledge, but valuing self-reliance; and tuned into the significance of the human spirit, but training hard and eating right.

When local students began to pour into the studio at five o'clock, Vikki handed me a slip of paper with an address.

"From now on, you will train with me at my home. It's private, better for my family, and better for you," she said.

I was training with Victory George, the humble superhero; I relished every second of it.

I stopped by UCLA on the way home and picked up our lab supplies from Dr. Semisi Alofa. He helped me carry everything to the loading dock so I could pack it into the back of the pickup truck.

"I was hoping Rose would be with you," Semisi said.

"She's busy today. I'm sure she will be around sometime soon, though," I replied.

"Take good care of her, Andrew. She's a good woman, and she means a lot to me."

"I will," I said.

"I would have fallen for Rose in grad school if she would have let me, but she's a mystery. She never let anyone get close to her. Rose must really like you if she has let you into her life, so take good care of her, okay?" I nodded my head. He was right; Rose is a delicate flower. *She probably deserves better than me.*

"My people are Samoan," Semisi said. "We have a love/hate relationship with America. Many of my people believe that we'd be better off if our islands never came under your control because your culture is wiping out our identity: But not me. I don't regret it. I've found opportunity in your lands. Mostly, I've come to know love here. I'm willing to die for Rose, but more importantly, I'm willing to live for her."

Semisi handed me a slip of paper—a bill. I noticed that he had under-billed for his time. I gave him another three thousand dollars to cover the balance, and we shook hands.

"Thanks for the advice, Doc. I'll take it to heart," I said.

"Good. Let me know if you need anything else," he said.

I turned over the engine and drove back to our hotel. While I carried everything up the back stairs, Rose set up the equipment. I didn't dare use the elevator since it would draw unnecessary questions. Being paranoid, I found the head housekeeper and gave her a healthy bribe not to raise any questions with management regarding the additions to our suite, and she assured me she would come and find me if there were any problems.

"How did it go today?" Rose asked.

I grabbed Rose, brought her in close to me, and kissed her lips for the first time. A jolt of electricity traveled from my feet to my brain. She kissed me back and then held me in her arms.

"Great, Victory George has accepted me as her student. If I can last two weeks, she will train me for a full year."

"That's great." She smiled.

"But I'll have to come up with a million bucks before the year is up."

"You didn't negotiate?"

"No, I sensed that I needed to come with my best offer right off the bat."

"Don't worry, you'll think of something," she said. I needed to. I didn't want to risk going back to New York City for Grandfather's gold.

We found a seafood restaurant for a quick and simple dinner. After that, we tracked down a mom and pop's bookstore. I bought every book they had on the subject of post-World War Two politics and Israeli history. The proprietor agreed to order several other relevant titles for me, but informed me that turnaround would take several weeks. Without the aid of Google or Yahoo!, traditional research would have to do as I refined my plan of action. Worried about how I was going to raise the million dollars for Vikki, I bought a copy of every newspaper the bookstore had for sale, too.

Rose bought several chemistry tomes, medical treatises, and novels to keep her busy.

"This would be so much easier with David and Eva," she said.

Across the street from the bookstore was a music shop. I couldn't resist a visit and promised I'd be brief. Forty-five minutes later, I was the proud owner of a Fender Stratocaster and Marshall amplifier.

When we got back to the hotel, I studied the financial sections of the newspapers. I had to be honest with myself: I didn't know anything about investing. I didn't come back in time with an investment scheme in my head like Grandfather.

I plugged in my new guitar and wailed on it in my room for a bit while Rose worked in her new makeshift laboratory. The crunch from the amp's vacuum tube assembly was inspirational, and playing again reminded me that the power of music was something my body and spirit needed every day in order to have a clear mind. *Music is my natural maintenance cocktail.* In the controlled chaos of sound, I made a mental list of information that I knew could be useful. I might not be an investment nerd like Warren Buffet, but I was a baseball nerd and proud of it. I could name every World Series winner from 1950 onwards, a project begun in elementary school that I carried into adulthood. What can I say; baseball fans love baseball history and statistics. I knew that this October, the Oakland A's would be world champs, and they'd repeat in 1973 and 1974. In 1975 and 1976, Cincinnati's 'Big Red Machine' would double up on championships. This was information I could leverage in Las Vegas.

And then there were movies. Being lonely most of my life provided lots of time with the big screen. I don't consider myself a movie geek like Roger Ebert, but I could name several films that would secure the Best Picture Oscar in the coming years. *The Godfather*, one of my favorites, was the big winner this year. I didn't know release years, but I was certain *The Godfather Part II, Rocky, Chariots of Fire, Platoon,* and *Dances with Wolves* were in the pipeline for the coming years. For certain, anything was fair game for a bet in Sin City. It's a shame I didn't know much about music awards, but their system was too confusing for me to pay a whole lot of attention to, even more so since most of my favorite acts rarely seemed to win many awards anyway.

The summer transitioned to fall, and for six days a week, I woke up early and went to the home of Victory George. The mornings were full of runs, jump roping, flexibility exercises, medicine balls, push-ups, heavy weight training, and many juice concoctions. Vikki enjoyed testing her nutritional ideas on me because she saw me as her equal during the training routine. She had never seen anyone who could keep up with her, save Bruce Lee, and this gave her the opportunity to observe as a scientist. In turn, I would share nutritional and training insights I had acquired in the present. I felt myself getting fitter and stronger with every workout. Together, we were like two machines, two pistons in the same high-powered engine. It was wonderful to satisfy Vikki with my results, but I could not have been more surprised myself. Motivation coupled with tangible results proved to be both gratifying and addictive in a way I'd never experienced in my life before.

The afternoons consisted of combat training. In those sessions, I learned about stance and footwork and how they lead to balance and economy of motion. Vikki instructed me on how to attack. It was important to think of my arms and legs as fluid instruments, not unlike a foil in fencing, which would allow for surprise in real combat, as my opponents wouldn't be able to anticipate my next moves. She taught me how to punch using my whole body to create force and speed. It's amazing how much power can be generated from even one inch with this technique. With a lot of practice, I learned to guide my hands like a whip. An assortment of kicks was given to me: Front kicks, inverted kicks, and Bruce Lee's ultra powerful side kick were added to my growing arsenal. Blocking and countering, trapping, and grappling were all used to round out The Way of the Hyena's core concept that if I was fast and sharp, I could beat any opponent to the punch.

Above all things, Victory George believed sparring was the best tool because true Combat cannot be simulated; it can only experienced, and in this manner, we concluded every afternoon in battle. As her private student, I was afforded the opportunity to fight the best. To say I was overmatched would be an understatement. Vikki relished the beatings she gave me every day. I was reminded that she's a master, not from the bruises, but by the grace she extended to me. Even though I was inferior to her in skill, she treated me as her equal.

Evenings were spent with Rose at the hotel. We had acquired more equipment and lab supplies so that she could continue her work on a cure for the Schneider's Lymphoma. It was clear to me that she exerted herself in the lab with the same intensity I applied to my training, and it was not lost on me that her work was all for my own personal benefit.

I was careful with her. It would have been easy to let our love smolder into a passionate, physical storm. Instead, I opted to stoke the fire slowly by investing in quality moments. If my plan worked, I felt like there would be an opportunity for us to be set free from the obligations that held us back.

Sundays, on our day off, Rose and I often took day trips to Las Vegas, and I spread some money around the city's sports books on the World Series. 1972 was the year of the Miami Dolphins' undefeated season and Super Bowl victory: So I had seventeen easy football games to bet a massive parlay on. I also placed bets on *The Godfather* to win the Academy Award for Best Picture. Rose advised me to branch out and make some traditional investments, so I owned a piece of Intel Corporation, which was a brand new company in 1972, and several other tech companies. By the end of March of 1973, I had three million dollars in cash in the bank, more than enough to satisfy my obligation to Vikki on the back end of our deal.

Vikki had so much confidence in our arrangement that she

dropped out of the filming of *Enter the Dragon* with Bruce Lee, her mentor. Now, she planned to travel the world in style with her mother and nephew once she completed her obligation to me. Vikki said that Bruce seemed disappointed, but understood. By finding another path, her lifeless body would not have to be retrieved from a dumpster outside an opium den in Hong Kong near the *Enter the Dragon* set. Victory George's family would not be deprived of her company. I felt like a hero.

E ven though I saw Victory George six days a week and I
    counted her as a friend, our conversations rarely strayed from
my training or our business relationship. One afternoon in April, we
broke into new territory.

"You're a driven man, Andrew. I've never known anyone before
with your focus, except myself. I would like to know more about what
drives you," Victory said to me.

"If I told you, you'd think I'm crazy," I said.

"I already know you're crazy, my friend. Please, I don't wish to
impose on your personal affairs, but if you're willing to share, I want
to know more about what inspires you to search so desperately for
your spiritual and physical limits."

"I've been thrust into a war that's not of my own choosing," I said,
not knowing where to begin.

"And this war requires skill in martial arts?"

"My back's against the wall. I have family fighting for both sides,
and I can no longer hold onto hope that we'll all find a way to survive.
There's just one chance. If I can become something bigger than
myself, then I may prevent death to innocent people."

"So you speak of actual war?"

"Yes, potentially. It seems inevitable."

"Do not fear death, my friend, for it comes to us all. A blessed warrior meets the end in battle fighting for an honorable cause. And there's nothing more honorable than love," Vikki said.

"I've been given so much over the last ten months, Sifu. I know that I have a chance. I'll be a force to be reckoned with because of your training."

"You'll be the call of the hyena," she said. I bowed to her out of gratitude.

"I know I can trust you. What I have to tell you is unbelievable," I said.

"I see only truth in you." I took her at her word.

"Okay. Here it goes. I'm from the future. I feel insane even saying it."

"Please, continue," Vikki said, without judgment in her voice.

"My grandfather's a scientist, and he accidentally discovered time travel. Grandfather shared the discovery with my dad, who's the number two man at his company. After a disagreement, Dad gave the time travel technology to people willing to weaponize it. My dad and Grandfather are now bitter enemies, and they've dragged me into the conflict. I've been forced to kill to protect myself and others."

"That's terrible. I'm sorry, Andrew."

"It's quietly become a world conflict, and it's my intent to go back to where it began and stop it before it happens."

"It seems you have come to the right place to train, my friend. Your quest will require the transcendence of self if you are to defeat your enemies, for you're on the river that leads to inevitable confrontation. You've been given tools and training by me and others, some good and some flawed. Only you can know that reality. When the time comes to act, you'll have to make decisions that have lasting consequences, but remember to trust in the truth within you, and you'll not be disappointed in the outcome."

"Thank you, Sifu. You're a most trusted advisor and friend." I bowed again.

"When do you leave?"

"In two months, when we're done with my training," I said.

After we finished for the day, I stopped on the way home and picked up the gift I'd ordered earlier for Rose. It was her birthday, and I had been planning to do something meaningful for her for a while. The gift needed to be special, but it couldn't be a ring. I loved her, and I was certain she knew that, but it didn't seem fair to place the weight of an engagement onto this emotional Everest. Rose was already fighting for my life, and what she had been asked to accomplish could end up being impossible under the circumstances. I was headed to the battlefield as a lone soldier; if I died, I was afraid our unrealized love would crush her. The beauty of her bloom was too rare for me to accept that. As much as I loved her, I felt that we had to wait to see if I would survive, and if I was given the chance to live, I would find a way to come back in time to her. *I would forfeit my life in the present to live in the past with her.*

Not too far from our hotel, I had found a specialty jewelry store and commissioned a necklace. The chain was made out of interlocking hearts while the pendant was a larger heart, accented by two golden spirals that interlocked to form a secondary heart. I was very particular about the mathematics of the spirals being correct, and it turned out better than I imagined.

Once at the hotel, I brought out the cake and candles that I had purchased for her. I sang "Happy Birthday" to her, using my guitar for accompaniment, and when I was finished, I handed her the gift.

"No matter what happens in the future or in the past, my heart will be next to yours," I said to her, while she removed the wrapping paper and opened the box.

"It's both beautiful and intellectual. It's absolutely perfect," she said, tracing the spirals. I put it around her neck, and we went to the rooftop terrace to enjoy the warmth of the setting spring sun.

A few days later, I was with Vikki doing jump rope training in her backyard when three masked men with guns jumped over the privacy wall, leaving little time to react. The first thug fired his handgun at Vikki, but she anticipated the move by grabbing a twenty-pound plate from the nearby weight bench and blocked the incoming bullets.

I grabbed two five-pound weights, spun, and launched them at the second intruder who had drawn his gun. The first weight was off its mark, but the second hit his wrist and sent the gun out of reach.

Like lightning, Vikki navigated the distance and advanced on the first gunman while he reloaded his weapon. An inverted left kick disarmed him. A side kick with her right foot sent him backwards into the stonewall with the force of a tractor-trailer. I was certain the thug's back was broken.

The second intruder pulled out a combat knife as I descended onto him. He lunged at me, but I caught his wrist. I pulled him forward and threw my knee repeatedly into his face. The knife dropped from his hand as I swept his legs and sent him tumbling hard to the ground. A jumping heel stomp to his head left him incapacitated.

I looked up. Vikki and the third intruder were locked in hand-to-hand combat.

A loud scream erupted within the house. I grabbed the combat knife off the ground and ran for the door. Inside, to my horror, I found a fourth intruder using Vikki's young nephew as a hostage and human shield. The thug opened up his Uzi on me. I dove out of the way in time behind the solid hardwood kitchen table. The table wasn't so lucky. As the splinters fell around me, I saw an opening and dove to my left and flicked the knife at his exposed lower leg. It was risky, but the boy was in danger. The knife hit its mark and pierced the thug's calf. In the confusion, Vikki's nephew ran from his attacker. I jumped over the rubble and unleashed a chain of punches to his face and ribs and then grabbed the handle of the knife and used it as a lever to sweep his feet from underneath him.

Vikki appeared and her nephew ran to her arms. Outside, I could see the three motionless attackers. The thug beneath me stirred. I looked down in time to see the fourth intruder slip a chocolate into his mouth. He disintegrated, leaving nothing but a pile of his clothes on the floor. Time travel. Vikki and her nephew saw it, too.

"Is your grandmother upstairs?" Vikki asked her nephew.

"Yes," the boy replied.

Vikki picked him up and ran up the stairs, returning a few minutes later.

"Mom is okay. She was hiding in a closet," Vikki said.

"Good," I replied.

"She called the police. They're on the way, so you should go."

This attack is my fault. I hadn't thought that Dad would still be after me. I hadn't been careful enough. Vikki was right: I should run, but that was not the honorable thing to do, not this time, not with innocent people being targeted.

Vikki and I tied up the three other thugs before they could ingest chocolate, and then the police arrived and asked a lot of questions. They were upset that I was unable to provide proper ID, but Vikki made sure that they didn't give me too much of a hard time. Anywhere the police went, the media was sure to follow; a wall of unwanted attention grew outside.

After a couple hours of investigation and questioning, the police left Vikki and her family alone. The local news channels wanted an interview, but Vikki declined. The media and curious neighbors swarmed by the front door. We were trapped. It was late, and I was worried about Rose. Did they find her, too, I wondered? I didn't dare call in case the phone was being monitored.

"Do you think they'll come back?" Vikki asked me.

"No, not with all of these people around. Not tonight."

"What're you going to do now?"

"I'm going back to 1946 tomorrow, and I'm going to put an end to all of this," I said.

"Good. You're ready. You proved that today." We had escaped

tragedy, but she was right: I had performed well under the stress of combat.

"Thank you, Sifu."

"I'm going to pack a bag. I'm going with you," Vikki said.

"What?"

"This is my fight now, too. No one comes to my home, threatens my family, and escapes."

"Sifu, the way time travel is achieved is dangerous. I'd have to give you a strain of cancer that there's currently no cure for. My partner is working on a treatment, but there's no guarantee of success. Even if we're victorious, we may still die."

"I'm not afraid of death, but I'm afraid of living in fear of my limitations. I cannot be in many places at the same time, but my enemy can. Good people cannot allow evil men to use this technology to commit atrocities. I'll accompany you even if it leads to death. Everything I have come to believe requires me to do so. My mother and my nephew...they could have been killed today."

Victory made some telephone calls, went upstairs to pack a bag, and spent some precious time with her family. A half hour later, students and masters from *The Way of the Hyena* studio arrived and pushed their way through the crowds outside to the door. They were there to protect Vikki's family and would remain until her return.

In the confusion, Vikki and I hopped over the privacy wall in the backyard. I parked the truck on the side of the house close to the back gate. Fortunately, no one noticed us getting in and driving away.

W e made it to the hotel and rushed up the back stairs to my room. I went inside and was relieved to find that Rose was safe.

"What's wrong?" Rose asked. "Is everything okay?" I pulled her in close and hugged her.

"Victory's family was attacked today, but everyone's fine."

"Thank God you're all right," she said.

"Hello again," Vikki said. "You must be Andrew's partner."

"Yes, I'm Rose."

"I remember you from the demonstration with the apples. You had the best reaction."

"Thank you, you're so sweet," she said. Rose shook her hand and then bowed to her.

"So, we're going to move up the timeline to today. We can't take any more time here," I said.

"No. We can pack up and move. Can't we can relocate and resettle? Then you can go when you're ready," she said.

"No, it has to be now," I said.

"I'm just not ready to say goodbye yet," Rose said. She hugged me again.

"Me, either, but in a perfect world, you won't even know I was gone, right?"

"If you say so," she said through tears.

"Vikki has decided to come with me."

"At least you won't be alone," Rose said. "I'll take solace in that."

She packed cocktail doses for us in an ice pack. She weighed us and then prepared the time travel pills for each of us to arrive in 1946. I gave the primer of bets, trades, and transactions to Rose.

"What's this?" she asked.

"If I am delayed, use this information to raise funds for the research. If I don't return within one year, take the money and disappear if you can," I told her.

I took her into my bedroom and showed her the boxes where I was storing the cash and stock certificates we accumulated. I packed a banker's box with five hundred thousand dollars in cash, the balance that I owed to Victory George.

"Make sure that Vikki's family receives this money as soon as possible to settle what I owe."

I gathered up some clothes, my fake IDs, and some traveling cash. Rose prepared a culture of the Schneider's Lymphoma cells.

"Are you sure about this, Ms. George? Has Andrew explained to you that this will kill you? It's like suicide."

"I have faith that Fate will have her say in all of this," Vikki said and extended her arm. Rose gave Vikki several injections containing the lymphoma.

"The clock is ticking. Be safe," Rose said. I handed her the keys to our truck, gave her one last hug, and kissed her forehead. We lingered in our embrace for a long minute, afraid to let go.

"I'll be back, I promise," I said.

"I know."

We had the receptionist call a cab for us. Before long we were at Los Angeles International Airport, and I used the traveling cash to buy two round trip first class tickets to London, England.

Fifteen hours later, Vikki and I were booked into a suite at the Dorchester Hotel in the heart of the city. I took the time to review my strategy in private with Vikki and to do some reconnaissance. We rested the remainder of the afternoon, and when the evening finally arrived, we put the plan into motion.

At seven p.m., we took the Tube to Knightsbridge. Harrods, the magnificent seven-floor department store, was a short walk from the station. We went inside and found the utility closet that I had determined was out of range of the store's Closed Circuit Television system. Modern London is covered with thousands of these silent eyes. I took out the two time travel pills that Rose had prepared and handed one to Vikki.

"This is going to feel really good, just so you know," I said. Vikki nodded her head.

"It's been an honor training you, Andrew. No matter what awaits us, we'll fight with honor for those we love. You go first, my friend," Vikki said.

I put the pill in my mouth and swallowed hard. The familiar exhilaration and elation of a chemical high swept over me. My skin began to tingle and disappear, followed by my flesh and bones. The last thing I saw was the shock in Vikki's eyes. I don't suppose anyone could get used to watching this performance, especially a friend. I opened my eyes, and I was still in the closet except I didn't have any clothes on. Thirty seconds later, Victory George appeared next to me in the motionless air, as nude as the day she was born. Rose's mixture calculations seemed to be spot on. We needed to confirm the date to be sure, but we had arrived together, which was encouraging.

"I feel really good," Vikki said. "Really, really, powerful."

"Just wait until you hit someone," I said, taking a peek at her physique. I couldn't help myself. *Wow*. Vikki noticed.

"Mind your eyes. You don't need any distractions," she said, half kidding; yet I caught her checking me out from the corner of my eye.

We exited the closet with caution. We didn't have to worry about any CCTVs, but we did have to worry about security guards. The lights were low and the store was closed. A clock on a wall read three a.m. *So far so good.*

Clothes. We sneaked around the store, dodging an occasional guard. In the semidarkness, we found a floor plan by the elevator. Like ghosts, we floated through the displays until we arrived at the men's department, which was filled with rack upon rack of business suits. The store had the feel of a surreal graveyard. First things first, Vikki located the underwear and soon we were no longer indecent. She had no qualms about dressing in men's clothing. We both selected sharp suits, crisp shirts, neckties, and the most practical dress shoes we could muster: We had to have hats to fit in. Vikki opted for a classic Fedora, while I chose a Homburg. It seemed like a Halloween or a costume party as we finished up our outfits with heavy overcoats. I felt like Michael Corleone.

It was still only five a.m., and the doors wouldn't open for several hours, so we snooped around the store some more. In a restaurant, we made some sandwiches and helped ourselves to some chocolate bars for later. In the hardware section, we examined the selection of tools. I didn't know what kind of resistance to expect, but I knew that it would be hard for our enemies to procure guns in the U.K. British citizens do not enjoy the right to bear arms like their American cousins. I took a hammer and placed it in my overcoat, while Vikki was more industrious, choosing a large heavy wood dowel, a handsaw, some screws, a screwdriver, a box of nails, and some chain. On the way back to our closet to hide and wait for the doors to open, I found a sturdy umbrella for myself and raided a cash register for some coins.

I sat in the corner and ate while Vikki went to work sawing away on her dowel until she had four equal length pieces. She cut the chain into two pieces and connected them with screws to the four dowels. I couldn't believe it: Vikki had made herself a pair of nunchakus. She withdrew to the far corner and tested the weapons for about twenty minutes. I couldn't help but smile. *Victory George is the most resourceful warrior in the history of mankind.*

When the store opened, we mixed in with the crowd and exited Harrods without incident. I walked over to a newsstand and purchased a copy of the *Financial Times* and scanned its salmon colored pages. Friday, February 1, 1946. We were right on target.

The streets bustled with men and women on their way to work. According to the research I had conducted over the last year, the three members of the Jewish-American Delegation had arrived in London the night before, and they were staying at the Dorchester Hotel in the very same suite that Vikki and I booked in 1973. Newspaper accounts stated that they went missing sometime after leaving their hotel in the early afternoon, and they never made it to the Anglo-American Committee of Inquiry to present their evidence and make their case for the creation of New Israel in Florida. Our plan was to shadow them on their trip from their hotel to their meeting and intercept at the first indication of trouble.

Vikki and I took the Tube back to the Dorchester. We waited in the lobby and did our best to remain inconspicuous. At twelve thirty, like clockwork, the three members of the Delegation appeared downstairs. Their leader, Nathan Levinson, retired Major League Baseball star of the Brooklyn Dodgers, whom I idolized in high school, was flanked by his two lesser known delegates, Abraham Cohen and Miriam Pearlman, who from my investigation I knew were up and coming lawyers. Levinson, now in his sixties, still sported his wild hair and beard, more grey than I remembered seeing in the old sports reels.

When the Delegation went outside, Vikki and I left our position of anonymity and trailed about ten yards behind them. It was a cool wintery day, but the sun was shining.

"Shall I hail a cab?" Abraham asked.

"Yes, thank you," Miriam replied.

"No, let's take public transportation. I want to stretch my legs after all that traveling," Levinson said.

"Are you sure?" Miriam asked Levinson. I agreed with her even though I couldn't provide any input; it would be safer to take a cab.

"Yes, my dear. I want to be among the people today." They started to walk. The Hyde Park Corner Tube Station wasn't too far away. Vikki and I followed behind them, but they were unaware of us. I didn't see any obvious signs of danger, and before long we were underground and in the station. *So far, so good.*

We all paid our fares and went through the turnstiles. The Delegation consulted the Tube map, while Vikki pretended to tie the laces on her new shoes. The platform was crowded. For a moment, we lost the Delegation, but after some maneuvering, we ended just a few people away from them at the edge of the platform.

The train arrived.

"Mind the gap," a conductor said.

Fortunately, we were able to get into the same crammed car as Levinson and the rest of his group. None of us had seats. *This is not an ideal place to make a defense.* Abraham studied the map on the wall of the train car.

The train stopped at the next station. Abraham was indecisive as some of the passengers left the train car.

"We need to change lines," Abraham said to the others. The Delegation disembarked, just before the inflow of new train riders began. Vikki and I were too far behind to avoid the incoming passengers. I opened my umbrella and used it like a weirdo to force people out of the way: *No one wants a spoke in their eye.* Eventually, I lost my umbrella to the eager crowd, but Vikki and I powered our way through the last few people and out of the car into the foot traffic on the platform. *Considerable distance between us and the Delegation now. Too much distance.*

Up ahead in the tunnels, a beautiful blonde stepped in front of them.

"Mr. Levinson, can I have your autograph? I'm a big fan," she said. I couldn't believe my eyes. It was Jennifer Dennison, my best friend. *What is she doing here?*

"Of course," Levinson said, taking the pen and paper from her hands.

Before Vikki and I could close in, four burly men in suits surrounded the Delegation.

"Mr. Levinson, you and the rest of your troublemaking friends are coming with us," their leader demanded.

"What is the meaning of this?" Levinson asked.

"Yes, we demand an explanation," Miriam added.

"Shut your mouth, woman, or I'll cut you open right here in front of everybody," Jennifer said, showing her a knife inside her handbag.

We were close enough now to react. I smashed the first perpetrator's head against a metal support post. He fell like a sack of potatoes to the filthy floor below. Vikki's powerful front kick to the back sent a second perpetrator into the wall. The third man sent his fists towards my face, but I blocked them, and my elbow cracked his nose open. I grabbed his wrist, spun, and hurled him into the side of the nearby train. Vikki finished the fourth perpetrator with a chain of punches to his stomach and a head butt. Over by the wall the second perpetrator attempted to get back to his feet, but I came up behind him and knocked him out with a fist to his skull. The first attacker found his knees by the support post as Vikki went up to him and side kicked his head into the post.

Crunch.

Jennifer stood in a state of panic and surprise through the fighting. The Delegation was also in shock.

"Andrew, I can't believe that's you," Jennifer said. Miriam slugged Jennifer in the head with her own handbag, sending her to the floor, knocking her unconscious.

"No, you shut your mouth," Miriam said.

"Who are you guys?" Abraham asked.

"Our guardian angels," Levinson answered for us. "We need to get to our meeting," he said with urgency.

"We will escort you," I said.

"Good, let's get to street level and get a cab. It'll be safer," Abraham said.

"No, there could be others waiting there. Let's get back on the train," I said. I led everyone down a series of tunnels until we were at the correct platform. There was a lot of commotion among the other commuters, but no one wanted to interfere with us, and I didn't blame them.

The train arrived, and we loaded into a car and were off. I couldn't believe Jennifer was involved in this. *She is my friend: How could I leave her down on the ground in the station?* Miriam had hit her hard, but I knew that she wasn't seriously injured and would be unconscious for only a short period of time, long enough for us to get ahead of our enemies, I hoped.

"Who're those people?" Levinson asked.

"People that don't want you to succeed today," I responded.

"You know the girl," Miriam said. "Who is she?"

"She was a friend," I replied. Levinson reached over and squeezed my shoulder. "You have my word that we'll get you to the meeting," I said.

"Andrew," Vikki said. "They'll be expecting us to get off at Westminster Station. Let's go to Embankment and walk back to Parliament and hope they don't expect that. With some luck, we may be able to slip by anyone who may be waiting."

"You're right. It's worth a shot."

We passed the stop for Westminster and proceeded to Embankment. I held my breath hoping for the best, and when we arrived, we exited to the platform. It was mostly empty. Outside, I heard Big Ben chiming the one o'clock hour. Vikki and I led the Delegation through the long series of tunnels towards the stairs and exit. Soon we could see a hallway that opened up into the lobby that connected to the outside and freedom, but the way was blocked. Vice President Hamilton Sherman, Dad, and Grandfather obstructed our escape with seven more thugs.

"Andrew, what're you doing here? How did you get involved in this?" Grandfather asked me.

"You got me into this," I said.

"What? I did?" Grandfather asked, genuinely confused.

"Andrew, I don't know why you're here, but you're interfering in government business," Dad said.

"I'm here to set things right," I said. *This is not my dad and grandfather of the present, but of sometime in the past.* "What you're trying to do will have horrible consequences."

"Who's this punk, Mr. Acheson?" Vice President Sherman said.

"He's my son," Dad answered.

"Well, I don't care who he is. I don't want him interfering with the arrangement you and your father set up." The two closest thugs drew shotguns from their trench coats.

"Stay behind us," Vikki told the Delegation.

"This doesn't have to end in a bloody tragedy, kid," Sherman said.

"It'll end for you when I pay you back for what you did to my Aunt Eva," I said.

"Men, take them down," Sherman said.

"Didn't anyone ever teach you to never bring a pet dog to the jungle to fight lions, boy?" the first gunman taunted Vikki.

With an inverted kick, Vikki sent the first gunman's shotgun towards the ceiling. It discharged. I somersaulted in the direction of the second gunman, removing the hammer from my jacket in the process, and struck the second gunman's throat at my apogee. He collapsed, gasping for air, while Vikki advanced on the first gunman. She retrieved several iron nails from her jacket pocket and placed them between the fingers of her closed fists: makeshift claws. Vikki swept the gunman's legs before he could react and descended upon him, punching him in the stomach and legs with her weapons. "Tame your tongue, lion," she said and deposited her helpless victim on the ground in a bloody heap. The remaining five thugs drew clubs and knives.

Vikki drew her homemade nunchakus and began swinging, and I gripped my hammer. *Thor has nothing on me.* We were outnumbered, but not outmatched. The third thug advanced with a club, but Vikki struck him down with blows to his teeth and groin. I spun out of the way when the fourth and fifth advanced on me, dropped to my knees and tripped the fourth with my hammer. I jumped back to my feet and sent high left and high right kicks to the fifth's head. He fell down near the Delegation. Abraham and Miriam wasted no time beating him unconscious.

Vikki was engaged with the sixth and seventh combatants while the fourth one was back up on me. He managed to slice open my shoulder with his knife. When he lunged at me a second time, I caught the blade in the claw of my hammer and twisted it out of his grasp. He threw a couple of punches at me: He was fast and landed one in my stomach, which caused me to lose my hammer. I plunged forward and tackled him. I punched him three times in the groin and once in the head. *Number four wouldn't be able to walk out of this train station.*

"Now we're even," I said to him and found my feet.

Vikki had relieved the sixth combatant of his club with her

nunchakus. Using misdirection, she shattered his knee with a quick kick. Another inverted kick from Vikki left the man incapacitated. With this, Vikki let out a loud, intimidating laugh and dropped her weapons. Number seven was frantic. He threw a series of punches at Vikki, but she blocked them all. The thug lunged at Vikki, but she moved like a cat and jumped right over him. She was fast—speedier than in any of the YouTube movies—I was afraid to blink. Vikki then side kicked number seven, who flew down a large flight of stairs.

Another aggressive hyena laugh.

Victory, the awesome, invincible warrior. Seven up. Seven down.

"Time to dance, Sherman," I said.

Dad threw a punch at Vikki, but Vikki drove him back against the wall where he cracked his head and was disoriented. Miriam picked up the loaded shotgun and aimed it at Dad.

Grandfather stepped in front of Vice President Sherman.

"Now wait, Andrew. Let's talk about this," Grandfather said. I pushed him out of my way and advanced on Sherman who backed away from me like coward and popped a piece of chocolate into his mouth. In anger, I side kicked his disappearing body into a wall.

I grabbed Grandfather by the collar and pushed him against the same wall.

"Tell the truth. Was all of this your idea?"

"What? What do you mean, Andrew?" Grandfather asked.

"Intervening. Sherman said this was your idea: Preventing the creation of New Israel?"

"I have no choice. The American government is prepared to go to war over the pending annexation of Mexico and Central American by New Israel."

"All of this over economics?"

"No, it's not that simple," Grandfather said. "It's about money, and it's about power, but it's more than that, too. The Feds are tired of being pushed around in their own hemisphere by New Israel. Sherman is the leader of a powerful political entity that believes Americans are God's chosen people and it's their 'manifest destiny' to rule. They see New Israel as a direct obstacle to achieving their God-given mandate. Sherman and his backers are obsessed and can't be stopped. They'll kill to get what they want. You have to understand that New Israel doesn't stand a chance in open war against the United States. If New Israel never exists, then there is peace and, our people, the Jewish people, survive. Besides, with the changes to the timeline, the Jews will get the Holy Lands and be content there. It makes more sense, don't you think? That alternative is better than all-out war with the U.S. Who can stand up to America? Sherman is prepared to wipe New Israel off the map. I can't live with that. Listen, I don't agree with Sherman's politics, but there's something poetic about Jews regaining possession of the Holy Lands after what we, our people, endured during the Holocaust. Don't you think? Remember, I'm American, too. I don't want to see a long bloody conflict between two very proud nations. Sometimes you have to dance with the Devil in order to sing in God's choir." *Clearly, Grandfather of the past and Grandfather of the present don't see eye to eye.*

"You're a fool, Grandfather. You've accomplished nothing. The only thing you've done is ensure our death and the slaughter of many innocent people. Just because you can change history, doesn't give you the right." I never thought words like those could escape my lips.

Out of the corner of my eye, I saw Dad eat a chocolate and phase to disappearance. I turned and watched. While I was distracted, Grandfather lifted a chocolate to his lips and began his journey forward in time. I was left holding his empty shirt. I ripped it in half in frustration.

Miriam and Abraham were speechless.

"We're not all the way there yet, Andrew," Vikki said. "We have to get the Delegation to the meeting. Time's running out, my friend."

"It's a short distance from here," Levinson said. "Leave your weapons here so you can pass through security."

Vikki and I rushed to straighten our clothes. We needed to look presentable. The five of us burst onto the sidewalk and rushed towards Big Ben and the Parliament buildings. No one followed us, and we made it to the entrance.

"Mr. Levinson, we've been expecting you and your group," the security guard said.

"Yes, this is Miriam Pearlman and Abraham Cohen, my associates. These other two folks are our bodyguards," Levinson said.

"Yes, come right this way for the security check," the guard said.

The pat down was cursory and quick, no issues. We received directions and walked with purpose towards the meeting room. At the door, we stopped to say our goodbyes. Abraham and Miriam rushed inside.

"Thank you, my friends," Levinson said, shaking our hands. "I don't know how to repay you."

"Making your speech is payment enough," I replied. "Oh, and don't tell anyone about what happened in the Tube today. There'd be an international panic if an investigation is started. Let's just say your buddy Einstein's theories on time travel are right."

"We'll wait out here until the meeting's complete," Vikki said. "Just in case." Levinson joined his group inside the conference room.

I sensed motion behind me. I turned and watched Sherman speed by, taunting me to follow. We made eye contact as he entered a nearby stairwell.

"You go after him. I'll stay here and make sure the Delegation is safe," Vikki said. "I hope to see you back in 1973." I knew following him was brash, but I felt emboldened by our success in the tube, so like Alice in Wonderland, I followed the white rabbit straight into his trap.

I hit the stairwell and took off after Sherman. He was running and a story above me, but my age and training allowed me to catch up. I was right behind him when he exited into an empty hallway where he fumbled at a door. I gave him a hand and kicked him through it. He fell onto the floor inside. Seated at the far end of the large office were Dad and Grandfather. By Grandfather's frail condition, I surmised that this was the Grandfather of the present and not the recent past. Dad and Sherman were dressed differently than they had been just minutes before, so I knew they were from the present as well.

"You followed the bait," Dad said to me. He indicated Sherman on the ground. "Your friend Jennifer has been an incredible resource to us; she's the one who helped us track you to San Bernardino and Los Angeles. Jennifer knew something was off when she read in *The Hollywood Reporter* that your buddy, Victory George, had dropped out of the production of *Enter the Dragon*. Jennifer and Geoff make a good team. I mean they *did* until you killed Geoff."

"The guy was top notch, well worth the price we paid him," Sherman said.

"Blood money," I said and kicked Sherman from his knees and back down to the floor.

"You know, assaulting the Vice President of the United States is a federal offense," Sherman said.

"So is terrorism," I replied.

"Andrew, let him up," Grandfather said.

"I can't believe you let Jennifer get involved," I said to my family.

"It was Geoff's idea. He thought it'd be a good opportunity for her, the historic research they could do together," Dad said.

"And you agreed?" I asked Grandfather.

"Yes," he said.

"You should've told me," I said.

"I didn't think you'd forgive me for it," Grandfather said. He was right.

"Don't worry. She's still alive: She's grieving for Geoff," Dad said.

"Don't give her someone else to mourn," Sherman said, getting to his feet.

"Your grandfather has had a change of heart about his collaboration with his government. After your family agreed to alter history, sending the Jews to the Middle East, and nixing the Florida plan, it became clear that David was hiding important additional research from us. Apparently, he's withholding a second breakthrough. It's a shame he's not as cooperative as your father," Sherman said.

"I don't know what you're talking about, Sherman. I don't know anything about another discovery," I said.

"Bull," Sherman said and punched Grandfather in the mouth.

"After we captured your grandfather in San Bernardino, we tortured him. We know that he told you about the encrypted data at the Company. He isn't willing to tell us the key code, though. Now, I've had to drag him here back in time as a hostage, just so I can threaten you. We need that data," Sherman said.

"Son, make this easy," Dad said. "Like I told you before, let's run the Company together as a team. You may not agree with what we're trying to do, and I applaud you on your success in stopping us today, but it doesn't have to be this hard. Join Sherman and me, and we can make decisions together, decisions that are good for everybody."

"I'm not up for screwing with other people's lives. It's wrong."

"I've had enough of this. Give us the code or your grandfather dies," Sherman said. He drew a knife, and Dad pulled Grandfather closer to him.

"Dad, you can't let him do this. He's your father," I said.

"He gave us a disease that has no cure, and now he's hiding data from us," Dad said. "At least he gave you a choice on whether to take the pill or not. I wasn't given the same opportunity." I looked over at Grandfather. "That's right," Dad continued. "We were out to dinner one night, arguing again about the technology, whether he was delusional or not. I became violently ill and passed out. He drugged me. I woke up at his house. He said he was giving me medicine—a shot of vitamins and some painkillers—and then there I was, swept back in time. The funny thing is, he knew I'd come around to his point of view. The time travel is addictive."

"Yes, he told me that. He told me that you've made hundreds of trips together."

"But did he tell you that there's a chemical dependence? The back and forth in time is intoxicating. You'll find out that your body can't live without it," Dad said.

"Grandfather, is this true?" I asked. By the way he hung his head, I knew it was. I already knew it deep down; *the feeling when I took the pills is too familiar.*

"Enough, Andrew. Tell us what we need to know, or your grandfather dies," Sherman demanded.

"He doesn't know," Grandfather said. Sherman stepped past Dad and stabbed Grandfather in the stomach with his knife.

"No," I yelled and caught him in my arms. "Grandfather, I'm sorry. I failed you."

"No. Don't be sorry, my boy. I wanted to save our people from another Holocaust and not let the Jews suffer again by *our* hands this time. Sherman will wipe them out if he has his way. But I was wrong to interfere in this manner," Grandfather said with great effort. I laid him on the floor and pushed my fist against his wound to try and slow the bleeding. He began to lose consciousness.

"Grandfather, stay with me!"

"If you never let go of your faith in love, everything will be okay. I get to be with Maria now. Remember the golden rule, Andrew," Grandfather said, before fading away in my arms. I laid his head on the ground and stood up, removing my jackets and shirts until I was bare-chested. I placed my clothes over Grandfather's body. Anger swelled like a tsunami wave inside my chest.

"You're mine," I said, pointing at Sherman. Dad hit me in the face with a right cross, which busted my lip open.

"You forgot that I walked on to the boxing team in college, didn't you, son?" Dad said.

"Let's see what you've got, old man."

Dad threw a combination of punches at me; one landed on my ribs. It hurt.

"Don't underestimate me," Dad said. I threw a couple of punches at his face as a diversion and kicked his thigh, but he stayed upright.

"I can't believe you stood there and let Sherman murder him," I said. I landed a couple of punches on his ribs. Dad winced in pain.

"Wait till you see what I'm going to do to you," Dad responded. He was fast, too fast, and landed another combo. I fell to the ground. He placed me in a chokehold and started to pound me in the face. "You can either help us or you can die, too. Death's coming whether you want it to or not. We all need a cure for the lymphoma. I think dad figured it out. I think he knew how to beat the cancer. What can you do with the data on your own? You're not a scientist. You're just my ungrateful son, and I'll deal with you back in the present." He took a piece of chocolate from his pocket and tried to ram it in my mouth, but I resisted. Dad then tried to beat me into submission. I blocked his next volley and punched him again in the ribs. The move stunned him long enough for me get my legs wrapped around his neck. Before I could choke him out, he landed a fist on my groin, and I was forced to release him. We both found our feet, and he came for me, but I was ready. I connected on a long series of punches to his stomach and face. A side kick to his chest sent him hurtling into the wall. I released a Victory George hyena laugh and picked up the chocolate bar from the floor. Dad struggled to breathe.

I forced the chocolate bar into Dad's mouth, wrapper and all. I squeezed his jaws and made him chew. The time travel process started and he started to disappear.

"Do not pass 'GO'. Do not collect $200," I said, as the process completed. Sherman hit me in the side with a chair and prepared to stab me with his blade. The pain was immense. Two security guards busted into the room before he could impale me.

"What's going on here?" one of the guards shouted. I had to make a move. I collected myself and sprinted into Sherman. The force of the blow carried us to the window and through the glass pane. We fell like stones into the Thames below.

For a moment, we fought below the surface of the water. I wanted to drown him: He deserved death. Sherman cut through the murky water and sliced my stomach with his knife. In the muck, he swam away from me.

In my pants pocket, I found the chocolate bar I took from Harrods. I didn't want to time travel in plain sight so I took a bite underwater. Instead of the feeling of ecstasy and delight that I had come to expect, I felt sick to my stomach. My skin and bones disappeared and reappeared. I felt desperately weak: I couldn't move my left arm. Somehow, I pushed my naked body to the shore with my last crumb of energy before I passed out.

A pain in my shoulder shot to my spine and transmitted an excruciating jolt to the rest of my body as I regained consciousness. I was naked and lying on a stretcher with IVs flowing into my veins. An older woman dressed in all black stood over me, flanked by two large men in dark suits. I was fixated on the IV.

"Let the drugs do their work," the Woman in Black said to me. I didn't know what was in the IV or why these people were holding me; I could only think of escape.

I pushed myself forward with all of the strength I could muster. The two suits advanced on me and tried to hold me down on the stretcher, but my string of desperate punches and elbows sent them to the floor, disoriented. *Never back a cat into a corner.* The Woman in Black retreated to the far corner of the room. I removed the needle in my arm in a matter of seconds, as my feet hit the floor, and I searched for my bearings.

"What are you doing, *Andrew?*" The Woman in Black asked. I stepped closer to her and raised my fist.

"Give me one reason not to," I said. As she shrunk down into the corner, I saw something peculiar: A heart shaped necklace with two golden spirals forming a second heart. When she pulled her knees in close to her chest, I saw a large diamond on her left ring finger.

"Rose?"

"Yes, it's me, Andrew," she said.

"Why didn't you just tell me it was you?"

"We're trying to prevent you from going into chemical shock," Rose answered.

"Why does my hand hurt so bad?"

"You dislocated your left shoulder during your fall. My team pulled you out of the Thames fifteen minutes ago," Rose said. I pulled her up to her feet. "My bodyguard just relocated it for you while you were still unconscious. We're just trying to help you." I tested my left shoulder: It was sore, but I had full range of motion. I also had bandages on my stomach from where Sherman had cut me.

"How did you know I'd be there?"

"Vikki came and found me when she returned to 1973. You were successful. You and Vikki prevented the timeline change," Rose said. I believed her, and the wings of relief touched my soul. "New Israel's safe, for now at least."

"What about Grandfather? Did he make it?"

"According to newspaper reports in 1946, a man fitting David's description was stabbed in a Parliament office. He was admitted to a hospital, but died of his injuries."

"What about Dad? Where is he?"

"He's running the Company now. When you get some rest, I want you to consider organizing an offensive against him." I let her words sink in.

"Is there a cure yet?" I asked. A heavy pause lingered.

"No, but we've made some advances to the cocktail. I'm holding onto hope," she said.

"So, you got married, huh?" I asked, indicating her ring. Rose nodded her head. I gave her a hug and felt the familiar warmth of her spirit. "Congratulations." Three things would not leave my mind:

Relief. I learned that there is a release that comes with victory. I had restored some order to the world. Victory George had helped me get the attention of Dad, Sherman, and others who thought they could revise history to suit their own agenda. They knew that I would not sit idly and allow them to wield such power. Now, I am prepared to lead such confrontations; I am a brick wall because I have learned how to believe in my own inner strength. I knew I would have to face my father again here in the present, probably sooner than I wanted, but I wasn't afraid anymore. If there was a chance that I could still save Dad, I wanted to press for that opportunity. Some people do not understand the difference between love and hate. Let them go to New Israel and Palestine. Some say we must embrace violence and death in order to procure our freedom. Let them go to New Israel and Palestine. Some say the present is defined by the past. Let them go to New Israel and Palestine. New Israel and Palestine have to be protected at all costs, even if it meant my having to end my own father's life.

Remorse. Lives had been taken in this conflict, some by my own hand, and I was not proud of this. The questions lingered: *Am I no different from my enemies? Am I the same kind of monster?* The answers were elusive, perhaps by my own choosing. *They will haunt me for my remaining days, lurking, waiting for the chance to cripple my patchwork spirit once again.* I could already feel it in my bones, but it wasn't a craving for the drugs of my youth any longer. The craving was time travel. I wanted to go back. My body told me I *needed* to feel that high again or else. Grandfather had not been forthright about a lot of things. He knew my history, yet brought me into this conflict anyway. *Could it be because he had taught me that recovery was possible, and he believed in my ability to find a way to overcome addiction? Or had he callously used me despite the dangers of my past?* He was dead now, and I might never see him again to determine the truth.

Regret. Although I was happy that Rose had survived and found love to comfort her in my absence, I was sorry I had not been there for her the last thirty-odd years. I knew that I could go back in time and change things, but love is not a selfish proposition. *No.* She dwelled in my heart. Her presence there would be felt with my every breath, but she was not my prisoner, held fast by a bony cage. I believed that one day, love would find me again, and I'd be okay. *Somehow.*

Despite the evil he had been doing at his death, my unshaken love for Grandfather made me hope that he had found his way to heaven. I wanted to think of him there, surrounded by angels singing the Norah Jones tunes he had enjoyed in life, his ears dining on sweet dessert. Perhaps, I could redeem his life? Could I return to the past and prevent his betrayal of New Israel as well as his untimely death? Could I save my father from his misguided alliance with anti-Semitic and morally depraved Sherman? The loss of Rose stung, but my resolve hardened: New Israel, Palestine, and my family were worth fighting for and dying for. The man I had become in the past year would not give up. This is not...THE END.

ABOUT THE AUTHOR

Husky Harlequin is an emerging author of science fiction. This is Husky's first book. Stay up to date on new releases by joining his mailing list:

www.HuskyHarlequin.com/contact.html

Like the book? Leave a review at your favorite retailer.

www.ingramcontent.com/pod-product-compliance
Lightning Source LLC
Chambersburg PA
CBHW020634260626
47157CB00008B/2733